THE BLOND TIGER

THE BLOND TIGER

LESLIE BOYLAN

PALMETTO
PUBLISHING
Charleston, SC
www.PalmettoPublishing.com

© 2024 by Leslie Boylan
All rights reserved.
No portion of this book may be reproduced, stored in a retrieval system, or transmitted in any form by any means–electronic, mechanical, photocopy, recording, or other–except for brief quotations in printed reviews, without prior permission of the author.
This is an historical work based on real people and events. Some names, places, and situations have been changed.

Paperback ISBN: 979-8-8229-4082-6
eBook ISBN: 979-8-8229-4083-3

It may or may not be true, but it definitely happened.
Edward Rotkoff

DEDICATION

To my parents, Natty and Eddie and to relatives
I never met or was too young to remember.

CHAPTER ONE

1930

The delivery was bloodier and more painful than Gussie had expected. Goldie, the midwife a neighbor had recommended, pulled the boy out like she was pulling a brisket from the oven. She chatted and fussed as if Gussie were listening. Gussie turned her face away when Goldie started cleaning the newborn enough to place him in her arms.

Gussie didn't want him. He was her fourth child and she was sick of children. As it was, with this Depression that everyone was talking about, she could barely feed the ones she had. She forced herself to look down at him, small and prune-like, eyes closed against the early sunlight. She knew she should feel lucky about surviving the delivery of another boy. Her sister Sadie had died in childbirth after delivering a healthy boy, and the father, a builder, was raising him on practically nothing. Gussie's mother, Yetta had hidden her three boys in Poland while the pogroms raged in their shtetl. Gussie was alive and healthy, and didn't need to hide her children. Those were the good things she could say about America. There were very few good things she could say about anything.

Sam wanted to name the baby "Edward" after his father. They'd argued but Sam rarely put his foot down, so she took him seriously.

Gussie scolded Goldie for not cleaning everything up right away. She wanted the room neat and clean, despite the birth. Even when she worked as a seamstress in Poland, she made sure to keep her work area tidy.

The bedroom was one of three rooms, including a tiny kitchen. The furniture was sparse but well made. Sam, a carpenter, had built or refurbished everything they had. Gussie gently touched the amulet that hung above her head on the hard wooden headboard Sam had carved out of a tree that had fallen in the yard. The scrap of paper in the amulet was covered with Hebrew letters she could not read, but the amulet comforted her, as did the pin she'd placed under the cradle blankets before the birth. She was not happy about having another baby, but she didn't want the angel of death flying away with him.

Gussie had thought she was done with babies and this pregnancy surprised her. Gussie hadn't believed she was pregnant until her clothes began to tighten around her waist. She never allowed herself to gain a pound, as strict with her diet as with everything else in her life and everyone else's. She'd left Poland before her mother was old enough to be done having babies or to explain to her when that might begin. That made Gussie think of the old women in the village. No one knew their exact age, least of all the women themselves, but they couldn't have been more than forty-five. They wore babushkas, head scarves, in public, and had wrinkled faces and sad eyes. Many were permanently stooped and had gnarled hands from too much work. Gussie thought the women in Brooklyn were so different. Even those with little money and a lot of children looked younger and less careworn.

Now Gussie lay spent after twelve hours in labor. She relaxed in the beautiful but worn handmade quilt, clean sheets, and plumped pillows. At forty, her light blond hair lay loose on the pillow. This was one of the few times it was loose. She only ever took the pins out when she prepared for bed. During the day, she wore a crown of two blond braids wrapped around each other.

She could still feel the sweat on her scalp despite the vigorous washing by the midwife. But it was early April and prematurely warm. The window was closed to ward off the evil eye. Despite the unexpectedly long labor, it had not been a difficult delivery. As much as she hated having another child, pregnancy and delivery were things she did well. She considered herself to do most things well. She couldn't read or write in any language but she knew all she needed to know and what she didn't know, didn't matter.

Another thing she knew she was good at was cooking. Even her worst enemy had to admit that. She made all the recipes from the old country, picking the feathers from the chickens she got from the kosher butcher before she boiled the meat in a large pot on the stove. She remembered watching Yetta make meals from whatever she scrounged from the earth in their tiny garden in Poland.

That brought up another sour thought: It was not hard to observe the old country ways and follow kosher rules here in Brooklyn, but her children were Americans – casual about tradition, religion, and customs she considered vitally important to maintaining Jewish life. Sam had also become an American. He had completely assimilated into "the land of opportunity." She held it against him and never let him forget it.

Gussie wished she knew the time. She had labored off and on throughout the night. The sun shone through the closed window curtains but it could just as easily be dawn as noon. She realized she was hungry, having had no food since before labor began. She decided she didn't care what time it was as long as there was something ready to eat.

Goldie was used to being in charge during home births, but not this time. As soon as the labor pains began, Gussie had made it clear she'd had three children without any problems. She knew what to do and had bossed and ordered Goldie throughout the labor, barely stopping to catch her breath between spasms of pain. *There's no telling this woman anything*, thought Goldie. Gussie's reputation for nastiness was well known in the neighborhood. Goldie knew the type – strong willed and difficult.

Goldie usually loved working with pregnant women. She'd learned midwifery from her mother, who'd delivered countless newborns in damp barns and on dirt floors in Poland, but gave birth to Goldie by herself in Brooklyn. Most of Goldie's clients were also poor women, but now and then her name found its way to a society matron who wanted to deliver at home on silken sheets with an experienced, undaunted attendant. Most women, no matter how strong willed, let the midwife take charge once they began labor. Even the rich ones who were used to telling everyone what to do, gave themselves up to Goldie's ministrations. Gussie was another matter altogether. She refused to listen and directed the labor and delivery the same way she ruled her family, like a tsar.

Goldie knew her appearance helped with most clients. She was a harmless looking woman, middle-aged with scraggly graying hair piled on top of her head, a substantial bosom, and strong hands When she visited her clients, she dressed in a way that would make them comfortable. With society matrons, she wore a dark navy-blue uniform she had created herself. With Gussie, she wore a clean faded housedress and thick soled shoes. She charged the rich women three times more than the poor ones and used the money to buy little things for her poor ladies, things they couldn't afford for their babies, like extra cloth diapers or bottles or food for their other children.

Goldie smiled inwardly and finished cleaning up. She'd washed Gussie, removed the soiled bedding and towels, and Baby Edward was settled quietly in the cradle. An aura of tranquility had settled over the room. It was the time both women secretly liked best, just after a birth when everything was clean, the baby was quiet, and the chaos of the household was held at bay on the other side of the door.

******

The few moments of tranquility didn't last long. The newborn was crying. Goldie stopped gathering her things as she prepared to leave and went to tend to him. He had soft yellow curls and a newborn's blue eyes. He seemed healthy and robust to her experienced eyes and hands. She was pleased that Gussie observed the old-world traditions as she shifted the pin to ensure that it wouldn't prick the baby. She believed strongly in these traditions and encouraged all her laboring mothers to observe them, except for those who lived uptown and scorned the old ways.

Goldie picked Edward up and tightened the blanket around him, then passed him to Gussie to nurse. At first, he had some trouble understanding what he was supposed to do, but soon caught on. Gussie peered down at him in disgust. *Another mouth to feed, another little animal wanting things,* she thought.

"See what's in the kitchen," she said to Goldie. "I'm hungry, too."

Goldie left the room. Miriam, eleven and Edna, five, tiptoed in with some bread and a glass of hot tea. Miriam closed the door quickly so her father and brother wouldn't see their mother's naked breast. Gussie motioned them to come alongside the bed. She switched the baby to the other breast and ate the bread with her free hand. When he was finished, she gave Edward to Miriam to place back in the cradle while she drank her tea. Edna handed her mother the worn cotton bed jacket so she could cover herself.

Gussie looked at her daughters and decided that once he was weaned off the breast, they could mother him, allowing her to pretend her progeny stopped at three. She found her daughters barely tolerable, but she could rely on them. They'd already taken on a lot of the housework and some cooking.

Before this pregnancy, Gussie had reached a point in her life when she could begin to dream about a future after the children were grown. With everyone gone during the day, Sam and Mac at work, and Miriam and Edna at school, she'd managed to carve out a little quiet time for herself after the cleaning and shopping were done and before the laundry and cooking began. She mourned the loss of that little piece of quiet time, knowing with Edward's birth, it was gone for many years to come. She blamed him for delaying the rest she felt she'd earned.

Goldie returned to the room and said, "I'm ready to go now, Gittela," using an affectionate form of Gussie's name. She didn't like the way Gussie had treated her but she made a rule of wiping the slate clean after delivery for all her mothers. She knew even the most devoted mother rarely looked forward to yet another pregnancy, especially when money was scarce.

"You're lucky to have such helpers. What pretty girls. Is there anything else I can do for you? I'll be back tomorrow to see how you are," she said in Yiddish, aware that Gussie knew very little English. Goldie smoothed the quilt over her patient, "Why don't you get some sleep?"

"Eh, I'll sleep if I want to sleep. My husband will pay you," replied Gussie gruffly in Yiddish.

"Danka," said Goldie softly. She'd put the dirty linens and cloths in a large flour sack in the kitchen and took it with her to launder. That was always part of her service. With a wink and a smile for the girls, Goldie left the room to collect her pay from Sam.

Miriam knew her mother expected her to see to everything, now that the midwife had gone. She checked the baby who was tightly swaddled and sleeping soundly again. She decided to call him Eddie. She gently touched his cheek, silently vowing to protect him from their mother. Edna followed Miriam about, mimicking her every move.

Sam walked in after paying Goldie and seeing her on her way. He stood in the doorway to gaze upon his new son. Then, he tiptoed to the cradle to touch the boy.

"No, no, you must wait," Gussie said, waving him away. "You'll wake him! Don't touch him," she commanded in Yiddish.

5

Sam winked at his daughters, smiling despite his disappointment. He knew his wife; there was no sense arguing with her. He went to the bed to kiss Gussie, who turned her head so he barely bussed her cheek. Then he and the girls went back to the kitchen to drink coffee with Mac and toast the birth. Sam drummed his fingers on the wooden table that he'd made shortly after getting married. He tapped his feet on the floor, anxious and impatient, but in good humor, happy the baby was healthy and that all had gone well.

"Edna," Gussie called through the open doorway from the bedroom to the kitchen, "Give me my brush and pins."

"Look Mama, now we both have babies," said Edna in English rushing to her mother, doll in hand. "Can I brush your hair, Mamma?"

Gussie nodded, tilting her head back and closing her eyes as Edna brushed out the silky hair that reached to Gussie's waist. Gussie enjoyed another moment of peace, then grabbed the hairbrush from her startled daughter and started to braid the damp hair. Gussie's hands moved swiftly, intertwining her hair from muscle memory. There was no mirror in the room. Edna held out the pins as Gussie coiled the braids around her head, jabbing the pins into her own scalp as punishment for having another baby.

When the baby began to fuss, Gussie signaled that Sam could now touch his child. Since finishing his coffee, he had been pacing with hands in his pockets, mumbling Hebrew prayers for the health and happiness of his new son. He didn't mind Gussie's obsession with the old-world rituals, but he didn't believe in them. He'd left all that behind in Russia.

He moved to the threshold of the bedroom, noting the amulet tied to the headboard before striding over to the cradle he'd made fifteen years ago for their first child, Mac. He could remember pulling the cradle out of storage and carefully re-sanding its wood to ensure nothing would hurt the new child. That was his way of protecting the newborn, better than amulets or pins.

"I think we should call him Eddie, Pop," said Miriam in English, standing behind her father as Sam reached down to pick up his wriggling son. He cradled him with the gentleness and assurance of an experienced father, talking to him in English, then Yiddish, then Russian, each word a nothing that people the world over murmur to babies.

"Yes, Eddie is a good name. What a handful he is, a good strong boychik."

Loud grunting came from Gussie, who'd turned her face away into her pillow to avoid the happy scene. "Take him in the other room and let me get some rest."

*****

Eddie was always hungry, and loved the comfort from the blankets swaddling him and the warm arms of people who adored him. Miriam realized he seemed to sense Gussie's disdain. He fed eagerly from her breasts but once satiated, he didn't want to remain in her arms any more than Gussie wanted him there. When Miriam, Mac or Sam held him, he was content until it was time to eat again.

On the eighth day, the bris, a ritual circumcision was held in the tiny living room. Mac found a mohel to perform the ritual. Miriam and Mac informed family and close friends and invited members of the synagogue on the corner to attend. Although the synagogue was right on the corner, Sam didn't attend it or any other. Gussie constantly scolded him for this, saying "It's a shanda," a disgrace. Sam told his children that he believed in the almighty, but had no interest in attending services.

Gussie remained in her bed; she was not expected to attend the ceremony or look after the guests. Miriam and Aunt Fanny prepared the food and greeted everyone. Sam told them to spend lavishly for the occasion. Against Gussie's wishes, he told them to make treats that the guests would not soon forget. He rarely defied her but this day was special.

The other women, dressed in their best clothes, stood in the background as the black suited men recited poems and sang Yiddish songs. Everyone laughed at the familiar tunes.

> *I know a good thing, it's good for everyone: chicken*
> *Go to a celebration, a bris, don't eat meat or fish, just chicken.*
> *You'll never complain, it won't knot up your stomach,*
> *It won't give you heartburn.*
> *Dear people, obey my plan, you'll be happy and healthy: eat chicken.*

Eddie was given a little kosher wine before the circumcision. Afterward, he was brought into his mother to nurse. Sam regaled the guests with stories of Mac's bris and childhood years. The relatives had heard the stories before but Sam had a way of retelling them that made them funnier and more entertaining every time. It was a joyous occasion.

"So then, Mac took my old cigar box with the tooth powder and one pair of his underwear and set off down the block! He kept looking back at me to check if I was watching him. He didn't watch where he was going, so he fell flat on his face!"

Mac, standing next to his father among the male guests, laughed, "I remember that, Pop. My nose bled for an hour. You didn't say anything about me running away. You just carried me home and put some ice on it. Then we had ice cream at the candy store!"

Sam laughed too. "You were so serious. I had to keep from laughing at your stern little face. It was a good thing your mother wasn't home. But later…"

"She really let you have it later, Pop. Like it was your fault!"

"I don't think she's forgiven me yet," laughed Sam, short and stocky with a square face and an ever-present cigar hanging from his lower lip.

After everyone had gone, Sam went to the bedroom to check on his wife and newborn son. Miriam, Fanny, and Edna were cleaning up.

"I heard you talking about me. Do you think I can't hear everything in this tiny apartment? Making fun of your own son! I was right to be angry and yes, I still am," said Gussie quietly, afraid of waking Eddie.

"It was just a joke, Gittela," said Sam, as he removed his suit jacket and replaced his one pair of good shoes with slippers. Before she could reply, he went into the kitchen to grab whatever food was left. He hadn't had time to eat during the celebration.

Sam tolerated Gussie's henpecking without comment, and frequently managed to coax a small smile from his diminutive wife when he shared a new Yiddish joke he'd heard. Gussie made sure the family was fed and clothed, and set high expectations for the children. But she rarely showed them any affection. Sam was the hugger, had a wonderful sense of humor, and made sure to find time to listen to his children.

"Mac went to get us some bread. We're all out," said Miriam, who'd changed out of her good dress into one of her mother's old "shmatas," an old house dress. She was drying the dishes as Fanny washed them. Edna was putting away the silverware and tidying up the living room.

"Here's some leftover lox, Pop," said Miriam handing it to her father on one of the clean plates. "Aunt Fanny made it."

"It's delicious, Fan. Thanks for being here and for all your help," said Sam giving her a quick hug. "I'll take over the dishes. You go on home now. We'll see ya tomorrow."

Fanny grabbed her dark blue cloth coat and matching handbag from the hook by the door. She was anxious to go home. Her feet hurt from standing all day. She threw kisses at the girls and left quietly.

Sam told his children to go rest. As he washed the dishes, he thought about how lucky his family was. His father, a shipbuilder, had taught him carpentry, then insisted he leave Russia and live with relatives in Scotland.

"Get yourself to America," his father had said after Sam's brother was killed in a pogrom. "Don't come back." His father gave him a few coins he'd saved and accompanied him to the dock. He remembered his mother, Miriam, crying and tearing her clothes, as if in mourning. She and other mothers in the shtetl had to let go of their children to save them.

It had been a shocking change for a fifteen-year-old, but his father wanted him out of Russia after the Tsar overturned the Revolution of 1905.

He'd gone to Scotland first, since there was family there with whom he could stay. When they sailed to America to go into Vaudeville, he'd moved to Blackpool, England, and worked on the docks saving money for his own passage across the Atlantic. He hadn't found the work hard, since he was used to physical labor and liked working with his hands. Sam laughed to himself when he remembered having to learn English in three very different dialects. His children teased him about his Yiddish, Russian, Scottish, British, American accent.

He'd met Gussie shortly after arriving in New York. Her brother-in-law, Fanny's husband, had hired him to work in his construction business. Sam liked living in the Brooklyn apartment building with Gussie and the kids. His Jewish, Irish, and Italian neighbors were friendly. Everyone helped each other, especially now, when so many of the families were using their savings to get through the week.

CHAPTER TWO

1932

Miriam fell in love with her baby brother. By the time he was two, everyone they passed on their daily walks commented on Eddie's golden ringlets. She made sure he was well fed with soft food she made herself and dressed in clean bright clothes appropriate for the weather. She tucked him in with a thick knitted baby blanket of bright blue and then off they'd go to the park or just around the block. Eddie seemed to enjoy these outings. He was quick to smile at passersby and babbled as if in serious conversation with anyone willing to pay him any attention.

Her mother didn't like the attention Eddie received. She was clearly bothered that this inconvenient child was admired and coddled when he was such a nuisance to her. Miriam suspected her mother blamed him for the extra weight she still carried and for once again being tied to her home by endless laundry and child care duties.

"Miriam, you fuss over him too much," her mother scolded in Yiddish. "Just sit him in the carriage on the porch. He doesn't need you to walk him around all the time." Ma stood in her faded gray housedress and house slippers waving at Miriam as if there were flies buzzing around her.

"But Ma, he loves the walks and it's such fun to watch him wave to everyone," Miriam replied pleasantly, willfully ignoring her mother's behavior.

To avoid confrontation and make her own life easier, Mirriam pretended that Ma was like other mothers. She knew she was smarter than her mother, and not just because Ma was a peasant from the old country. Miriam prided herself on carefully observing the world around her but Ma seemed to pay no attention to the larger world and lived in her own little cocoon of family and tradition.

Gussie turned her eyes away from Miriam and Eddie. *My mother would never have tolerated this.* Yetta had insisted that Gussie do what she was told and work hard with her sister and brothers while their father, Coseel, sat in Torah study all day. *My father was hardly ever home and work? Work? I don't think he knew the meaning of the word. Mama slaved all day and so did we, once we were old enough.* Yetta taught her how to be strong and survive despite the ever-present fear of pogroms and hunger. She knew this had made her too distrustful of people but without that strength, she'd never have made it to America on a ship alone at the age of just seventeen.

I was so beautiful then. There were lots of parties on the ship to America. I've never felt so carefree. Maybe, I should have stayed on the ship! My life has been nothing but work since. But it was much worse for Mama.

Gussie thought back to a story her mother had told her about how, following custom, Yetta met her prospective in-laws for the first time at supper in their house. Coseel's and Yetta's parents had tentatively arranged the marriage. Yetta wore her best dress, saved for Shabbas and holidays.

When Yetta arrived at Coseel's small wooden house, he was at the shul with his father. His mother and sisters barely spoke to her and were neither warm nor welcoming. Coseel's mother met her at the door, and told her to sit down and wait for the men to arrive. Hoping to make a good impression, Yetta soon crept to the small kitchen area to see if she could help with supper. She saw a broom lying across the packed dirt floor. The floor itself, while packed earth, was as clean as anyone could expect from a shack in the shtetl, but beside the broom sat a pile of dirt someone must have carefully gathered and placed there.

As Yetta looked at the broom, she noticed out of the corner of her eye that Coseel's mother and sisters had gathered in the small doorway. Without looking at them, Yetta picked up the broom and swept the dirt into her hands. She carried the dirt outside and scattered it in the fields. She brushed off her hands, one against the other, reentered the tiny home and placed the broom beside the door. Finally, she turned toward the women in the doorway. One by one, starting with her future mother-in-law, they silently approached Yetta and gave her a gentle hug. They now knew what kind of wife she would be. Together, they finished preparing supper. Gussie had not been put through that test when she met Sam because, like so many other traditions, it had been left behind in Poland.

Her mother was always proud of Coseel and never complained, but when the opportunity arose to emigrate to America, Yetta took it and left her husband behind. No one knew exactly why she'd done that or why her husband hadn't followed her. *Maybe she got tired of doing all the work and him, sitting in shul all day.* Yetta lived in Fanny's house until she died; a sad, lost, lonely refugee.

Gussie often felt that way herself. *What do my children know of hardship?* They made fun of her old country rituals behind her back but she was smarter than them in the ways that really mattered. She could keep the family fed on very little. She could make matzo balls in a hearty broth to fill the belly. She knew how to use the cheapest cuts and free marrow bones from the butcher to make a filling stew. She had a talent for making something nutritious out of nothing. *What do they know?*

CHAPTER THREE

1935

Sam's business, the Rugby Structural Corporation, had stayed afloat during the Depression, but constantly had to evolve in order to stay in business. Back in the boom days of the 1920s, the company had started off building warehouses and wharves, then moved on to building houses. Then, in '29 the stock market crashed, and within a few months a lot of people lost their jobs, and those who were still employed couldn't get mortgages because so many banks had collapsed.

No one was buying houses anymore, and instead, people had to move in with family or share small tenement apartments. So, Sam had shifted into building and repairing bridges and large public and commercial buildings. It helped that many of those were government projects. Even so, Rugby had barely scraped by and there were two winters when the family had to wear newspaper in their shoes to stay warm because Sam couldn't pay for enough coal to keep the furnace going all day. Then in '34, Roosevelt had set up the Federal Housing Administration; it gave Rugby steady work building private homes in the suburbs. Things were definitely looking up.

Mac helped him with the business and worked alongside his other employees, but he was best at drumming up new business. Mac was short and stocky just like his father, but with light blue eyes instead of brown. He was handsome, charming, outgoing, and could talk most people into most things. Mac had no accent, so the gentiles seemed to take right to him. It didn't hurt that he had Sam's sense of humor and "hail fellow, well met" personality.

Mac was a good brother to Miriam although they were four years apart. Any man interested in her would have to go through Mac! Sam knew his son was as protective of the family as he was, and it felt good that his eldest son was following in his footsteps, learning the trade that would serve him well. He silently thanked his long-lost father for passing it on to him at a very young age.

Sam's thoughts turned to Miriam or 'Mimi' as he liked to call her. He worried about her breathing problem but she was as smart as any man he knew and it was she, more than himself or Gussie, who held the family together. For someone so young, she was remarkably sensitive to what other people needed and was always keen to make up for her mother's lack of interest in the family. *It's too much of a burden. It might eventually wear her down. But how can I tell her to stop and enjoy being a child while she still can? The truth is, I need her to help manage the family.* He had several children to feed and, while Gussie fed them well, she was too ignorant to fill their heads with useful knowledge and too cold to make them happy. He and Mimi would have to fill the gaps as long as either of them had the strength.

Edna, his younger daughter, his 'kanadle' or dumpling, was already very pretty at age ten, red haired and blue-eyed. Gussie told him Edna and Eddie sang songs as they skipped the three blocks from home to school. He wished he could watch them but his work started early. There was so little joy in the household when Gussie was around. Everyone was so afraid of upsetting her that they stifled their humor and rambunctiousness except when they couldn't help it or Mac was around. Gussie loosened her stays, so to speak, when her eldest was home.

Now Eddie, his 'tattele', his little papa, was his favorite. The first time he'd seen him, Sam felt a new feeling of strength rising from within him. He loved all his children intensely but he thought of Eddie as a wonderful, unexpected gift.

He felt like he wore an invisible shield to deflect the poisonous arrows Gussie shot at all of them.

******

There were ten children in Eddie's class. He could count them. Eddie knew his kindergarten teacher, Miss Marcus, liked him best. She always ran her fingers through his hair, and let him sit on her lap and draw with crayons while he waited for someone to pick him up after school. He liked being the last one to be picked up. It meant more time with Miss Marcus.

Miss Marcus watched Eddie's large brown eyes flicker between the other children and their mothers who burst into the classroom, one after another, like princesses at a ball. He watched them reach for their children, hugging and kissing them, and asking what they did in school that day. She knew his sister, Miriam, the one he called Mimi, was a nice young lady who often left her high school at lunchtime to pick up Eddie because their mother didn't like coming or had no time to. Miss Marcus had only met her once; the woman hadn't been interested in what Eddie was learning. Instead, she wanted to know if he was behaving himself.

Miss Marcus was plain faced and squarely built, only recently out of teacher's college. She wore a bit of makeup to soften her rather masculine features. She'd chosen teaching because she loved children and didn't think she had much chance of having any of her own. She tried to content herself with the kindergarten children and did whatever she could for them. Some lacked basic needs like food, clothing or, like Eddie, motherly affection.

"That's lovely, Eddie," said Miss Marcus as she scrutinized Eddie's latest drawing. It was a picture of a woman with curly hair and large eyes.

"Is that me, Eddie? I think I'll have to take this one home. Is that alright? What a good artist you are!"

Eddie was pleased. Yesterday, Ma found him sitting under the kitchen table, drawing. She made him get out from under the table and tore up the paper. He was drawing a horse he had seen on the street. It was pulling a cart for the milkman. He'd been intrigued by the horse because it was brown with white spots and seemed to look straight at him. The milkman had let him pet the horse and the horse whinnied as if to say "Thank you."

Ma had yelled, "What are you doing Eddie? Don't waste your time. Go out and play. You're getting in my way."

Eddie waited until he was on the stoop to cry. He had gone under the table to hide from his mother but she had found him and taken away the piece of paper he'd found on Pop's desk. He had hoped to give the picture to him.

Eddie craved attention from Miss Marcus. Only Mimi and his father seemed to care for him as much as Miss Marcus did. She always smelled so nice and talked to the children in a calm voice, never shrill like Ma's.

"So sorry I'm late, Miss Marcus," Miriam said breathlessly as she stood at the classroom door. For years, the asthma had been getting steadily worse. Still, she had run all the way to pick up Eddie after stopping by home to get the lunch she'd forgotten to take to her own school. She'd found Ma in the kitchen cooking.

"What about Eddie? It's late, Ma. I thought you were picking him up today," she said to her mother's back hunched over the stove.

"I'm cooking. I can't leave the food on the stove. You go."

There was no time to argue; Miriam's exasperation made her breath come in short gasps but she forced herself to ignore it so she could hurry to the school. She ran the few blocks, worried Eddie would be upset. She had to stop a couple of times to catch her breath, bend over and grasp her legs with her hands to get more air.

"Mimi," cried Eddie, "I thought you forgot me."

"I could never forget you, my little Eddie. What did you learn in school today?" she said as she scooped him into her arms. She nodded to Miss Marcus, who was only a few years older than herself. Miss Marcus smiled in return. Neither of them needed words to explain her love for Eddie.

"Look, I made a picture! Miss Marcus will take it home."

"Yes, Eddie, I will. Thank you. I will look at it every day. Why don't you take a piece of paper and some crayons home with you. You can bring back the crayons tomorrow." Eddie's mood rebounded; he ran out of the classroom leaving Mimi to follow.

"Thank you, Miss Marcus. You know, Eddie really likes you."

"I like him. He's a sweet boy."

Embarrassed, she answered, "I'm sorry we're always late."

"Don't worry. He's a pleasure."

Eddie ran on ahead as Miriam, worrying about her asthma, slowed her steps heedless of how late she would be getting back to school. All she could think about was breathing. When she was short of breath, panic overwhelmed all other thoughts, except her concern for Eddie.

"Come on Mimi, let's go home. I'm hungry!"

"Slow down Eddie, wait for me."

Eddie turned, walked back, grabbed her hand, and pulled her alongside him.

"It's okay, Mimi. I'll help you." After walking awhile, Eddie leading her by the hand, stopped suddenly on the sidewalk and looked up at her. "I don't think I should bring the paper and crayons home. I didn't want to tell Miss Marcus."

"Sure, you should bring them home, Eddie. Maybe you can draw a picture to show me when I get home from school."

Eddie didn't want to disappoint her, so he nodded his head and they resumed walking at a slightly quicker pace so Miriam wouldn't miss school altogether. He decided to hide the paper and crayons under the cupboard in the living room. When Ma wasn't looking, he would draw a picture for Mimi.

She dropped Eddie off at the house and left quickly to return to school. Miriam walked slowly for a few paces and then quickly for a few, so she didn't run out of breath. She knew she'd be very late and would have to stay after school as punishment.

She didn't mind missing portions of her class. She found school boring, and preferred to read whatever she could lay her hands on at the library. She thought her mother was jealous because she'd never learned to read and thought books were mysterious and probably harmful. Sometimes she even hid the books Miriam brought home. Ma said she was raised to believe girls took care of the home and children while their husbands worked and prayed. Miriam didn't like housework, other than cooking.

Miriam enjoyed cooking because she was intrigued by how bits and pieces of food added up to make a meal. She had to hand it to Ma for making an amazing dish out of one free marrow bone. Yet, Ma was particular about following the old traditions about what you could eat and when. Miriam wanted to learn how to cook foods with more flavor and spice, and didn't care about preparing certain foods and meals for particular times of the day or for certain festival days. She was interested in the science of cooking, how a little of this and a lot of that could make a meal taste differently with the same ingredients.

Miriam hoped to go to college instead of marrying right out of school like so many girls did. College could open her mind to everything she thought she was missing like science and other cultures. She thought she'd love to travel and see other countries for herself.

She didn't want to marry until she finished college or at least, learned more about the world. Miriam found it difficult to understand the girls around her. They all wore similar colorfully printed cotton dresses and shoes with short heels. Someday, she thought, she would like to wear the tailored dresses worn by the rich, fashionable women she saw on the street. For now, she tried to accessorize with pins she placed on the tam she wore to school. She had one shaped like an arrow that she especially loved.

As she slowly made her way back to school, Miriam thought about what it would be like to go to college. She'd talked to Pop about it. He wanted her to go but the Depression had ruled that out. She knew she would have to work to help support the family, but Pop promised she would graduate from high school, no matter what.

Miriam stopped walking to bend over and take a few deep breaths. She felt tingling in her fingers, never a good sign. She knew it meant there wasn't enough oxygen getting to the tips of her fingers.

Miriam remembered the lunch she'd barely had time to grab on the way out the door to pick Eddie up at school. It was a homemade kasha knish, still warm and fragrant. She took a few nibbles but found it hard to breathe, walk, and chew at the same time, so she put it back into its wax paper wrap.

By the time Miriam got back to school, her breathing had calmed and she no longer felt tingling in her fingers. Feeling calmer, she slipped in among her classmates, practically indistinguishable from one another, who were already seated at their desks. The teacher quietly walked to her desk and bent down to whisper so only Miriam could hear, "You will stay late today."

******

At home, Eddie sat under the table drawing. Ma had barely said anything when Mimi dropped him off but put a sandwich and a glass of milk on the table. Eddie ate in silence, brought his dishes to the sink, and then went under the table. This time, Ma ignored his drawing. He was relieved. He felt sleepy and thought he'd probably close his eyes for a little while.

Ma never asked him what he'd done at school, so he made sure to remember everything until Pop came home. He would sit on Pop's lap while he and Mac drank their coffee and Ma set the table. Sometimes, when the weather was hot, Mac took him outside to play catch after dinner. Other times, they threw a ball against the stoop. Eddie loved his big brother.

Mac loved Eddie too, but the difference in their ages made it hard to spend much time together. Mac had become Pop's foreman; he preferred that to being a salesman. The men seemed to respect him for more than just being the boss' son. He put in a full day's work and pulled his weight. At work, Pop treated him like he did everyone else.

Mac liked working for his father but wanted more. He wanted to be in charge someday, free to make decisions without needing Pop's approval. He knew men his age who'd been working their way up in big companies before the Depression hit. He didn't know what happened to them, but imagined many were spending their days standing in bread lines or waiting for meals at soup kitchens. Mac knew he was lucky to have a job and to be learning from his father. But at some point, he'd have to go out on his own.

He was dating a woman he'd met through friends, thinking more and more about getting married and having a family. He felt late off the mark with that, too. Other guys his age were already married with kids on the way. *Dottie might be the one.* She was blonde with freckles and long dark eyelashes framing bright blue eyes. She didn't look Jewish but her parents came from the old country about the same time his own had.

Mac had invited Dottie to their home for the Passover Seder. She agreed because it was a long shlep back to her parents' home out on Long Island and she wanted to see Mac and meet his family. She preferred to spend the night in the dormitory she shared with a few other girls, not far from where she worked as a secretary. Dottie had the second day of Passover off, but she planned to use it to catch up on her sleep.

After dinner, Mac had walked Dottie back to the dormitory. She allowed him to kiss her and arrange the next date.

"I'm living with my folks now but I want to move out, as soon as I have the cash," he'd told her, although she hadn't asked.

"That's nice," she had said, but nothing more.

"I mean, I won't always be living with them. I'm too old for that. I'm looking for another job in construction, away from my father. I know enough. I think I can do it," he said in a rush, explaining what didn't yet need to be explained.

She had given him a peck on the cheek then, and turned to go into the building. He hadn't known what to think. *What did she think?*

Pop always walked home from work with Mac. During their walks, Pop was like a stranger who suddenly becomes a close friend, changing his shape and tone to resume his roles as father and confidante. It took some time for Mac to adjust to this, but he understood why Pop had to be one way at work and another way outside of work. One evening, as they walked home for dinner, it was as if Pop could read his thoughts.

He asked, "So, isn't it about time you found a good woman and settled down? What about that cute girl you brought over for Pesach?"

Mac matched Sam's directness with his own. "Would ya like to get rid of me, Pop?"

"Ha! Of course not," Pop laughed, grabbing his son around the shoulders and hugging him to his chest. "I love you Mac, but you need a life of your own. You're not getting any younger. We can still work together or maybe you'd like to do something else?"

"How would you feel, Pop, if I worked for another company? Just to see what it's like?" asked Mac, tentatively.

Pop removed his arm from Mac's shoulder, not in anger but to gesture as he spoke, "I think that's a very good idea. It's time you learned how other companies work and took orders from a boss other than your father."

The more Pop talked, the more he tended to fall back into Yiddish. The farther they walked away from the work site, as Sam changed back from boss to father, his language changed from an odd mixture of British and American English and Yiddish to only Yiddish. By the time they reached the house, it was as if an actor had shed his costume along the way.

"Really, Pop? You aren't mad at me? I've thought about it a lot. I think Artie can be moved up to foreman. He's a good, honest man."

"You may be right, boychik. I'll talk to him soon. Now about getting a wife…."

"Well Pop," started Mac, matching his father's changes in language, "I think I like Dottie. It's still new but I have a good feeling about her."

"Gotseidanken, my son!! Gotseidanken! She's a pretty girl. A zwase meydl, a nice girl!" Pop said, patting Mac on the back as they approached the house.

As they made their way to the fourth floor, Mac and Sam nodded and greeted their neighbors, some of whom hung over the banister or sat on the landings.

"Moshe, how's your Sarah? Better, I hope. Mazel Tov, Adam. I hear little Shmuel is Bar Mitzvah in a few weeks. Mrs. Hoffman, you're looking well."

Pop smiled at everyone as he climbed the stairs with Mac a step or two behind. Mac marveled at his father who knew everything about everyone in the building. Unlike his friend's parents, it was not Ma who was the busybody - it was Pop. Everyone seemed to love him. Before they got the FHA work, when they had next to nothing, Sam repaired his neighbors' apartments for free. Miriam often went along, learning how to fix the plumbing and repair broken light fixtures. It amused Mac that the neighbors looked at her strangely, but he and Pop were proud of her.

******

"Ah my bride," said Sam as he entered the kitchen to peck Gussie on the cheek. She didn't pay any attention, and without turning from the stove, accepted the kiss like it was the brush of an insect.

"Eddie, my bubbeleh, how are you?" laughed Sam as he lifted Eddie from the floor where he'd been playing with Mac's old toy truck. Sam swung him around and then tossed him in the air to Mac who resumed swinging. Eddie laughed and begged to continue after Mac pretended to drop him while gently placing his brother on the rag rug.

Sam and Mac repeated the game with Edna, more gently and with less vigor. Edna had awaited her turn with grinning expectation. She too laughed and begged for more as Sam and Mac left the apartment to go down the hall to the bathroom to wash up for dinner. When they returned, Gussie said, "Miriam is late. Do you want to wait?" She was in the kitchen sweating from her exertions.

"I'm starving, Ma. Can we start without her? Let's eat, Pops," said Mac.

"It's up to your father and stop calling him Pops. Who do you think you are? Show some respect. Are you a goyim now?"

"Ok, Ma," said Mac reaching down to kiss his mother on the cheek, "Sorry, Ma," he said as he winked at Eddie and Edna, who giggled behind their hands.

Miriam came in well after the chicken soup had gone cold. "Sorry Ma, Pop. I had to stay late because I was late getting back to school after lunch," she said in Yiddish, throwing an accusing glance at her mother.

"I thought Ma was picking the bubbeleh up from school now," commented Sam as he finished the dregs of his soup, using a piece of challah to clean up the broth.

"I was cooking and couldn't leave," said Gussie, irritated at the veiled accusation. Sam glanced at Miriam in silent agreement that they would discuss this together at another time.

"I brought home some kugel. Trudy's mother made it. I didn't get time to finish my lunch today so Trudy shared hers with me. I brought some home to share. It's really good," said Miriam in English. She placed a small packet of wax paper on the dinner table.

Sam winked at her and spoke to Gussie, "Ma loves kugel, nu?"

"Is it kosher? Is this friend, Trudy, from a kosher home?" snapped Gussie.

"Of course, Ma. Would I bring home something to share that wasn't kosher?"

Gussie grunted and helped herself to a portion of the kugel. She loved the mixture of noodles, sour cream, cottage cheese and eggs. Trudy's mother had added raisins and cinnamon to increase the sweetness. After taking a bite, Gussie asked "Why kugel now? It's not a holiday!" She took some more, shaking her head as she chewed.

CHAPTER FOUR

1936

Gussie disapproved of Dottie because no girl could be good enough for Mac and she looked like a shiksa, not Jewish enough. Gussie forced herself to dance at the wedding and eat the food that she, Miriam, and Fannie had prepared. *She really is quite pretty,* thought Gussie. *My son deserves someone pretty. But can she cook? Will she cook? She's been working. Will she stay home now?* She convinced herself Dottie wasn't up to the job.

Gussie didn't mingle with the guests in the synagogue hall. Instead, she sat grim faced at the round table where Dottie and her mother had placed Mac's family. She picked at the food on her plate. She'd spent weeks keeping whitefish alive in the water filled bathtub, killing each one with a rolling pin to the head before marinating it. She'd boiled several chickens after plucking out the roots of feathers that stubbornly stuck to the prickly skin. The feet she put to boil for soup. Fannie and Miriam had baked till their hands were sore. Gussie grudgingly admitted to herself that the two of them had done well.

Gussie watched couples dance, and her son and his new wife making the rounds of the guests, greeting each one with wide grins as if they were the only people in the world who'd ever been married! Sam was also glad-handing in the hall, tailed by Eddie who adored his father. Miriam and Edna were entertaining their cousins in the synagogue's backyard. Gussie wondered why she was always left alone. *I am just a laundry woman and cook to this family.* No one really cared except Mac. *His wife better not change his mind.*

*****

Dottie was happy when Mac found them an apartment of their own. But it was near his parents' apartment and Dottie was not happy when Gussie visited most days while Mac was at work. She criticized Dottie's cooking and her housekeeping. Dottie kept kosher, but Gussie insisted she was not kosher enough. When Gussie visited, she brought her own pots and pans to cook for Mac. Dottie begged Mac to talk to her but she knew he was afraid of Gussie. *Imagine, afraid of an old lady, and a dumb peasant at that!*

Mac told her he hoped to move them out onto Long Island so Dottie could be closer to her parents and further from his, but they needed to save some money to make it possible. Dottie did what she could to put money aside.

CHAPTER FIVE

1938

They'd all heard Roosevelt on the radio saying the Depression was over and it was time to start balancing the budget. But it turned out that the Depression wasn't over and construction companies were folding again as the government money dried up. The company Mac worked for told him to stay home most days, so his paycheck was shrinking alarmingly. He couldn't ask his father for help because Rugby was having problems of its own.

With all of his plans for the future at risk, Mac decided to join the Marines. At least he'd always have a job and be able to pay the rent and support Dottie until things got better. Mac planned to discuss his decision with his father before talking to Dottie.

It was Rosh Hashanah, the Jewish New Year. Mac and Dottie had gone to the synagogue on the corner, the evening before. They were getting ready to go back to the shul with Eddie and Edna, who were off from school for the holiday. Miriam and her fiancé Ez planned to meet them there.

"Kids," said Mac to his siblings, "grab sweaters. The shul gets cold after sitting a while. I don't want to hear any complaining about having to leave because you're cold."

Eddie stuck his eight-year-old tongue out at his brother and then smiled. Mac never treated him like a baby and was always eager to look at his drawings. Mac grabbed Eddie around the shoulder in a quick half Nelson. Dottie, wearing a belted, flowered dress under a coat with a fake fur collar, gently took Edna by the hand and they all walked toward the door.

"Bye Ma, Pop," said Mac over his shoulder.

Gussie stayed home with Sam to prepare apples and honey for a sweet new year and the dinner. They said private prayers. He, in the living room standing by the window, wearing his yarmulke and tallit and she in her kitchen preparing to cook.

Sam prayed for a sweet new year as he watched the swirling fall leaves outside the window. He was worried about his children, his business, and what was happening in the world.

Mac approached his father the day after Rosh Hashanah. He knew one was not supposed to talk about business or other non-religious matters during the ten holy days that end with Yom Kippur, the Day of Atonement, but he knew Pop would not be offended by the discussion. His father was religious in his own way but he'd left the rituals behind in Russia.

"The Marines, Maxilla? Why the Marines?" asked Pop from his easy chair in the living room.

"I want to enlist and the Marines sound like the perfect place for me. Besides, there's not much work in construction here now."

"There's talk of a war in Europe. What if we get involved? Are you prepared to risk your life?" replied Pop in his unique blend of Yiddish and English.

"I hope we don't get in a war. But if there is one, I want to fight Hitler."

Hitler had invaded Czechoslovakia and both knew war could break out any day. Mac sat on the sofa across from his father, anxiously awaiting his blessing.

"Pop, I don't think we're gonna get involved. Roosevelt and Congress won't let that happen. Besides, Hitler hates Jews. I think we should fight him if it comes to that."

"What about Dottie? What does she say? You're not married that long."

"Won't you take care of her, Pop? I haven't told her yet. She probably won't like it but it's something I need to do. You understand, right?"

"You're a grown man. It's your wife you have to answer to, not me. I'm not going to stop you. I love this country. It's given me everything. I'm proud you want to serve, but I'm afraid of war."

"Where would you have me be if war comes, Pop?"

"I guess you're right and I'm a little jealous. I wish I could kill that Nazi bastard with my own two hands." With that, Pop rose from his chair. Before he went into the bedroom, he turned to Mac with one final comment on the matter.

"You must tell your mother," He said with a snigger. "Better you than me!"

Sam sat on the edge of the bed. For the first time, he sensed what his own father must have felt when he sent him away to build a new life away from poverty and death. Mac was leaving for his own reasons, but for a father, the pain was the same. He could no more ask Mac to stay than he could convince his father to let him stay in Belarus.

Sam had heard little from his family since he left Russia over twenty years ago. Of his family there, only his father could read. Sam sent letters in Yiddish and Hebrew but heard nothing. He was not close to his mother, but thought about his father almost daily. He could not count how many times he wished his father was working beside him.

Sam prayed daily that his family was alive and well. Since the pogroms in Russia, he had not felt as close to God. He constantly struggled with the question of whether he still believed or not. *Why is the world so fakakta, so screwed up? Let people live their lives! The bastards!*

He quickly pushed these thoughts away to focus on the matter at hand. Gussie would not be happy about Mac's news. *Mac is her favorite child. She might worry herself into an illness. Maybe she'll take the news better from Mac than from me. If he tells her, she'll blame him. I can only take so much of her yelling and kvetching.*

Mac watched his father rise from his chair and go into the bedroom. He worried about Pop. He wasn't the kind of man to hold his kids back, but agreeing to let Mac leave Rugby had been a real sacrifice. Pop had depended on Mac as one of the few people he could trust completely. *Who will he talk to when I'm gone?* But none of them would have anything if Pop had stayed in Russia and he'd probably be long dead. *Pop is a survivor, that's for sure.* Mac wasn't sure about his mother though – somehow, she'd survive anything.

What will I say to her? She'll think I'm abandoning her. Ma has no allegiance to anyone or anything but she might listen to me. Then again, she might never speak to me again. He figured he'd better get it over with, so he waited until the end of the High Holy Days and told Ma before he spoke to Dottie.

"I've enlisted in the Marines, Ma," said Mac without preamble. The children were at school, but Pop was in the bathroom, shaving before walking to work. Ma was sitting at the kitchen table drinking coffee. She'd already put up her hair. Her clean yellow housedress hung in loose folds. A pot of water simmered on the stove. Mac stood in the doorway holding the cup of coffee she had handed to him.

Ma looked down into her coffee cup, pretending she hadn't heard. *Maybe he'll take it back.* She would give him the chance to pretend he'd never spoken.

"Ma? Did you hear me, Ma?" said Mac, hoping Pop would rescue him if she yelled at him. Then he thought, *I'm enlisting in the Marines. I'd better be able to handle my own ma!* Then, *I'm not sure even the Marines could handle my ma!* He laughed to himself.

"What are you laughing at? I heard you," Ma said clearly irritated, as she stared up at him, mouth set in a straight line. "I HEARD YOU!" she said again, much louder this time.

Now she was livid, screaming in Yiddish, "You ungrateful son! You don't care about your mother! All I do for you and you want to leave me!" She rose from the chair and seemed ready to throw the still warm coffee in his face, but seeming to think better of it, placed it on the tiny counter.

Gussie, no taller than his chest, grabbed him by both arms and yelled up at him, "My children are all worthless. No one cares about what I want. Go. Go ahead and leave me. What about your Papa? You're leaving him. What will he do without you?"

"Ma, Ma," Mac said in a soothing tone, enfolding her in his arms and kissing the top of her head. She continued to scream into his chest and beat him with her fists.

Back in Poland, no one wanted their sons going into the army. Gussie remembered hearing about Jewish boys as young as thirteen or fourteen being drafted by the Russians. Yetta had told her about fathers who cut their son's trigger fingers off so they couldn't shoot. Others knocked out their son's two front teeth, so they wouldn't be able to tear the old paper rifle cartridges. Many families hid their boys.

Sam came up behind Mac. When Mac turned his head to look back at him, Sam signaled that he would take over and try to soothe his wife. He nodded at Mac to leave the kitchen.

"How can you let him do this to us? You know what things were like. Speak to him. Tell him he can't go!" commanded Gussie as she wriggled from Sam's grasp. He knew what she meant. *But that was Russia and this is America,* he thought. He stood by quietly as she moved to the stove and started fussing with the pot that was now boiling. He heard her grumbling as he grabbed his jacket and hat.

Mac met him outside. He'd long suspected that his parents' marriage was not for love but convenience - two lonely immigrants from the same region who needed one another. When Ma yelled at Pop, Pop generally tried to lighten the mood or he left the room.

The two walked silently out of the neighborhood. Someone walking behind them would have seen two men, one older, one younger, walking slumped over with both worry and relief. They worried about Gussie and how she would be when they got home. Mac thought it funny that that's what he knew they were worrying about rather than the prospect of him going to war. The relief came from having good excuses to be away from Gussie for several hours. She couldn't keep them from work.

When Dottie found out Mac had told his mother about joining the Marines before telling her, she predicted it would be this way until Gussie died. She knew Mac both feared and loved his mother. He didn't seem to fear Dottie, *but maybe he should!* She was no more thrilled by his news than Gussie had been but realized he was determined to enlist. It was best done with before they had any children who would miss him.

CHAPTER SIX

1938

When she was ready to graduate from high school, Miriam's teachers encouraged her to go to college. Her father had some work but the family still had trouble making ends meet. She knew she'd have to work full time; She found a job in a secretarial pool at The Baxter Corporation two miles from home. She decided she would give half her money to her mother and save half for college.

"College?" Ma asked, looking at her daughter as if she were a street urchin planning to live in Buckingham Palace.

"Yeah Ma. I'd like to go to college. What's wrong with that? Just because you want to stay ignorant, doesn't mean I shouldn't try to do better!" said Miriam as her voice rose.

"Feh. You'll be too busy having children, if any man will have you. Do something with that hair and men don't like women who act so smart," Ma walked out of the kitchen and straightened the chairs in the living room. Eddie had slept on them since he was too old for the cradle. He could still fit, with his head and chest on one and his legs curled on the other.

Ma put his blanket and pillow in the closet and called back to Miriam, "You keep a dollar a week from your salary and give the rest to me!"

Miriam grabbed her sweater and left the apartment quickly, making sure to bang the door on her way out. She would have liked to rush out onto the street and run until the tears in her eyes dried to crusts. But running caused breathlessness and her asthma was getting worse. It made some kinds of work impossible, but fortunately, she could do secretarial work with her eyes closed. It was rote and repetitive and most importantly, sedentary.

Miriam walked slowly out into the street and down the block. She was used to Ma's endless criticism but the words still stung. Miriam knew she was plain but she wasn't ugly and Pop said she had a good sense of humor. She wasn't coy like other women and doubted she could flirt with any success. But marrying the right person might be her ticket to going to college. He would have to be an unusual man who was willing to give up having dinner on the table promptly at five and a houseful of children, at least for the first few years. She needed a man who didn't need a wife with movie star looks but who could brighten a room with her wit. He'd have to respect her intelligence and treat her as his equal. She laughed to herself, *Oh Mimi, what a fool you are! He doesn't exist!*

There were several nice, Jewish boys in the building where she began working as a secretary the week after graduation. She sat with several other girls in a large, ugly room in the office building in Brooklyn. They sat at small desks with typewriters and seemingly endless piles of paper. Absent was the sense of accomplishment she felt when she cooked or helped her father with building repairs. When she left work every day, the piles of paper were just as high as when she'd come in. She felt like an easily replaceable cog in the wheel of a factory that produced a surprising amount of letters, invoices, and inventory lists.

She got to know a few of the girls but most of them were empty-headed and sat day after day waiting for a husband to discover them beneath the piles of paper and take them to an altar and install them in a kitchen. Most were prettier than Miriam and those who weren't, had style. They managed to put together outfits from the Five and Dime store that looked fashionable. Miriam had no role model for fashion, certainly not her mother, so her clothes were more practical than stylish.

Despite her deficiencies compared to the rows of hopeful girls, there were boys who occasionally asked her out but she wasn't attracted to them. After a couple of dates, she knew what they were looking for and wished she could point out any one of the hopefuls with whom she sat day after day.

"Try Susan," she imagined herself saying, "she's just what you're looking for." Or, "Martha has been waiting for a guy just like you. She's sitting over there with the pink blouse."

Maybe I should be a marriage broker, she thought. *Some families still use them. I could spot a perfect match in a heartbeat. At least I'd get some respect!*

She and Dottie had become close. Miriam thought people took Dottie for granted because of her good looks. The two women had hit it off when they started talking about books and how they'd like to travel. One day, much later, they met for coffee after work.

"What are the girls like where you work, Dottie? I feel like the girls at Baxter are just waiting for marriage," said Miriam. "They have nothing to talk about other than clothes and men."

"Not much different where I am. I like working. I think I'd be bored at home but I'm sure children will keep me busy enough, when they come along."

Miriam noticed Dottie's hairstyle and thought she might try it with her own hair. The front and sides were swept up into rolled curls with larger curls at the base of her neck. Miriam was wearing a light green snood that matched her dress. It was easier in the morning before work.

"Don't you want to get married, Mimi?" asked Dottie as she sipped her steaming black coffee.

"I do, yes, and I want to have children. But I'd love to go to college and travel first or travel with a man willing to let me do what I want before having kids."

"Well then, you just need to find the right man. I'm sure he's out there somewhere but not easy to find. I'll keep my eyes peeled for you," said Dottie with a laugh.

They both laughed. The conversation moved on to how Dottie liked being married and how she felt about Mac joining the Marines.

"I really love Mac. He's a good husband but I can't bear that he's going away so soon," she said taking a bite of a bagel.

"He's not leaving you, Dottie, as much as he's trying to find out who he is," explained Miriam. "You didn't grow up in our home. My mother is impossible to live with and although she favors Mac, I think he's always felt like he was carrying the weight for the rest of us. My pop too."

"What do you mean, 'carrying the weight'?"

"Well," started Miriam chewing on Danish as she pondered how to explain. "Well, Mac's the eldest. I think he's always felt a responsibility to protect us from Ma, to sort of take her anger at us and smooth it down so Ma wouldn't hurt us so much. We've never talked about it but I think he feels like he can hand that responsibility off to me, now that he's married."

"But why volunteer to go away?" asked Dottie as she brushed crumbs from her dress.

"Because, it's not just getting away from Ma that he needs. It's proving himself. I think he wants to be worthy for you. I also think he's very upset about what's happening in Europe and wants to try to do something about it."

"I suppose there's something to that. Let's just hope he doesn't have to fight," agreed Dottie.

"If it comes to that, all the young men will be going," she said solemnly. On a lighter note, Miriam said "Besides, you'll have me and Edna, and Eddie. We'll try to keep you laughing!"

"Okay, it's a deal," answered Dottie as both women got up to take their checks to the register.

At the risk of seeming frivolous, Miriam asked, "Dottie, how'd you get your hair that way? Do you think I could do it? Would it look good on me?"

"Of course, darling. I'll come over one night this week and show you. You'll knock Mr. Right dead."

"If ever he shows himself!" laughed Miriam.

She met Ezra Feldman at a dance in the synagogue. She spotted him dancing with another girl and used her wits to engage him in conversation. She didn't have the breath to swing dance. But if she could catch his interest, maybe they could dance together when the band played a slower tune. Miriam walked by Ezra as soon as he and the other girl finished their dance. She had a glass of water in her hand that she "accidentally" spilled on his shirt.

"Oh! Look what I've done. Oh, and on such a nice shirt. Honey, can you get a napkin please? What a dear," said Miriam to Ezra and the girl. As soon as the girl left, Miriam grabbed his hand and led him to the side of the room out of the way of dancers ready to do the Conga.

She pulled her handkerchief from her purse to dab his shirt, "Your girlfriend must have gotten tied up in the crowd. Here, this should take care of it. You must think I'm so clumsy!"

"That's quite alright," said Ezra, speaking for the first time. "No harm done." He took her hand holding the handkerchief, put his other arm around her waist and moved them into the crowd of dancers.

"What's your name, doll face?" he asked.

She wondered if he was serious. Only Pop had ever made her feel beautiful. *He's beautiful,* she thought. He looked a few years older than her, tall and slim, and movie star handsome. He led the dance like she weighed no more than a feather. She told herself to conserve her energy and let him lead. She hoped the dance wouldn't last long so he wouldn't see her turn blue. He moved so easily. It was love at first sight. Her list of requirements for a husband never entered her mind.

"Miriam. What's yours, handsome?"

"Everyone calls me Ez. My name is Ezra but I never use it. Hey, you're a good dancer Miriam."

Miriam saw the girl Ez had danced with out of the corner of her eye. She felt a bit guilty for stealing him away but consoled herself. *She's so pretty; she can have anyone here.*

The dance exhausted Miriam, so she said she was hungry. Ez took her to a nearby café where they ordered coffee and sandwiches. She'd worn an A-line black skirt and short sleeved pink knit sweater with low black heels. Her little sister knew much more about fashion than she did. Edna had told her what to wear. She removed her short white gloves and her pink hat with the upturned brim before sliding into the booth. She fluffed her hair, pleased that Dottie had shown her how to curl it properly.

"So, tell me about yourself, Mimi. Can I call you Mimi?" Ez asked, after they ordered.

"My little brother and my Pop call me Mimi. I like it. Well, I'm a secretary but I hope to go to college."

"College? You must be one of those girls with looks AND brains. Am I right, Mimi?" said Ez leaning across the table. His light brown hair fell over his forehead and into his eyes.

"I don't know about that. But I love to read and learn about stuff."

"Yeah? I might be too dumb for you, since I only finished high school."

"I'm sure you're not dumb," answered Mimi, bowled over by this man's interest in her.

"Well, I'm not nearly as smart as my Ma. She came from Lithuania when she was very young. She takes in sewing. She learned how at the orphanage for Jewish children. She learned English there, too."

"What about your father? Did he come from Lithuania, too?'

"My dad died when I was seven. He was a cigar roller in Russia. I don't remember much about him."

"How about your family? Are they as smart as you? What does your father do? Do you like working as a secretary?" Ez usually didn't babble so much with girls, but this one seemed smart and that was a little intimidating. He finally trailed off when he started thinking about his mother and how she'd aged before her time. He wanted to keep this conversation light.

"My father came from Russia, too. I guess you could say the same about Ma. She came from Poland but really, what's the difference? They met once they got here. Pop has his own construction company. Rugby Structural Corporation. I don't imagine you've heard of it. What do you do for work, Ez?" Mimi took a bite of her egg salad sandwich.

"I sell matchbooks for the Lion Match Company," Ez took a matchbook out of his pocket to show her. "The company's owned by White Russians who refer to themselves as dukes and counts! Lucky for them, they escaped to New York after the Tsar and his family were murdered and the revolution took off. They have family here." He added more sugar to the coffee. "It's funny to listen to them. They speak Russian, English, and Yiddish all at the same time! I like working there. I get to travel all around the city. I guess I'm a good talker."

"My Pop's like that. We tease him about his Russian, Scottish, British, American, Yiddish accent! He lived awhile in Scotland and England before he came here. Anyway, you're lucky. I don't think much of my job. I sit in a big room with a bunch of other girls. We type all day. It's endless. I count every minute till I can go home."

"Let's not think about that. Hey, do you like jokes? Do you know who Burns and Allen are? I heard this great bit on the radio. Burns says: 'Do you like to love?' Allen- that's his ditzy wife- says: 'No'. Then, Burns says: 'Like to kiss?' Then she says: 'No'. Then Burns says: 'What do you like?' Allen says: 'Lamb chops'. Burns says: 'Lamb chops. Could you eat two big lamb chops alone?'" Ez started laughing and had to catch his breath to continue. "Then ditzy Allen says: 'Alone? Oh, no, not alone. With potatoes I could.' Isn't that great?" asked Ez, finishing the last of his coffee and signaling to the waitress for more.

"You're funny," said Mimi. "My whole family likes to laugh, except for my mother, that is. I don't know if I've ever seen her laugh!"

"My Ma loves to laugh. I think it's what keeps her going," said Ez. Then he reached across the table and grabbing Mimi's hand, said, "I like you, Mimi. I'd like to see you again. Okay with you?"

Mimi looked down at her lap, thinking, *He's so handsome. I'm in over my head. I should've left him to the other girl. How could I have stolen him away like that?*

"Really?" she said, suddenly realizing she shouldn't have said that out loud.

Ez responded by kissing her on the cheek. She'd never been kissed by a boy before and never imagined it would be by someone so handsome. *Wait till I brag to the girls at work.*

After that night, they went to the movies and to dinner and dancing. It was nice to date someone with real money for a change. After two months, Ez brought Mimi home to meet his mother, Leah. They were very close. He was also close to his sister Ada, but she was rarely around.

Mimi was not yet prepared to tell her mother, or anyone, about Ez. *Who would believe it, anyway?* She asked Ma to make over one of Aunt Fanny's dresses for her to wear to work. Instead, she wore it to meet Leah. The dress, along with a hat and gloves, made her feel properly dressed. She didn't want to embarrass Ez.

He waited for her at a pre-arranged spot, in front of the soda shop by Miriam's house. They walked to his apartment together.

"What a beauty, you are!" he said on first seeing her. Ez seemed to have a sixth sense about what a woman wanted to hear. She tried to respond with nonchalance.

"I'm looking forward to meeting your mother. What have you told her about me?"

"That you're ravishing and brilliant and the best thing since sliced bread," he said, laughing.

"Oh no, you didn't. You didn't, really? Did you?"

"Of course, I did, Kid. Why not? Don't worry. Ma can be tough but she's also very sweet. You'll like her."

Leah was standing at her door when they came in downstairs. As they ascended the staircase, they could see more of her. Miriam could look her over before they were formally introduced. Leah was as round as she was tall. She was shorter than Miriam and had a large round face and ears that stuck out from her head. Her graying hair was cut short and swept back from her forehead. *She isn't entirely unattractive,* Miriam thought, but imagined Ez must've gotten his looks from his father. Once Leah spotted Ez on the staircase, Miriam saw her mouth widen into a tremendous smile; it took over her entire face. She held her heavy arms out to him, ready for a hug, seeming to care less whether it might wrinkle the carefully ironed light blue dress she wore.

"Miriam!" she said, after hugging her son for several seconds. Leah reached out to the girl to give her a hug. Miriam could feel Leah's heavy bosom crushing her own carefully ironed dress. "Come, come, inside, dinner is ready."

"A pleasure to meet you Mrs. Feldman," she said as she was pulled through the apartment door.

"Call me Leah, Širdelė," said Leah, using a Lithuanian endearment. "Now, come, sit on the couch, and tell me all about Miriam. Then, we'll eat," Leah ignored Ez, as he went into the kitchen to check on the food. He and his mother were used to cooking, cleaning, and eating together.

Miriam looked around the room. The third-floor walk-up seemed very small, which was a little surprising since she thought Ez was making good money. If that were so, surely he wouldn't keep his mother in such a tiny apartment. Maybe, she had it all wrong. Still, it was nicely decorated and cozy. Miriam could tell the couch she and Leah sat on was probably the sofa bed where Ez slept. It was dark blue. A matching wing-backed chair sat in the corner beside a telephone table. Miriam was surprised they had their own phone. That was proof that he was doing well.

He came around the corner from the kitchen holding a small tray of deviled eggs and placed the tray on the oblong, wooden coffee table. Then, he sat down in the chair.

Miriam said, "I don't have much to tell. Ez probably told you everything."

"What do boys know about the important things? Bubkes, nothing. Where are your parents from?"

"Russia and Poland. They met after they came here"

"And the rest of your family? Who are they, what do they do?"

"Ma is a seamstress but mostly takes care of all of us," Miriam thought to herself, *more likely she puts up with us.* "Pop has his own construction business and my little brother and sister are in school. I have an older brother in the Marines."

"Ma, Mimi will start to think you're the police! Let's eat. I'm starving," said Ez. *I'd better rescue her or we'll be here all day,* he thought.

"Seems like a nice Jewish girl," Ma said to Ez after he'd returned from walking Miriam home. He helped her wash and dry the dinner dishes.

"You like her then, Ma?"

"She's not as pretty as most of your girlfriends but she's funny and smart. I thought you only went for the movie stars!" she said, as she put the last dish away in the cupboard and began to remove her apron.

"I think I'm ready to settle down and looks only last so long - except in your case, Ma. You'll always be a looker!"

"Such a good boy and a good liar," said Leah, pinching his cheek. "I'm off to bed."

*****

Soon, it was Ez's turn to meet Mimi's family. She spoke to her father first. "Pop, please don't let Ma scare him away. You know how she can be."

"Bubbeleh, don't worry. Even your Mama couldn't scare him away. Where else will he get such a beauty?"

"I mean it, Pop."

"So do I, my child."

She need not have worried. Ez charmed Ma from the moment he stepped into the apartment. "Mrs. Roth, how good of you to make time to have me visit. What a lovely home, you have," the charm oozed out of him. Only Ma was taken in. Even Edna and Eddie thought it was too much. They giggled behind their hands.

CHAPTER SEVEN

1941

Miriam was preparing for her wedding when they heard the news on the radio. Some naval base in Hawaii had been attacked by the Japanese. On that Sunday morning, they were all sitting around in the apartment upstairs listening to music after lunch when the announcer broke in. Edna had been chasing Eddie in and out of the rooms trying to get her hairbrush back. Now, the two stopped to listen.

Alright now, listen carefully. The island of Oahu is being attacked by enemy planes. The center of this attack is Pearl Harbor, but the planes are attacking airfields as well.

"Vayesmere," said Pop rising from his chair.

"What? What?" asked Edna and Eddie in unison, alarmed at Pop's expression. He had been laughing just a few minutes earlier.

"What does it mean, Pop? What will happen now?" asked Miriam. "I'd better call Ez."

"I don't know. I don't know," Pop said, as he slumped back down into the chair.

"What's going on?" asked Ma in Yiddish. "Is Mac okay? Tell me," she said as she pulled on Pop's shirt. The radio announcer continued:

We are under attack. Do not go out on the streets. Keep under cover and keep calm....Now keep your radio on and tell your neighbor to do the same....Please don't use your telephone unless you absolutely have to do so.

"Ez is on his way over," Miriam said. "I'm scared. He shouldn't go out but he won't listen to me."

Miriam was worried for all the people in Hawaii but when she stopped to think, she realized her wedding might have to be postponed. When Ez arrived, he brought Leah; He gave Miriam a quick kiss and sat down by the radio. Leah paced anxiously.

"I didn't want her sitting home alone," Ez said to everyone by way of explanation. Pop had explained what was happening to Ma, who promptly went into the kitchen to prepare more food. Leah went with her. Miriam sat down next to Ez and took comfort in his closeness.

"I don't get it," said Eddie. "What should we do?"

"Why don't you and Edna go downstairs and play a game or read. We'll let you know what's going on when we know more, okay?" said Pop, trying to sound normal.

"Okay, Pop. Can someone bring us some snacks?" asked Edna.

"Sure. As soon as Ma has some ready, one of us will come down. Now go on!" said Pop a little more forcefully than he had intended.

*****

They decided to go ahead with the wedding, as planned. Ma made Miriam's dress of white rayon with a rounded collar and long sleeves. The veil fell from each side of a beaded cap and was trimmed with a thin piece of lace. She dyed her shoes white. Ma used some left-over fabric from other clothes to make a going away suit of pale pink.

They days they spent preparing the wedding clothes, seemed to Miriam like the only time Ma ever took any real interest in her. Ma gushed over her accomplishment, less so over her daughter. "He's too good looking for you," she said to her in Yiddish. "He's liable to run off with some shiksa."

Miriam ignored this as she removed the veil and dress so Ma could make final alterations. Anything she might say would only make things worse. She was happy and excited; she didn't want to let Ma ruin it. Instead, she thought about Ez and how he supported the idea of her going to college.

"Sure, anything you want," he'd said. *Somehow, I've captured a prince!* Even Ma liked him. If he could charm her, he could go far and she'd be right there with him.

Miriam was glad Eddie and Ez got along. Mac had been away so long, Eddie said he hardly remembered him. Eddie liked playing ball with Ez, who seemed to like his drawings. Ez told Mimi he knew artists at the Lion Match Company and had shown them some of Eddie's art work. They'd told Ez, "The kid's got something."

They all missed Mac and wished he could be at the wedding. The war in the Pacific had begun and Mac was sure to be in the thick of it. Yet, the one letter they got from him before the wedding was mostly devoted to a joke he thought they'd like.

Dear Pop,
I hope you and the rest of the family are okay. I think about you all the time. I'm okay. Please tell Ma I wrote her a separate letter. It's on its way.
I've got another joke for you. I'm not sure if this one is true. I heard it from a guy in my outfit.
A company of guys just got back from a 20-mile march. They're standing in formation ready to go clean up and get some chow. So, their CO says to them- you know they're all hot, sweaty, dirty, and very hungry- the CO says: "Hey men, we can show everyone we're the best damn company in the battalion if we turn right around and go on another 20-mile march. Whaddya say? Anyone who doesn't think he can do it, take two steps backward." So, guess what? All the guys, except one, take two steps backward. So, there's only one guy up front and the CO says to that guy: "You're a fine soldier, an example to your peers. I'm proud of you son, but are you sure you want to do the 20-mile march alone?"
Get this, Pop. The soldier says: "No sir. I'm just standing here cause I don't have the energy to take two steps backwards."

It was typical of Mac to do that rather than write about things that might upset them. Yet, in the months to come, there would be less and less in Mac's letters that Sam would be willing to share.

The wedding was simple. Ez wore a black suit, yarmulke, and tallit. He and Miriam stood together, holding hands, under the white chuppah.

Dottie watched Mimi and Ez, hoping they would always be as happy as they appeared. She had a few doubts about Ez but kept them to herself. Dottie thought back to the conversation they'd had before Mimi met Ez. She recalled how important going to college and traveling were to her sister-in-law. It seemed Mimi had thrown all of that out the window. In the end, Mimi wasn't so different from the girls she complained about who were only interested in finding husbands. Dottie had a feeling Mimi would eventually come to her senses and realize she hadn't gotten what she'd wanted but hoped she was wrong. Both families watched as Ez stomped the wine glass signaling the end of the ceremony.

"Mazel tov," said everyone in unison. They laughed and hugged each other.

Eddie tugged at Pop's jacket and whispered, "Why'd they do that, Pop? Everyone is so excited about Ez stomping on the wine glass."

"Because, Eddela, it's a very important tradition. It reminds the couple how fragile relationships can be and to nurture and treasure theirs."

"Is that what you and Ma do, Pop?"

Sam scratched his chin and smiled, thinking how astute little Eddie was, "Yes, that's what we do." Sam didn't like to lie but his relationship with Gussie was complicated and not what he wanted to think about at his daughter's wedding. "Smashing the wine glass also reminds us that even when we are happy, we should remember the destruction of the first temple. It reminds us to remember we are Jews."

That seemed enough for Eddie who went running off to find some sweets to eat. Soon, Ez and Mimi were rising in the air on matching straight backed chairs as their friends and family danced around them. Looking back, Miriam would remember her wedding as a few rare hours of untainted joy and anticipation.

*****

They moved in with Leah, who quickly replaced Ma as an overbearing mother. Instead of hovering all the time waiting to criticize, Leah's attentions were warm and friendly, but intrusive, nonetheless. She made it clear in whose home they lived and that her word was final. Leah and his sister Ada, doted on Ez, who could do no wrong. If he and Miriam argued within Leah's hearing, which was almost certain in the small apartment, Leah put her hands up signaling there was to be no more of that and that Ez was right, no matter what.

"Why do you and your mother live in such a small apartment?" Miriam had asked one day, before the wedding. "I thought you were doing well at the Lion Match Company."

"Because it's her apartment. She pays for it from what she makes sewing. She won't let me pay the rent but likes having me live with her. She always said I'd get married someday and move out. She didn't want to be stuck with a large apartment to have to clean herself."

Now the wedding was behind them and Miriam was ready to move. Whenever she asked Ez how soon it could happen, he'd shrug and answer, "Soon, honeybunch."

CHAPTER EIGHT

1942

Miriam's marriage to Ezra wasn't going well. They'd argued frequently. Ez had been staying out late and she, still working as a secretary, arrived home tired and frequently ill. Ez had wanted to go dancing most nights or to the clubs, while she had neither the will nor the energy. On more than one occasion, anxiety and stress had sent her to the hospital for difficulty breathing. She'd throw herself into a taxi barely able to say the word "hospital" to the driver, who figured he needed to get the lead out or have a dead passenger on his hands.

Ez had been overly solicitous when she was ill, but as soon as she got better, he'd resume gallivanting all over the city. He seemed to have friends and business acquaintances everywhere and an urgent need to visit them.

When she asked what would happen to them after he returned from the war, he answered, "When the war's over, everyone's gonna wanna hire vets. Maybe Lion will give me a promotion or I can get work somewhere else that'll pay more. I'm a good salesman. The contacts I'm making now will help out later."

She believed him. With his charm and good looks, he could go far. Maybe they could get a place on Ocean Parkway someday. Maybe some time away from each other would be good for their marriage. She decided to ignore the niggling doubts.

*****

Miriam was still walking to work, two miles each way to save trolley fare. Pop had since bought a one-family house on east Fifty-Third Street in Brooklyn and renovated it into a two-family house. He'd planned on renting out the first floor but with Ez leaving, he proposed that she move in. The first floor had two bedrooms. He and Ma lived upstairs in three rooms with Eddie still sleeping on two chairs pulled together and Edna on the couch in the living room. Miriam thought she would invite Eddie to sleep in the extra bedroom whenever he wanted. Maybe, Edna could come downstairs and stay with her. Both kids would be much more comfortable.

Miriam thought about her younger sister. Edna was like a vivacious butterfly, striking to look at and fun to be with. Unlike Miriam, she didn't aspire to an education beyond high school. Academics were too challenging and of no interest. She planned to work and marry as soon as she could after graduating from high school. There was no shortage of boys interested in her. Miriam thought of her as one of the stylish girls in the endless rows of typists she encountered day after day. Edna was a "hopeful," as Miriam had dubbed them. They were the women who sat patiently at their typewriters waiting for a man to take them from one life of drudgery to another.

Although Eddie and Edna were closest in age of all the siblings, they weren't close otherwise. Edna seemed too busy with school and her friends to care much about her little brother and did not want to be seen with him. Neither was she close to Mac, who must have seemed from another generation altogether. Edna told her he was old-fashioned and seemed more like an uncle than an older brother.

Miriam's own relationship with Edna was much closer, but tinged with a bit of envy on both sides. She loved Edna and admired her health, her beauty, and especially her carefree ways. Miriam wished she could live that way herself because she'd been burdened by cares and worries for as long as she could remember. She made Pop laugh when Ma was too much to bear and she'd mothered Eddie since he was born. She'd taught Mac manners until he had a wife to do that for him and also acted as Edna's confidante. She could say anything to Pop or her siblings, but her mother only knew how to be critical and Ez only knew how to flatter. Neither of which helped Miriam. Maybe she could learn something from her younger sister, although she didn't know what.

Miriam had been shocked when Edna told her 'out of the blue' that she admired her brains and would trade her own prized red hair just to have a small bit of them. She'd said, "People listen to you; they only look at me.".

*****

The war was not going well. The Japanese were running amok in the Pacific. Rommel had routed the British in North Africa – again. The Nazis were advancing rapidly in Russia, and U-boats, lurking just off the east coast were torpedoing ships by the dozen. Beachgoers out on Long Island could often see the smoke billowing out of burning ships just offshore. One tanker went down within sight of Rockaway Beach, barely ten miles from Brooklyn. With the war so close to home, Ezra had decided that he had to 'do his bit,' and join the Army.

Miriam understood Ez' reasons for signing up and honestly was not all that sad to see him leave. *Maybe going to war will make him grow up, she thought, and realize what's really important in life – his wife and home.* Yet, she simply could not imagine that he'd ever be killed, or even get injured. Ez moved through life with such ease and confidence that he seemed invulnerable to the dangers and frailties that threatened everyone else.

"I'm going to move back home while you're away," she said to Ez a couple of weeks before he reported for duty. Leah stood at the kitchen sink far enough away to give them privacy but close enough to hear every word.

"I thought you didn't like living at home. It'll be much quieter for you here with my mother. You can both rest after work, listen to the radio, take long walks."

"You're welcome to stay Mimi," said Leah poking her head around the corner. "I'd love the company," she said half-heartedly.

Miriam replied, "Thank you, but I'd like to spend some time with my family and it's closer to work." She took Ez's hand and led him outside, away from Leah. They stood under a leafy tree in the front yard. Ez took his hand from hers and pulled her into an embrace.

"You told me we would move to our own place. What happened? Now, I have to choose between your mother and my mother. Not much of a choice!"

"At least you'll be near Edna and Eddie, and you'll have your own apartment!"

Miriam laughed wryly, "That's a laugh. You know my mother well enough to know she'll be downstairs every day to spy on me!"

"You can always stay with my Ma. She's not so bad, is she?"

"No," said Miriam, "Your mother is a lovely woman but the apartment is too small. I'll never have any peace."

"Whatever you want, Kiddo. I'm sorry I have to leave but you understand. I'll send money you can put aside for college. How 'bout that? Something to look forward to when all this is over."

That made her smile. *Maybe things will be alright. Maybe he will miss me so much, he'll want to stay home in the evenings after the war.*

Then, he said, "I have to start packing. Will you help me?"

*****

Gussie thought about the new household arrangements. *Edna is seventeen now. She can move downstairs with Miriam while Ez is away. That will make things a bit easier for me.* Gussie remembered how she felt when she was seventeen and had just stepped off the boat at Ellis Island. *Edna's a child. She couldn't have traveled alone across the ocean. She's spoiled and coddled. Sam spoils all the children. I work too hard for them. She can be Miriam's problem for a while,* although she intended to make frequent visits to the girls downstairs to make sure they were doing what she expected of them.

Sam's family surname, Ryzhiy, meant red in Russian, but when he arrived in America, the name was unpronounceable to the intimidating men at the military style desks on Ellis Island, so it became Roth. Edna's red hair was proof that some long-forgotten Viking ancestor once sailed down the Dnepr River. Gussie warned Edna that she was pretty enough to get herself into trouble but Edna ignored her.

Before he left for the Army, Ez had to finalize some last-minute details at the Lion Match Company. He invited Edna to go to the city with him. Ez liked having Mimi's little sister around. He and Edna were a lot alike: good looking, rule breakers, and preoccupied with having fun. Unlike Mimi, Edna loved looking at the fashions in the department store windows. She said she especially liked Lord & Taylor and dreamed of having enough money to buy a dress with a matching hat there. Ez got a kick out of watching her window shop.

He suggested she sit on a bench in the lobby of his building while he went upstairs to his office. "You can have fun watching everyone rushing here and there," Ez said.

She sat on a bench, one leg crossed over the other, demure but provocative. Her brilliant red hair hung loose, parted on the side in Veronica Lake style. It shone in the light streaming through the front window. She was wearing a light blue pleated dress with a pocket over each breast and a matching belt at her slim waist. She examined her nails to see if they needed trimming and a new coat of polish.

In between thinking about her nails, she thought about where she'd like to go for lunch. Ez had said it was her choice "within reason." Ez was generous, perhaps too generous given he hardly ever seemed to take Miriam out anymore. She debated whether to prioritize her sister's finances or her own taste but decided Ez would soon be away in the service so she was doing him a favor by lunching with him.

She couldn't help but notice a young man rushing back and forth across the lobby. There were several women, probably secretaries, and older men in suits who passed her as she waited, but this man was young and incredibly good looking. She watched him sneak glances her way until he finally stopped right in front of her.

Aaron Cohen had been dashing around the building, crisscrossing the lobby, as he ran errands for his boss and conferred with colleagues in other parts of the building. He noticed Edna but was too preoccupied to initiate a conversation. Finally, it was nearing lunch time. He was walking more slowly as he headed back to his office to get his sandwich. He planned to sit outside and enjoy the cloudy summer day. He didn't mind the clouds, since they took the fire out of the typical New York hot summer days.

Now, strolling slowly through the lobby, Aaron had time to take a proper look at the girl. He admired her hair, then her legs, then the tiny white squares that accented her dress and the sharply cornered collar. He usually didn't pay attention to women's clothing, but this time was different. He wanted to remember every detail even if he never saw her again.

Aaron was twenty years old, tall, and handsome with a moustache that made him look dashing and daring. Yet, he was quiet, introverted and typically shy around girls, even those who tried everything to get his attention.

Knowing that he'd kick himself later if he didn't at least try to talk to the girl, Aaron stopped in front of her and blurted out "Hello," steeling himself against the possibility of rejection.

Edna was surprised by his effrontery but flattered by his attention. She liked to think of herself as flirtatious but now she heard Ma's voice in her head warning her about how dangerous boys could be. She loved pretending she was a movie star although she knew she couldn't act so confident in real life. The truth was that, although some people thought she was brazen because of her looks, Edna felt a little intimidated by guys, especially one like this who was not really a boy anymore. Without looking up at him, she rose from the bench to move to another several feet away and stared at her nails as if they were all that mattered in the world.

"I apologize for being so bold, Miss, but as they say, 'nothing ventured, nothing gained.' If I don't talk to you now, I might never see you again. I'm Aaron."

He stood still, not venturing to move to where she now sat on the other bench. He wanted her to have an easy getaway if that was her plan.

Just then, a man came off the elevator and walked toward the beautiful girl. He stopped when he saw Aaron. They looked at each other like cowboys at a gunfight. Aaron took a few steps back, ready to put on his hat and make an embarrassed exit. The man looked like he was wavering between introducing himself to Aaron and taking the girl away. Finally, he took the girl's hand and walked with her past Aaron, out of the building and onto the street. Aaron straightened his tie and jacket, chalked this one up to bad timing, and followed them into the street to find a bench and eat his sandwich. He was suddenly too depressed to enjoy the weather, but couldn't bear to go back to his office just yet.

"He's quite handsome, Edna," teased Ez as they walked up the block.

"He's cute, but a bit too forward. You know, at heart I'm not as modern as some girls. Besides what would Ma and Mimi say if I had a date with a stranger?"

"Isn't every new person a stranger at first? If you want me to find out who he is and a little about him, I can probably do that. It looks like he works in the same building. Are you interested, Kiddo?"

"Let me think about it over lunch. Where are we going?" said Edna, squeezing his arm, excited to be escorted by her handsome brother-in-law and pretend he was her boyfriend.

Ez didn't have much time to fulfill his promise. He was shipping out in a few days. After lunch at the automat (Ez's choice, not Edna's after all), he put her on the subway and walked back to his office building. When Ez reached it, he saw Jack, the black elevator operator, discreetly trying to have a smoke, leaning casually against the stone wall. He'd known Jack since he'd started working for Lion.

"Hey Jack," he said.

"Hey, Mr. Feldman! How was your lunch? Pretty girl but aint you married? Don't worry. I won't tell the missus," He laughed, flicking ashes from his uniform.

"She's my sister-in-law. Sweet, too. Listen, Jack. Did you see the guy flirting with her in the lobby? Tall, thin, looked a bit like Errol Flynn?"

"Yeah, I saw him. Nice fella. Quiet, but always says hi. Like you. Most people round here act like I'm parta the wall. What if they had to take the stairs?" He laughed.

"Too much work- the stairs- right Jack? Hey, do ya know anything about him?"

"You gonna slug the poor guy for talking to a pretty girl?"

"She liked him. Wants to know who he is. She doesn't go out with just anybody. Her mother would kill her and so would I!" Ez offered Jack another cigarette. He pocketed it for later.

"Yeah, he's a nice fella, like I said. Name's Aaron Cohen. Works for the paper company on the sixth floor. Tell him Jack put in a good word!"

"You got it. Thanks, Jack. Wanna take me up there, now that you're done with that smoke?"

Ez spoke to a few folks on the sixth floor who all seemed to like Aaron Cohen, whom they described as not exactly friendly, but "a nice guy."

"I don't know," he said to Mimi, that night after Edna had gone upstairs. "What d'ya think? Should I introduce the two? Give it my blessing?"

"I think you should tell my Pop and let him decide. You've got plenty to do in the next coupla days. You're not her father, ya know," she said.

"'Spose you're right, Kid. What will I do without you? You're the brains a this operation," he said, imitating Bogart, the actor.

"That's right and don't you forget it," she said. "When Edna comes down, you go on up and talk to Pop. But don't let Ma hear you. She likes you and Mac, but no one else!"

Sam didn't trust Ez very much but if Edna was interested in this man, he saw no harm in a date or two. Ez told his friend at Lion to find Aaron on the sixth floor and tell him "You can call the redhead you met in the lobby. Her Pop gave you the okay."

*****

When Edna brought Aaron home after dating him for a few months, Gussie thought, *he's just as handsome as Ez, but so shy! He's barely spoken a word to me or Sam. But… he has a job.* She looked at the ceiling and muttered to herself, "Gottze dank, thank you." This boy was younger than Mac or Ez but looked older. *Something around the eyes,* she thought. Even so, she didn't like him. He didn't charm her like Ez had. He hardly paid her any attention!

Gussie liked Ez better than Aaron because he brought her small gifts and wasn't so standoffish. "You can't trust handsome men," she told Edna while pointing out that Ez was the exception. Miriam who overheard the comment had laughed, saying, "When I married Ez, you told me he'd probably run off with other women because he was too good looking for me!" Gussie scoffed. She had grown stout since Eddie's birth but Ez always complimented her in Yiddish, and teased her like she was a beautiful young thing just off the boat.

After they'd met, Sam was skeptical of Edna's choice, but he thought Aaron a better sort than Ez, whom he'd guessed from the start would make Miriam unhappy. For all Miriam's intelligence, she fell for the first handsome guy who'd swept her off her feet. Whether or not she realized it, Edna had picked someone who was a good match for her ebullience, someone who could ground her.

CHAPTER NINE

1943

Gussie objected loudly when Edna announced that Aaron had proposed. But here she was making over Miriam's wedding dress for Edna. Edna wanted a new dress but Gussie said the fabric was too expensive and a new one was a waste of money. Wartime rationing made buying something new to wear only once beyond anyone's comprehension. Even getting enough fabric for a dress could be difficult.

The newspapers were full of news about the devastation in Europe. In February, Germany had been defeated at Stalingrad. Americans rejoiced. In May, the allies finished off Rommel's army in North Africa, and in July, the Americans and English invaded Sicily. Benito Mussolini, the Italian dictator, was overthrown and Italy switched sides. Now people said, *"That's one down and two to go,"* referring to Germany and Japan.

There were good reasons to be hopeful and Aaron reveled in them while Edna suffered her mother's efforts to prepare the wedding dress. Ma grabbed Edna at the most inopportune moments to tell her to try on the dress. She scolded Edna as she pinned and tucked. Sometimes the pins stuck her as Ma hurriedly adapted the fabric to her frame. Edna cried out each time she felt the sharpness of a pin and cried whenever Ma screeched at her about how uncooperative she was or how little she seemed to care that Gussie was being taken away from other chores to alter the dress. Like her sister, Edna knew better than to argue. She counted the days until the wedding.

They married in September. Aaron hoped to stay out of the war. He'd been promoted to salesman. He was marrying a beautiful woman and his life was finally taking off.

Like Mac and Dottie and Miriam and Ez, Edna and Aaron married under the chuppah in the synagogue on the corner. Sam walked Edna down the aisle. Mac sent a telegram congratulating the couple and money to pay for a bottle of champagne.

Aaron moved Edna into his bedsit while they discussed where to live. Edna didn't want to work as a secretary anymore. She'd waited dutifully for a husband. To go back to secretarial work would not only mean drudgery but the other girls might think she was still single or worse yet, a failure at marriage. She preferred to take in sewing to augment Aaron's salary. In this, Gussie had been a willing teacher. She took great pride in the tailoring she'd learned in Poland and remembered how hard it was to learn, especially with icy cold fingers in the winter.

Gussie had been teaching her daughters the art of sewing since they'd learned to walk. She required an hour of practicing every day, time they would have preferred to be outdoors, playing tag or jumping rope. Aunt Fannie had taught both girls to cook. Once a week, she went over to the apartment or the girls went to her house and Fannie gave them cooking lessons. She was no more creative with spices and ingredients than Gussie was, but she helped the girls understand how to take basic ingredients and make them into something mouthwatering. Miriam never took to sewing but she loved to cook. Edna was a natural seamstress. By the time she was ten, she was updating her clothes in the latest fashion.

CHAPTER TEN

1944

Aaron held out as long as he could against pressure from friends and relatives to enlist, but was drafted into the Army anyway. He would be going to England and couldn't tell Edna exactly what he would be doing there. He didn't know himself. After his induction, the Army gave him aptitude and intelligence tests, and told him he'd be doing secret work. He warned Edna his letters would be sporadic, but he gave her a contact she could call to confirm he was safe. Aaron said he'd likely be safe behind a desk.

"I don't see why you have to go at all," whined Edna.

"I have no choice. Besides, it's the right thing to do. Hopefully, it'll be over soon and I'll be home before you know it."

"But you won't be here. That's the important part. What will I do while you're gone?"

"You could move back in with your sister. Ez is sure to be away a long time yet. I'd like to know you're with your family while I'm away. Won't you continue to sew? With all the rationing, it seems like there are a lot of women who want you to sew for them. But you don't have to. I'll be making decent money."

"I haven't told my mother I'm sewing. I'm worried she'll try to take over and correct everything I do. It's getting harder to hide it from her."

"I can't help you with that, darling. But I trust you'll manage. You always do," he said lifting her off the floor and smacking her on the lips.

*****

Edna and Miriam shared the first-floor apartment in their parents' house. Eddie frequently came down and flopped on the couch in the living room. He used the bathroom upstairs so his sisters could have the one on the first floor. One corner of Edna's bedroom was reserved for her small tailoring business. She had a metal mannequin and a basket of assorted brassieres and shoes her clients could use while trying on clothes. Whenever she heard her mother on the stairs, she threw a blanket over the mannequin and pushed the basket and whatever she was working on into the closet. Ma would be proud she was sewing but would want to inspect every stitch.

Eddie's job was to gather the loose threads that stuck to the thin rug every day and throw them in the incinerator. Miriam couldn't hide her cooking and Ma always showed up just as she started to assemble her ingredients. Gussie inspected every vegetable, marrow bone, and spice Miriam proposed to use, tossing some in the trash, others back in the cupboard, and finally a few in a pot she'd brought with her.

"Neyn, neyn," said Gussie, shaking her head dismissively.

"Ma, please. I'm cooking, not you. Please Ma, go back upstairs. Pop should be home any minute. He'll be looking for you."

"What do you know other than what I or Fanny tried to teach you? You know nothing. I'm a good cook, so I'll show you. Now listen and watch me!" Ma yelled in Yiddish.

Miriam threw her hands up. "I don't want to listen to you or watch you. I want you to please go upstairs now, Ma," she said quietly, reluctant to turn this into a shouting match.

"And you?" asked Gussie of Edna standing in the doorway of her bedroom.

"Please, Ma. Let Miriam cook. I like her cooking. You can cook for us when we come upstairs."

"Eh. You both treat your mama this way," Ma yelled again, throwing the cooking ingredients on the floor. "How did I deserve daughters like you? I'm ashamed."

Both girls were silent as Gussie shuffled to the door, making sure to step on the food that had fallen to the floor and bang a few pots before leaving.

"What'll we do next time, Mimi?" asked Edna. "You know she won't take no for an answer."

"No, she won't," laughed Miriam. "But it's funny to watch her get so mad."

Edna laughed with her as Miriam picked the food up off the ground, washed it in the sink, and prepared to cook.

*****

Eddie hid from his mother in the basement studio Pop had built for him. There, he could escape her endless criticism and didn't have to see her do embarrassing things. Whenever anyone came over, whether it was a neighbor asking to borrow something or one of the guys who worked for Pop, Ma did something embarrassing like swinging a dead chicken around her head while chanting some old Yiddish incantation. On the other hand, they were probably used to such things in their own homes. If Eddie was in the basement, he assumed Ma forgot he was home. He liked it that way.

The studio made Eddie feel like a real artist. Pop seemed to like Eddie's work and said he was proud of him. Sometimes, he visited Miss Marcus, still unmarried, at the elementary school to show her his progress. She was always encouraging, just like Pop and Mimi.

Gussie didn't like Eddie having a studio or Sam encouraging him in a useless profession. She wanted him to work selling things, down the block at the Robert Hall department store. She growled when Sam and the girls gushed over how talented he was.

She was glad to have only one child at home but, on the other hand, she didn't like the loneliness- a new sensation. Sam stayed out later than before and Eddie came home or upstairs only for food and sometimes, to sleep. She didn't mind when her neighbors stopped by to ask for a missing ingredient for one of their recipes but she didn't invite them to sit or have coffee. She didn't know what to say to them.

Other than Mac, she didn't like her children but she had become used to the noise they made. Now, she was mostly home alone. When Sam came home, he tried to hug and kiss her but she would have none of it. *Who does he think I am? Some floozy, waiting for him to come home?* She was in bed, turned away from his side and silent as he got undressed. She always waited till morning to yell at him for drinking. He never said a word or yelled back at her. He just looked at her and left for work.

She remembered how angry she was when Eddie was born that the peace she craved would have to be put off for another several years. Now that she finally had it, she felt old and unsure of herself. Her daughters didn't appreciate her efforts to help them. Mac, Ez, and Aaron were gone. She worried Mac would die in the war. Already, people on the street had received the dreaded telegram informing them of a son's death or injury. She knew because she sat by the window in the afternoons and watched the Western Union boy deliver them.

One day, when the boy rang the bell downstairs, Gussie began to run around her apartment, frantic. It was mid-morning. She was still doing her housekeeping chores. No one else was home. She began to cry and pull at her hair. The bell kept ringing. Finally, she pressed the buzzer to allow him in and walked slowly down the stairs to greet him.

He was young, about thirteen, too skinny. Under other circumstances, Gussie would have given him a knish to take with him to fatten him up. She had a soft spot for other people's children, if they looked ill or unhappy. The boy's black hair hung over his eyes; he glanced up at her through the silky screen as she descended toward him.

"Good morning, Mam. Telegram," he started to say.

"Give me that," said Gussie, in broken English as she grabbed for the envelope.

The boy wasn't surprised. He'd been working for three months, delivering telegrams after school and on weekends. He studied the people to whom he gave telegrams. Some walked slowly down the stairs as this woman had. Others stood far apart from him as if the distance would prevent bad news from reaching them. Then, there were those who ran to him and grabbed the envelope, trying to get that first horrible moment over quickly. He felt invisible. But somehow, a coin was usually dropped into his hand when he got ready to leave. He wanted to reach out and give comfort but understood it wasn't his comfort they wanted. They didn't see him and wouldn't remember him although every other detail of this day from this moment forward would be burned in their memories forever.

"Read it," Gussie commanded. She handed the telegram back to the boy.

"The secretary of war desires me to express his deep regret that your husband Ezra Feldman was injured on his ship when it was sunk. He is alive. When further details or other information are available, you will be promptly notified."

Gussie had forgotten to grab a coin to tip the boy. She nodded to him as he left the building. Then, she slipped the telegram under Miriam's door. At least, for now, Mac was safe.

CHAPTER ELEVEN

1945

Germany had surrendered. Miriam and Edna grabbed Eddie and they rushed to Times Square to join the celebrations. There were happy people as far as the eye could see. They waved flags and hugged strangers. The excitement was palpable and seemingly endless. After a while, they got back on the subway with thousands of others and hung on till their stop. It wasn't till they were walking back toward the house that they began to talk about what it might be like when Mac, Ez, and Eli came home.

Eddie listened to his sisters' chatter about what they would wear when they first saw their husbands again and where they hoped to live. He was glad to see them so happy. People they knew from the neighborhood waved and stopped to hug them. Eddie wondered if so many people would ever be so happy at the same time again. But he also thought of the war with the Japanese still raging in the Pacific. He thought it might be a while before the men came home but at least now they could begin to plan for the future.

He loved his sisters and hoped all would work out as they were happily planning. Whenever he was home, he took time to talk with them and do whatever he could to help out. He and Pop often went downstairs together so they could be with the girls and avoid Ma's scorn.

Eddie stayed away from home now as much as he could. He went to the Police Athletic League after school when he didn't have Bar Mitzvah practice. His friend Babe Merola, an Italian Catholic in the neighborhood, invited Eddie to eat Sunday "gravy" with his family. Eddie laughed to himself when he thought about how Babe got his nickname. He had a round face like a baby and laughed a lot. He looked a bit like the actor, Edward G. Robinson. But when all his hair, even his eyebrows, came off when his father's dry-cleaning store exploded, that really clinched it. He became "Babe."

Babe didn't mind that Eddie was Jewish, although a lot of Italian and Irish kids thought Jewish kids were wimps and bullied them. Babe's mother made the traditional spaghetti and red gravy every Sunday, only for family. Eddie was thrilled to be considered family and to get a break from his mother's limited Eastern European repertoire. He felt ashamed that he couldn't reciprocate. His mother didn't welcome Eddie's friends and would certainly have gotten mad if he invited anyone to dinner.

With two other Jewish guys, Arnie Siegel and Norm Weisman, they made a foursome who palled around together trying to avoid going home until dark. They liked the Police Athletic League because there was always something to do and no one could beat them up there, except if it was in the boxing ring - which Eddie loved. He felt angry a lot. Boxing helped. He could punch someone else while pretending he was punching the person or thing that made him mad. But he didn't always know what that was that made his anger simmer until he felt like hitting someone. He fought with himself to control it. He followed the fights of Bummy Davis, a famous Jewish boxer from Brownsville who also seemed angry and was tough just like Eddie wanted to be.

Eddie thought he was pretty good on the parallel bars at the PAL's gym. After a few months there, he no longer felt like the scrawny Jewish kid who couldn't defend himself. When he wasn't at school or working on his drawing in the basement, he spent a lot of time at the PAL. He made sure no one in the family knew he was boxing but when Pop said, "Hey, the boychik has muscles!" Eddie felt proud.

He felt much better around the bullies at school and in the neighborhood but felt shy around pretty girls. Mimi said, "We don't bite, you know," when they were walking along and passed a girl who'd said, "Hi Eddie."

"You should have stopped to say hello. Girls like that," said Mimi, after he had walked by in silence.

"I don't think girls like me, Mimi. I'm skinny and not much to look at. They like the bigger guys."

"How'd you know? You're smart. Girls like that, too. Have any of them seen you on the parallel bars or looked at your drawings?"

"Nah. They don't want to see my drawings. Leave me alone, Mimi, will ya? Let's go to Katz' and get some rugelach, on me."

"Since when do you have money?" she said, but knew better than to expect an answer.

Eddie was fifteen with blonde curls and a nice nose, not yet misshapen by fists. He didn't tell Mimi that Pop slipped him a couple of dollars every now and then. Reading had become an addiction like art and boxing. He loved to go to the school and public libraries. Ma yelled at him for cluttering the house with books.

One day, the gym teacher asked him to give a performance on the parallel bars to the entire school. Eddie was flattered and thrilled to show off to the girls but anxious too, because he'd only ever "performed" in the boxing ring. He secretly liked to imagine he was a professional boxer and had even come up with his ring name - *The Blond Tiger*. So far, he'd taken a few beatings, but he never lost. How was he expected to perform gymnastics? It would be him alone in his gym clothes- a tank top and shorts. *Not a pretty sight,* he thought.

"Eddie's gonna show us how you're supposed to go on the parallel bars, aren't ya Eddie?" said the gym teacher, an athletic looking man with a stern manner. "Gather round," he said to the boys in the class.

The parallel bars were set up on a mat on the polished wooden gymnasium floor. Eddie heard a few guys snigger. "His hair weighs more than he does," said one. Now, Eddie was glad to show them what's what.

He dusted his hands with some powder the gym teacher gave him, stretched his arms and legs just for show, and mounted the bars. He grabbed one bar with each hand and extended his arms, then he swayed back and forth a few times before pulling himself up and swinging his legs up. He heard an intake of breath. Maybe it was one of the guys who'd made fun of him. He did a few flips on the bars before he came back to his starting position.

"Well done, Eddie," said the gym teacher. "Okay, now you guys try it." There was nervous laughter. Eddie loved it. A couple of guys shook his hand and said, "You're good," as he took his place in the crowd.

No, school isn't so bad, he thought. Home was another story. Eddie alternated sleeping across the two chairs in the living room and on the couch in his sisters' apartment. He frequently stayed with them for supper, laughing about Ma behind her back.

*****

Whenever he could, Sam went downstairs to see Edna and Miriam. They drank tea together and ate pickled herring and boiled eggs. The girls were concerned because he had become increasingly bloated. Tiny red capillaries decorated his cheeks. His nose was bulbous and his belly distended. Yet, the girls didn't blame him for drinking. They could escape Ma but his options were limited.

Sam cherished time with his children and missed the men in the family terribly. He prayed for their safety and recovery by the living room window. He wanted to go to synagogue and pray with the other fathers who missed their sons, but he could not bring himself to go. He knew it wasn't logical but he held God responsible for the death of his brother and other relatives and neighbors during the pogroms back in Russia. Sam had been saved more than once thanks to his quick-witted father who'd frequently put himself in harm's way to protect him. He had also been disgusted to see their neighbors simply accept what was happening to them instead of resisting or fighting back. The synagogue brought back those terrible times. He preferred to pray alone.

Although the war in Europe had ended, Sam still worried about Mac, Ez, and Eli. He also worried he wouldn't live to see Eddie, his favorite, the one who made his life worth living, grow up to adulthood. He could tell his strength wasn't what it used to be, and the alcohol wasn't doing him any favors. He tried not to let the liquor change his behavior. He was not a mean drunk. Instead, he felt more subdued, quieter. When he drank, he could feel his sense of humor dry up; he just wanted to crawl into a dark hole.

Sam harbored a lot of guilt. He'd escaped from Russia before the first World War, the Communists, and famine had devastated his family. He'd lost touch with them years ago. *Only the Almighty knows what happened to my family after the Nazis came to Russia four years ago. The newsreels and stories about the concentration camps are terrifying. What happened to my parents and the rest of the family? It's been so long. they might not remember me even if they are alive.*

Sam also felt guilty because he'd married a shrew and subjected his children to her endless screeches and nastiness, and because he knew he was drinking himself to death and wouldn't be around very long.

Sam worried about Miriam; she wasn't well. He knew about Ez's philandering, having spotted him at a bar with another woman shortly before he'd left for the war. He wasn't sure if Ez saw him but he held his tongue. He thought he should stay out of Mimi's marriage. He prayed that Ez had grown out of chasing skirts would return from war to be a good husband.

Sam felt guilty too, because he knew how smart Miriam was and that she wanted to be more and do more than to be a housewife and mother. He wished he had the money to get her good medicine and send her to college. He'd try to support her if her marriage failed. Mac would be okay. He was smart and tough. If he could only survive until the end of the war and come home even half the man he was when he left, he and Dottie and their future children would be alright. Sam thought he would leave his construction company to Mac. It would be in good hands.

He was not so sure about Edna and Aaron. They seemed a good match but someone in that family should have a decent brain. Maybe Aaron was smarter than he seemed to be. They didn't pick dummies for secret work, so he must have something upstairs. Edna was a doll in every way. Sam loved her very much, but she needed attention and coddling. She and Mimi seemed to get along although they were very different people. At least they had each other when Gussie became too much. They could escape by enjoying each other's company. Sam had no one to talk to about his life or about Gussie so he told his troubles to the bottle.

Gussie certainly had plenty to say.

"What's wrong with you?" she'd ask in Yiddish, following him around whenever he was home.

"Nothing, my dearest. I'm fine," he'd answer and turn away.

Gussie nagged him and Eddie more than ever now. She cried almost constantly, worried about Mac, still far away. Earlier in the year, he'd been in a horrible battle on some island called Iwo Jima. She knew that before that, he'd been lucky to survive another battle with the Japanese at Peleliu. *How long can his luck last?* She wondered. *Maybe now, he'll come home.*

Ez had survived the injuries he'd had when his ship sunk, but suffered a relapse of the tuberculosis he'd had as a child and was in some army hospital in Colorado. She worried he might not make a full recovery. Aaron remained in England and no one knew much about how he was doing. He rarely wrote; Edna didn't share much when he did.

*****

V-J Day came a few months after Germany surrendered. Now, with Japan's surrender, World War II was finally and completely over. *Now, Mac will come home,* thought Dottie. The last letter she'd received from him was after Iwo Jima, sometime in March. It was more of a note than a letter. In it, he said he was alright and hoped he'd be home soon. He said he loved her. That was all. His handwriting looked like a tired scrawl, but she was very relieved to get it.

After she'd read it a few times, she rode the trolley over to show it to Gussie and Sam so they'd know he was safe. Dottie read the note to them, but Gussie insisted on seeing it for herself even though she couldn't read. It wasn't until much later, when Dottie had her own children, that she thought back to that day and finally understood why Gussie needed to hold that note from Mac. It must have been as if his essence was still on the paper, that she could somehow inhale it or gather it into herself and keep it safe.

The day Mac came home, he went directly to the apartment he'd moved Dottie into before he'd left to join the Marines. He buzzed from inside the front door but didn't respond when he heard Dottie's voice asking, "Who is it?" She buzzed him in anyway.

Dottie didn't know who was coming up the stairs. She assumed it was a neighbor who'd forgotten their key. That happened often, as much to her as anyone else. She never worried about her safety during the day, especially on a beautiful Sunday in September. She was in the kitchen cooking for the week. She had attended Sabbath dinner Friday night with her family on Long Island and stayed overnight returning late Saturday evening.

She had a small brisket with a few potatoes and carrots in the oven and was preparing to bake some cookies for her lunch bag. Then came a knock she recognized, two hard taps and two light taps. That was the knock she and Mac agreed to when they married. It was also the signal they used when they wanted to leave his mother's place. One of them would tap on the table.

"It can't be," Dottie said out loud, swiftly removing her apron and touching up her hair, "It can't be," she said again, shaking and starting to sob.

"Oh yes it can, yes it damn well can!" yelled Mac from the other side of the door.

"I can't believe it! Mac, is it really you?"

"Yes, my love. Please open the door, already. People are starting to stare." All the neighbors were standing in their doorways; some were moving toward Mac. He didn't recognize them all. He'd been gone so long with only two leaves in the years since Pearl Harbor.

Neighbors started pushing each other to greet the returning Marine before Dottie had a chance to embrace him. She told herself that she would have him forever so she should try to be patient and let him enjoy a hero's welcome. She stood in the doorway to the apartment, wringing her hands, rocking up and down on her toes, smiling so hard she felt her mouth stretching wider than it had ever been.

Her dirty blonde hair was swept up into a ponytail to avoid getting it into her cooking. She was wearing a multicolored house dress that made her look bloated and obscured her hourglass shape. She wasn't wearing makeup because it was Sunday and she had nowhere to be. As she watched Mac laughingly greet the neighbors, many of whom he'd never had a chance to know before he left, she touched up her hair again and pinched her cheeks and lips. Mac turned to look at Dottie standing in the doorway whenever one neighbor who'd shaken his hand or given him a hug finally stepped away to allow another to take their place. Finally, the neighbors drifted away having enjoyed welcome news and some excitement on an otherwise lazy Sunday.

"Mac, why didn't you tell me you were coming? I look a fright!"

"Were you expecting someone else?" said Mac with a wink, lifting Dottie off the ground with arms so strong she felt her ribs becoming sore. They moved together into the apartment as Mac kicked the door closed behind him. He covered her with kisses and then stepped back to finally have a good look at her.

"You're a sight for sore eyes. Just as gorgeous as when we married."

"What? Oh Mac, look at me. I didn't know you were coming. I would have gotten dressed, put some make up on, run a comb through my hair!"

"You're perfect as you are. Natural, the way I thought of you all these years," said Mac, now subdued, his energy was rapidly fading.

"Here Honey," said Dottie, having recovered a little bit from all the excitement, "Let me take your jacket and your shoes. Are you hungry or would you rather go lie down? You must be so exhausted, I can't imagine."

"I don't know which I am more of, hungry or tired. Will you come lie down with me until I fall asleep? I just need a short nap." Looking around, he mustered a light laugh, "Where's the bedroom?"

*****

Shots rang out in the early morning in November, just before Thanksgiving. Mac and Dottie heard about it on the radio as they ate breakfast that Monday morning. Mac got up from the table and called Mimi, who'd been thrilled when Ez had a phone installed.

"Mimi, run upstairs and get Eddie," said Mac.

"What's going on, Mac?" Mimi asked.

"Don't worry, we're fine. Just get him on the phone, will ya?" Mac munched on his toast as he waited.

"What's going on, Mac?" asked Eddie, sounding a little out of breath. "I was eating. What's the emergency?"

"Did you hear, Kid? Turn on the radio," said Mac.

"No, Pop's still sleeping. Hold on. Mimi, turn on the radio," Eddie called out.

"Bummy Davis is dead, Eddie. He was murdered last night!"

Eddie was silent for a few minutes but Mac could hear the radio in the background. They'd moved on to other news.

"Did you hear me, Kid?"

"I can't believe it. What happened? Did they say?"

"They were robbers. They came into his bar. Davis punched one of em for being rude to another guy in the bar. They shot Davis three times! Three times, Eddie and he still kept coming. He chased em to their car but they shot him again. He died in the road."

Eddie gasped, "That's horrible. I can't believe it!" He was crestfallen that his hero was gone and ashamedly wiped away a tear that had appeared in the corner of his eye. But, in barely a second, Eddie had mastered himself and stood up straight again with his chest stuck out. "Boy was Bummy tough, chasing them off like that with three bullets in him. I want to be just like him. Thanks for telling me, Mac."

"No Eddie, you don't want to be just like him. Box like him, okay, but he was no good, Eddie. Look what happened to the guy. Please tell me you get it," said Mac.

Mac could hear Ma calling down the stairs for Eddie to go to school or he'll be late.

"I get it! I get it!"

"Sorry, Kid. I know how much you admired the guy."

"Yeah. Gotta go, Ma's yelling."

CHAPTER TWELVE

1946

Miriam went to visit Ez in the hospital in far off Colorado. She took one train after another, barely able to breathe due to all the smoke and coal dust. After three days, she arrived exhausted and sicker than she'd been in years. A bus took her to a boarding house Ez had found through one of the nurses. He'd written to Mimi that it was cheap, but clean, and that patients and family members often stayed there. Miriam knocked at the front door wishing she looked and felt more presentable.

A young woman, all in white, answered the door. Miriam almost fell into her arms.

"Oh my, you don't look well at all. No, not at all. Let me help you," said the young nurse as she helped Miriam into the sitting room.

"You're going to be alright," she said as she maneuvered Miriam into the most comfortable chair in the room, took her shoes off, planted Miriam's feet on the ottoman she dragged from the corner of the room and loosened her collar. The nurse did all this quickly and efficiently as she had been trained to do, muttering comforting words as she worked, noting Miriam's pale face and blue lips, her heaving chest, and her moist skin.

"I'm going to get you a glass of water. You just sit still there and catch your breath."

Miriam didn't know what hit her. The girl was like a whirlwind, scooping her up and putting her down again without so much as asking Miriam's name or why she had knocked. Miriam was grateful. Here was someone who simply acted when that was what was needed. She didn't stand around asking questions or contemplating her navel trying to decide what to do. She already liked the woman, who was younger than Miriam but as efficient and professional as anyone twice her age.

"What's going on Edith?" Miriam heard someone calling from deep inside the house. "What's all the fuss about?' The woman had a thick rich voice like an opera singer. Miriam found it soothing but also interesting. She wanted to know this faceless person. She heard mumbling in response to the faceless voice. It sounded like Edith was telling the other woman what was going on while she was running the water for Miriam. Edith hurried back into the room holding a jelly jar of water filled to the brim.

"Here now. You drink this. Not too fast now. Is that better? Are you feeling a bit better?" Edith paused to allow her patient to speak, as the woman whose voice Miriam had heard entered the room.

"What's happened? Who is this lady? Is she alright?"

"I'm fine now, thank you," said Miriam, trying to push a sentence into the space left by the two women. Her words came out in short gasps. She took another sip of water before trying again.

"Thank you for your help. I'm so sorry to be troubling you," she said to Edith who was bending over her, her fingers on Miriam's wrist. "Really, I'm much better now, thank you," Miriam said again beginning to rise from the chair.

"No, no, miss. You need a few more minutes of rest. No one is rushing you," said Edith as she gave the other woman a backward glance that said *All in good time.*

Miriam recovered and introduced herself. Edith was a nurse who'd come to the boarding house from the hospital to deliver a message to one of her patient's relatives. She had been about to leave when Miriam knocked on the door. Ruth was the other woman and the owner of the house. She'd been expecting Miriam and gave her a quick hug and a warm welcome. Ruth said that she had been a nurse herself, in the last world war. Now, she boarded hospital visitors or patients who needed to be close to the hospital while they waited for surgeries or treatments.

Ruth showed Miriam to her room. Edith called to them as they slowly ascended the stairs, "Nice to meet you, Miriam. See you later, Ruthie."

Miriam rested before washing and changing her clothes to visit Ez. "There's a lung specialist at the hospital. I could arrange an appointment for you, if you like. He's a good friend. He often comes for supper," said Ruth when Miriam came down the stairs.

"If it's not too much trouble, I'd be grateful. No one at home seems to know what to do with me. But I don't think I can pay him."

"He's a good friend and a good doctor. He won't expect any money. Don't give it a second thought. I'll know something when you're back here for supper."

Miriam dressed to remind Ez she was his wife and to ignore the pretty nurses he must see every day. Her navy-blue cross V-neck swing dress with white trim suited her hair and complexion. She wore a double string of faux white pearls with matching earrings she'd borrowed from Edna. For the first time in her life, she felt very fashionable.

She walked the two blocks to the hospital where she was directed to the porch. Ez was sitting up in a bed lined along the wall with several others, all filled with veterans, young men who used to be models of good health but were now gray and pallid, weak and wan. Ez was the exception. He sat up in his bed looking like he'd just won a pie eating contest. His cheeks were flushed, his smile broad.

"I've been waiting for you. The nurses keep telling me too much excitement isn't good for me but I can't help it." He wore green pajamas with thin white stripes. *Only Ez could look killer diller in pajamas,* she thought.

"Hey guys, this is my wife. Isn't she gorgeous?"

"Oh Ez, what have they done to you?" said Mimi, reaching out to hug him.

A nurse who looked like Rita Hayworth stood nearby scowling. "That's enough now, Missus. Ez, would you like to put on your robe and take a walk on the lawn with your wife?"

Ez practically jumped out of bed but the nurse handed him a robe and cane and told him to walk slowly. They walked onto the grass and found two chairs to settle in.

"Thanks for coming, Honeybunch. I'm sure it was a rough trip but I've dreamed about this day. It's what's kept me going," he grabbed her hand, looking around to see if any stern nurses lingered nearby. Surely, one could hold hands.

"How are you Ez, really? You look well. What does the doctor say? When can you come home?"

"I think it'll be a few more months. He said I'm getting better but I still get these fevers. I may look well but my rosy cheeks are from fever. The nurse gave me an aspirin just before you arrived. It should get better soon," he said quietly. Then with a laugh, "Let's not talk about me. I want to hear about you and all that's going on at home. Let's talk about what we'll do when I go home. How's little Eddie and your folks? How's your Pop's business going? Have you seen my mother?"

"Leah is fine. She talks about you constantly and can't wait for you to come home. She wants us to live with her again, Ez. Please, let's not. We need a place of our own. Anyway, Eddie's sixteen now, can you believe it? He's a good kid. He's been a big help. Whenever Ma scolds me, Eddie makes me laugh."

"Sixteen? I'm glad this war's over. It seemed like it would never end. Eddie might have been drafted! Is he still drawing? When I get back, I'm gonna see if my boss can get him a job."

"Really? He would love that. Ma can be so mean to him. At least he has a couple of places to hide from her, in the basement or in our apartment."

"How is my favorite Polish yenta, your mother?"

"Same as always. She still doesn't know Edna is sewing in the apartment. She must think we just have a lot of visitors! All the women who come for dress fittings!"

"That's all for now. It's time for the patients to nap, Missus. You can come back tomorrow," said the stern looking nurse who'd been on the porch.

"A nap," said Ez after the nurse left them to bother the next patient on the lawn, "they treat us like babies and God forbid there should be any variation in the schedule!"

"All I care about is that you get well and come home soon. You do whatever they say. I'll be back tomorrow. I'll try to come a bit earlier. My last train was late."

"I love you, Mimi," he said as they walked arm in arm back to the porch. Several nurses were shuttling the patients inside.

"I love you, too," said Miriam, handing him over to one of the nurses before she started walking back to the boarding house for another rest before supper.

*****

The next morning, she sat in the doctor's office. The office was large and lined with cases of medical books. A humidor stood next to the mahogany desk. The doctor extracted a cigar from it before sitting down behind the desk, his starched white coat open to reveal a brown waistcoat and a gold watch chain.

"Good morning, Mrs. Feldman. I'm Doctor Westland. I understand you're here visiting your husband in our tuberculosis ward. I know him. He's one of my patients. A fine young man. He keeps everyone's spirits up. I don't doubt he'll be joining you at home before too long. He's making good progress. As for you, well I wish I had better news to impart," He paused to prepare his words.

He never liked giving bad news to patients and often wondered how some of his colleagues seemed to enjoy the power they had when giving bad news. They managed to look serious and empathetic when they told a young mother her child was dying or an old man his wife of thirty years was terminal, but he knew they weren't always sincere. They were the doctors and knew best. He'd seen them deliver bad news, then quickly rise to leave the bereaved alone, until a kindly nurse sat down next to them to take one of their hands in her own. He knew that at one time they'd cared about what they were saying and many still did. But others had become callous after saying the same thing again and again until the words held little meaning for them. To the people to whom his colleagues spoke, the doctor's words were as exalted as those etched into the stone tablets of the ten commandments. They heard the words but rarely absorbed them until the doctor went away and the nurse slowly repeated them, word by word until they were understood. By then, it was too late to ask the doctor questions, even if they had questions to ask.

Miriam sat holding her gloves, legs crossed at the ankles. She'd worn her second-best dress, ready to visit Ez in the afternoon. She felt alone and cowardly.

"Looking at the X-ray we just took, I see that you have scar tissue on your lungs from asthma. I'm afraid it's only going to get worse. It's important you conserve your energy as much as possible," Doctor Westland said quietly. He believed in giving patients and family members sufficient time to understand what they were facing and to express their fear, however it chose to manifest itself.

He smiled and said, "There are new medicines in the works. I'm sure your doctor at home will make sure you have them when they become available. I wish I could do more but I'd be happy to have you visit again, anytime, if I can do anything to help you."

The doctor waited, "Do you have any questions?" Miriam was looking down at her hands with their flat nailbeds from too little oxygen for so many years.

"No, thank you for taking the time to see me this morning, Doctor," She said as she raised her head, stood, then straightened her dress, and stretched out her hand.

He saw the tears in her eyes. She blinked rapidly to dispel them.

"Someday, we'll have better treatments. Hang on, Mrs. Feldman. Please don't lose hope. I haven't."

*****

Aaron came home in 1946 and soon went back to work. He couldn't talk about what he'd done in Europe and hoped Edna wouldn't care. He was just glad to be home, safe and physically unharmed though he knew he was damaged inside. She wondered why he came home well after Mac had returned. Edna and her family thought he'd "flown a desk" but that wasn't true. The things he'd seen and done in France and Germany haunted him. He wasn't allowed to talk with anyone about them, so he had no outlet for his trauma or regrets.

Talking to people was difficult. He felt like pretending to fit back into the real world took more energy than he could spare. He used up a lot of it fighting back against the memories that swept over him like a tsunami and threatened to drown him. He wondered how many deaths he'd contributed to and if the lives he'd saved outweighed them. What little energy he had left for human interaction was reserved for Edna and his customers. Aaron only hoped that he could make a new life for himself and Edna, although he'd become a very different person than he was when they married.

Edna thought he looked as handsome as ever, if a little thinner and even quieter. Mac knew enough not to interrogate Aaron, but Sam and the women kept framing and reframing their questions hoping he would answer them and satisfy their curiosity. They finally stopped when he began to leave the room whenever anyone brought up the subject of what he did in the war.

Aaron moved into the first-floor apartment, where he and Edna shared the second bedroom. Aaron felt a little cramped and was uncomfortable having his sister-in-law in the next room and Eddie popping in and out without warning. One day after three months at home, Aaron said, "Let's move out to the suburbs, out onto Long Island. We can buy a house there." It was a Sunday. Neither of them had to work.

He and Edna, resplendent in a burnt orange dress that matched her hair, were sitting on a park bench near their home enjoying the scents of spring. Aaron had picked up potato latkes from the local deli. He slathered one with applesauce and handed it to Edna.

"Oh Aaron, I'd love a house, but can we afford it? My father says there are a lot of new homes being built out there. Do you think we could get one of those? How much do they cost?"

"Slow down, Babe. One question at a time," he said slathering the rest of the applesauce on his own latke. "We can use the money from the GI Bill plus some money I saved before the war."

"Maybe I could have a garden and a yard for our children to play in," said Edna becoming more excited.

"How 'bout house first, children after? Okay?" he smiled at her, pleased to see her happy. He'd known her family would take care of her but had worried about their marriage because they hadn't been together very long before he'd been drafted.

Edna stood holding her latke in one hand, the wax paper soaked with grease. She took a few steps through the grass and turned back toward him, her dress swirling around her shapely legs "What do you think we'll have, all boys or all girls or a few of each?'

"Now you're really getting ahead of yourself! Here, sit down and have a black and white. They were yesterdays, on sale!"

"You're so good to me. I feel like a queen eating latkes and cookies on a beautiful day with my long-lost husband! Did you bring any coffee to go with this delightful lunch?" She laughed and pulled him toward her.

"In public, no less. You really have missed me," Aaron gave her a loud kiss on the mouth. They laughed at first but then grew serious as they hugged and kissed on the bench until an old woman walked by tsking noisily. He was not so shy with Edna.

Once they'd made the decision, Aaron and Edna spent every weekend out on Long Island looking at houses. Dottie and Mac decided this was a good idea so the four of them often went house hunting together.

*****

Since Ez was still recuperating in Colorado, Miriam continued to live downstairs from her parents after Aaron and Edna moved out on Long Island. Miriam was happy for Edna and Mac, but also jealous of them. They were both back living with their spouses and had beautiful homes out on Long Island. Miriam continued to suffer from her mother's bullying and her asthma was getting steadily worse.

When she was admitted to the hospital, about once a month, she was given epinephrine injections. But there was very little else anyone could do. In a way, she envied Ez for being cared for on a tuberculosis ward. His letters were usually cheery. He spent most of his day resting outdoors, bundled up to keep warm. He had scheduled rest times and mealtimes. He was told when and how far he could walk each day and had a daily visit from a physician. All his needs were seen to by someone else *and all on the government's nickel!*

She knew it was no picnic. Many people died of TB, but she understood all too well what it was like to not be able to breathe. Yet, she still had to go to work, buy and make her own food, and do her own laundry. Ma was unsympathetic. Pop didn't know how he could help. Eddie spent as much time as he could with her but he was sixteen and in the throes of a hectic adolescence. He and his friends Arnie, Norm, and Babe, formed the Bijou Club. They'd wanted to join the Longfellow Club at school but apparently you had to be six feet tall. They were all too short except for Norm, who decided he'd rather be with his buddies. Eddie was surprised when Ma agreed to sew large letter "B's" on their sweaters.

Together, dressed in their best, they went to a jazz club on Fifty-Second Street. A new friend "Eppy," short for Epstein, played trumpet in the high school band. He introduced Eddie to Billie Holiday's music. After that, they listened to her records on juke boxes in the local soda shops. They were buddies Eddie could rely on. More than once, he used his boxing skills to get one or all of them out of a jam. In return, he could show up at one of their doors whenever he needed to escape his mother and see how happy families lived. While he loved Mimi, he thought he was too old to be seen hanging around his sister and she was too old to have her younger brother at her heels. But they still talked. When she was struggling to breathe, Eddie carried the groceries in for her, cleaned the apartment, and helped in whatever way he could.

CHAPTER THIRTEEN
1947

Miriam finally received notice that Ez was on his way home from Colorado. Although not quite hale and hearty, he was well enough to resume a normal life, whatever that might look like after a long war and a long hospitalization. She was hopeful they could start anew. Maybe the war and his illness had forced him to grow up and take responsibility. She was ready to have a baby, stop working, and devote herself to motherhood. Maybe when her children were older, she could pursue a career, if she lived that long. She was only twenty-eight but felt middle-aged. If Ez was well enough to go back to work, she could reserve her energy for child rearing.

Yet, Miriam was still anxious about how things would work out with Ez. *What does he want from me, anyway? Why did he marry me? He's tall and handsome. I am short and stocky and far from beautiful. He could have had any woman, including someone who had money, someone who would have been willing to support him in style just to have him escort her to the theatre and parties.* She thought he liked her wit and humor but that was not enough to keep a man very long. Not if he was aware that he was attractive and she was not. *Perhaps he met someone at the sanatorium. Maybe he's coming home to get his things and say good bye before leaving me forever.*

Miriam asked herself these questions as she walked home from work. She decided if there was to be a new slate then she must wipe the old one clean and erase her suspicions. She would give Ez another chance. The man was recovering from war and illness. He would need care and patience. No matter what happened before, she would help him remember that she could always cheer him and love him more than any other women had or would. Eventually, any others would lose patience with him and let him go, especially when he only had his looks to offer in return. *How long can they last?* Miriam laughed wryly, drawing curious glances from other people on the sidewalk. *We're still young. His looks will last until he's an old man,* she thought to herself. Hers were bound to worsen. She'd get stockier with each baby and her difficulty breathing would start to show on her face and in her body.

Miriam was nothing if not practical. Taking over her mother's role since childhood had forced her to be practical and dismiss trivialities as not worth her time or energy. She was the one who bolstered her father's confidence, comforted Edna and Eddie, and ensured everyone's needs were seen to before her own. She was also practical about her health. She didn't think she'd live very long and wanted to leave some legacy. She'd wanted it to be a product of her intellect, but instead it would be a product of her womb. If she got nothing else from Ez or this life, she would have children to remember her.

Now Mac was off picking Ez up from the train station. She found it ironic that after being in a war and hospitalized for a deadly disease, he was coming home and would resume a normal life, while she was doomed to tiptoe through whatever remained of her life, scarcely daring to move without worrying about breathing.

She'd stayed busy cooking all day the day before to prepare for Ez's arrival. Now, home from work, she started heating everything on the stove, washed her face, reapplied her makeup, and donned a new winter dress. It was November, cold and blustery. She decided to rest a while in a chair by the window. She was tired from anxiety about seeing Ez again, from her tedious work day, and from the years of loneliness she hoped to put behind her. The knock was very loud. Smoothing her dress, hair, and lipstick, she went to answer the door.

"I'm going to wait with you!" said Ma in Yiddish, pushing past Miriam into the apartment. "I want to see he's alright."

"It's his first day home Ma, can't you see him tomorrow?"

Ma, sniffing the air, said "What? You've been cooking? You should have let me cook. The man's been eating army and hospital food. Don't you want to give him something good?" Ma ignored Miriam, pushing her way into the little kitchen.

"What did you make? Oy, a brisket? Tzimmes? It's not Rosh Hashanah. Why'd you make tzimmes? What do you have for dessert? I'll go upstairs and get some pastry. I'll be right back!"

"No Ma, please. I'd like to have some time alone with him. He's my husband."

Her mother was out the door, climbing the stairs. Miriam could hear Ma's heavy tread above her. *She makes me so angry,* she thought. *But I know she's been worried, too. But, he's my husband for heaven's sake. We've got to find a way to move out of here!*

As she listened to her mother on the stairs, she heard the front door to the building open. She ran out into the hall. He looked as handsome as ever, as if he'd been on vacation. Ez scooped her up into his arms. Mac, standing behind him, dropped Ez's bags onto the floor and slid behind the couple and up the stairs. Miriam could hear him gently coercing their mother back into the upstairs apartment. Ez and Miriam moved slowly into their own and closed the door.

CHAPTER FOURTEEN

1948

Eddie had been dating Daisy, a cute blond from his English class, with more looks than brains. Whenever she asked the teacher a question, she raised her dainty hand and squeaked in a high voice, "Oh teacher. I have a question." Then, she asked something stupid like how to spell a word. Invariably, the teacher told her to look in the dictionary. Invariably, she responded, "But how can I look it up if I don't know how to spell it?" Eddie liked her because she was lighthearted and made him laugh even when she didn't intend to.

Eddie and Daisy broke up after the school holidays back in December. He had grown tired of her whiny voice and lack of anything interesting to say. It was an amicable split. Daisy had been making eyes at one of the boys on the football team. Eddie had become an excellent gymnast and was deceptively strong due to boxing. Yet, he was still skinny, his ears stuck out from his head, and his nose was perpetually swollen and bruised. The kid on the football team was big, brawny, and dumb, more Daisy's type.

Eddie and Sarah started going out shortly after the break up. She was auburn haired and sweet, and unlike Daisy, could hold her own in a conversation. In February, Sarah hosted a Valentine's Day party at her house, telling Eddie and everyone she knew to invite their friends. Eddie invited his Bijou

Club pals and they invited their girlfriends. Eddie and Sarah hoped to set Babe up with Sarah's friend Lisa. Neither one of them was a looker.

Eddie helped Sarah decorate the downstairs room with red hearts and paper roses. She and her mother baked cakes and cookies for weeks. This was Sarah's first party and her mother wanted it to be perfect. They owned the entire two-story house and were wealthy by Eddie's standards.

The living room and kitchen were full of people. Only some of the kids knew each other but they had a great time dancing to the music on the phonograph- *Buttons and Bows, Manana was soon enough for me* and Eddie's favorite- *How High the Moon*. He'd loved the song since he'd heard jazz great, Lionel Hampton, perform it after Eppy had let them sneak into a rehearsal at one of the clubs over in Manhattan.

Somewhere there's music
How faint the tune
Somewhere there's heaven
How high the moon
There is no moon above
When love is far away too
Until it comes true
That you love me as I love you
Somewhere there's music
How near, how far
Somewhere there's heaven
It's where you are
The darkest night would shine
If you would come to me soon
Until you will, how still my heart
How high the moon, Ahh
Somewhere there's music
How faint the tune
Somewhere there's heaven
How high the moon
The darkest night would shine
If you would come to me soon
Until you will, how still my heart
How high the moon

Eddie danced with a few girls while Sarah looked on, graciously refilling drinks and restocking the cookies. Norm danced with Arnie's sister Gloria, and seemed enthralled.

Eddie and his buddies looked like all the other young men at the party, wearing club sweaters over tee-shirts and dark solid-colored pants. Sarah and the other girls wore dresses with fitted bodices and flowered skirts. Most of the girls wore something red to the party and carried short white gloves. A pocketbook that matched the dress was a vital accessory.

It was a lively party. Sarah's father emerged from upstairs only once to ask everyone to "quiet down a bit and lower the music please." Sarah did as he asked. She knew her father to be an old fuddy-duddy but a lovable one.

The sparks failed to fly between Babe and Lisa. She took one look at this big bruiser with an upside-down sailor cap and no eyebrows and turned in the other direction.

"Sorry, Pal," said Eddie, putting his arm around Babe's shoulders. "What does she know? You can do better, anyway." Babe smirked and went to the buffet table to stuff himself. Toward the end of the evening, Sarah asked Eddie to walk two girls home, one he already knew and a new acquaintance, Natty Leibowitz.

*****

Eddie was working as a soda jerk, making ice cream sundaes and milk shakes at the local soda shop. He turned eighteen in April. One of the coaches at the PAL said he could get him some professional fights. His art teacher had given him a choice: ruin your hands for art work by boxing or give up boxing. The bouts he'd win would give him much more than what he earned at the soda shop. He wanted to save up money for art school.

He'd boxed young, inexperienced guys like himself at the PAL. But professional boxers were a different story. He fought as a flyweight and tried his best to exude confidence when facing an opponent but he was scared to death he'd be hurt. Eddie got pretty bruised but his mother didn't question him. He worked in his basement studio almost every day, although Ma often came downstairs to berate him and remind him he'd be better off working as a clerk. Pop and Mac noticed the bruises though, and Mimi fussed over him so much he had to tell them what he was doing.

"I don't like this, Eddie. You're made for better things than getting beaten up in the ring," scolded Pop.

"Yeah Kid, your face looks like a truck ran over it!" laughed Mac, more afraid for his little brother than he was willing to admit.

"I'm pretty good, even if I don't look it. You should see the other guy!" Eddie laughed. "Come see me fight. I'm called *The Blond Tiger!*"

"We will. Right, Pop?" asked Mac, ruffling Eddie's curls. "Blond tiger- some tiger," he said dodging Eddie's playful punch. Sam scowled but nodded his head.

Eddie often escaped with his Bijou Club friends. Each of them had a girlfriend, except Babe who was still bald and without eyebrows. The girls were sympathetic but not enough to date him. Some guys weren't at all sympathetic and threw insults at Babe, so Eddie threw punches back. Eddie and Babe fought alongside each other, laughing as if they were slapping at flies.

Norm was dating Gloria. Her father was an electrician who also worked in the local movie theatre. Sometimes the boys and their dates got in for free. They also went to jazz clubs, usually without their dates. Eppy played trumpet for one of the bands and hung out with them on breaks.

Eddie liked to babysit for Mimi's young son, Allan. He eagerly awaited the birth of her second child, due next year. Mimi, Ez, and Allan still lived in the downstairs apartment.

Ma made him walk barefoot or wear shoes in her apartment. He couldn't walk around in socks because she said he was tempting the evil eye. He also knew not to say anyone's entire birthday out loud for fear of attracting the angel of death. Usually, he rolled his eyes at Ma's superstitions, fighting the urge to argue with her like he had when he was younger. Now, he understood that she would not change and ignored her whenever he could.

Eddie thought Mimi was a wonderful mother. She took such good care of Allan, a dark haired, dark eyed kid who would look at home in Saudi Arabia or Egypt. Eddie tried to take him under his wing like Mac and Ez had done with him when he was little. Ez, wasn't around much lately. When he was, he showed his son great affection but he didn't know him like a father should.

Ez had been very attentive to Mimi after he came home from the hospital. He went back to work for the Lion Match Company and devoted himself to earning cash, so they could move out and start a family. But he soon took to gambling, leaving very little money to add to their savings. Eddie wished he could still feel good about Ez but he saw Mimi struggling to get by, giving up the dreams she'd had before Ez came home. It didn't help Mimi that most of the family liked Ez. Ma seemed to be constantly telling her what a good man he was. If Pop was around when she said that, he rolled his eyes.

Ez's sister, Ada, worked for famous movie directors. She was always there for Ez when he needed money and introduced him to beautiful women. So far, Miriam only suspected that he had trysts with other women but she wasn't sure. Like their mother, Leah, Ada spoiled him so much, Miriam couldn't compete. He needed to be entertained and fussed over, neither of which Miriam cared to do. She felt she was also entitled to a little fussing.

Eddie sat with little Allan whenever he could spare the time so Mimi could go out with the few friends she had or go to her doctor's appointments. Her asthma was worse than ever. But there was little anyone could do for her.

*****

Natty was a black-haired beauty with shining brown eyes and a big bright smile that showed perfectly white teeth. Natty laughed a lot but unlike Daisy, Eddie noticed, she was very smart and loved to read. He made sure to get her number before they'd parted after the Valentine's Day party, and it turned out that she was just what he needed to clear away the gloom that overpowered him at times. They were soon going steady.

"I'm sorry for Sarah," said Natty as they walked in the park one Sunday in March. "But not that sorry," she laughed.

"Me too, but 'all's fair in love and war.' She's a nice girl and I'm sure there'll be guys lining up to date her."

"Really? Sounds like you miss her already!" Natty teased.

"Sure, I do. She always brought me chocolate. When did you ever bring me anything chocolate?"

"Vanilla is the best flavor. How can you like chocolate?"

"You seemed to like it fine when I made you that special sundae at the soda shop! You even licked the spoon!"

"I was just trying to impress you," said Natty, pulling him around to face her. "Okay, tell you what? We're gonna march right over to Albert's and get you as much chocolate as your money can buy."

"My money? Isn't this your treat?"

"With what money? I can offer to sing. Maybe Albert's will give us the candy for free."

"Oh no. Ok, Ok. I'll pay. Just please don't sing," Eddie laughed, recalling Natty's rendition of *The Chattanooga Choo Choo*. It was ear splitting.

Gradually, Eddie heard about Natty's erratic childhood. Her father, Harry, was an attorney but for some reason he managed a store. She said she was very close to her father and had missed him terribly when her mother had taken her and her sister to Cleveland where Natty's grandparents and aunts and uncles lived. Her mother left her father in Brownsville and left Natty with relatives in Cleveland while she took Natty's crazy sister to see one doctor after another. No one knew what was wrong with her sister's head but that's how her mother, a nurse, spent most of her time.

Eddie got a chance to meet Harry when he picked Natty up for a date. They were going to the movies, but Harry insisted on giving Eddie money to take Natty to see the opera *Carmen* instead. After that, Eddie had become an opera buff. Just as Harry had introduced Natty to literary classics, Harry gave Eddie books to read that he'd never known existed or thought would interest him.

Harry liked this young man and was glad that Natty had enough sense to date him. Sometimes, Eddie slept on the couch in their living room, and he told Harry about his father's drinking and his fraught relationship with his mother. Harry understood that he needed to escape his family. And, as much as Eddie loved his father, he came to realize he had much more in common with Harry.

*****

Sam was relieved that Mac was running the business now. He sometimes felt his heart pound and race. He had to stop and rest, breathing deeply. He was a heavy smoker but his doctor said that wouldn't hurt him. The alcohol was the biggest problem. Sam was drinking more heavily now. He stopped at bars after work, often arriving home drunk and sleepy after everyone had gone to bed. He knew he was slowly killing himself but Gussie had become even harder to live with. She seemed to hate all her children except Mac, although she doted on her grandchildren.

Mac was glad his father had asked him to take over Rugby. Pop had told him he felt his heart getting weaker and couldn't work so hard anymore. He popped in the office now and then to check on things and say hello to his men. Then, he'd make his way to one of his gin mills.

Sometimes, Ez drove Sam and Gussie out to see Mac and Dottie, Edna and Eli, and the children. Gussie always brought her pots and pans to cook kosher meals because she didn't think her children were kosher enough. In the car, Ez kept up a running dialogue with Sam; Gussie only spoke to complain about the temperature or to tell Ez to slow down or speed up, whichever he was not doing at the time. Miriam rarely made these trips, saving her energy to clean the house and care for Allan. She hadn't worked since Allan's birth and had no regrets about giving up the secretarial job she'd always disliked.

Sam, Mac, and Mimi attended Eddie's high school graduation. Eddie was awarded the art medal and the gymnastics medal. He felt proud and enjoyed the attention. After the ceremony, he introduced his family to his art teacher who took Sam aside, "Mr. Roth, your boy has talent. He should become an artist. He's already very good."

"You don't have to tell me Mr. Snyder, but I'm glad to hear it from his teacher. What do I know about art?" said Sam, shrugging.

As they walked home together, Sam stopped all the passersby to brag about his son.

"Look, look at my son. He's going to be a famous artist someday!" He said smiling. No one could help but get caught up in Sam's glee and some stopped to shake Eddie's hand. He was embarrassed but accepted congratulations from men in suits hurrying by importantly, women pushing baby carriages or carrying groceries, young boys walking dogs, and old men playing chess outside cafes. Mac and Miriam stood by, silently laughing behind their hands. They'd never seen their father quite so happy, except when Eddie was born. They were thrilled for Eddie and basked in vicarious glory.

They went back to Ma and Pop's house to celebrate. Dottie and Edna were there with their children. Ez was setting up chairs in the basement studio, the only place large enough to accommodate the whole family. The food was laid out on Eddie's drawing table over a starched white cloth saved for special occasions. The children ran up and down the stairs into both apartments and back into the basement. All the doors were open. A fan stirred the dry basement air.

Eddie went upstairs first to show Ma his medals.

"Look, Ma. I was so surprised. I didn't expect to win anything!" said Eddie to his mother who turned from the kitchen counter to glance at the silver dollar sized gold-plated disks attached to red, white, and blue ribbons. She looked up at Eddie, then back at the crumbs on the counter and began to wipe them into the sink with a wet cloth.

Eddie turned from her as Ez walked in. "Wow, Eddie. Look at that shine! You make me proud," said Ez, grabbing Eddie around the neck, punching his belly gently. "Hey, let's go show Dottie. She loves gold." Ez turned Eddie away from his mother toward the stairs.

It doesn't matter what Ma thinks. What does she know about art or gymnastics? She's an ignorant peasant and always has been. Nothing I can do is ever gonna change that.

They stopped at Miriam and Ez's apartment to grab Allan and another plate of food from the icebox to carry to the basement. Ez almost tripped over his son, who was running underfoot, wearing his cowboy hat and the vest with the fringe. Allan looked back at them, pointed his toy pistol at his father. "Bang, you're dead," he said.

CHAPTER FIFTEEN

1948

Eddie went to work for his father right after graduation. Since he knew next to nothing about construction, Sam made him a foreman on a small job. Eddie agreed, but was unsure what the job involved.

"Okay, Pop, but what do I do?"

"Just make sure everyone's working - doing what they're supposed to do."

"You make it sound easy," said Eddie, skeptically.

"You'll be fine," Pop said.

Mac came by that evening. He pulled Eddie outside. Mac took something out of the car, he and Aaron shared.

"What's this? A baseball bat?" asked Eddie.

"It's a four by four I put on the lathe. Here, take it. It's yours now."

"Thanks Mac but I don't have time for baseball," said Eddie handing it back to his brother.

"Pop told me he was gonna ask you to be foreman on a job. Right?"

"Yeah, so? Pop said it'll be easy."

"So, take the bat, Kid. You're gonna need it. You think those guys working for us are sweethearts? Some of em have been to prison! They're tough and wanna get paid without doing any work"

"I'm tough too, but you expect me to hit em with a four by four?"

"Don't hit em unless you have to. Just threaten em. That's what I learned when I was foreman. You're a skinny guy. You're strong, but they don't know that. Carry a big bat around and they won't give you any trouble!"

Eddie looked at his brother. He took the bat and examined it carefully.

"Nah, not for me. I resign. Thanks anyway. I'll go tell Pop."

Eddie joined the Army instead. He needed to get away from his mother and wanted to get his military obligation out of the way. Under the Selective Service Act, he had to serve on active duty for twenty-one months. After that, he could either do another twelve months on active-duty service or serve thirty-six months in the reserves. He decided to do the extra twelve months so he couldn't be called up again. He wanted to put in his time and then go to art school. Arnie and Norm joined the Navy. Babe was considered unfit. Eppy was languishing in jail for mail fraud and playing his trumpet for his fellow prisoners.

Mac told him, "Good choice, little brother. In and out. You'll be home in no time."

*****

Natty made lamb chops and potatoes for Eddie and her father a few days before Eddie left for basic training in Camp Hood, Texas. Natty's mother, Rose, was in Cleveland again with Natty's sister Abby, whose mental illness was not getting any better. The men talked about opera and books while Natty cleared the table and cleaned the kitchen. The lamb chops had been over cooked and the potatoes underdone. During the Depression, Eddie had eaten shoe leather that tasted better but he was thrilled Natty had made a homemade meal just for him. Eddie knew something about cooking himself; he'd learned to make spaghetti and homemade "gravy." He ate at Babe's house most Sundays, and always snuck into the kitchen to watch Babe's mother add ingredients from memory.

"Babe, you write this down for Eddie so he knows what I'm doing," she said as she stirred fresh garlic and onions in olive oil. Eddie could see beads of sweat already forming on her broad, homely face crowned with graying hair pulling at haphazardly placed pins. She wiped her hands on her apron, clean but still stained from many Sundays.

"So, you see, I'm stirring the onions and garlic until the onions are sort of clear looking. Now, add the salt and pepper, a pinch of each and then the oregano," she spoke with a mild Italian accent. It sounded warm and maternal.

"I already peeled and mashed the tomatoes from the garden. Go ahead, Eddie, you mix them in the pot. Good, good. Now we add the sweet basil and the parsley and let it all boil together. Grate the cheese, Honey," she said to Babe who was carefully noting each item.

"We don't have a garden," said Eddie to Babe's mother. "We did during the war but now it's all overgrown."

"So, you go to the market and get what you need, but it must be fresh. Okay, now we add the Parmesan and let it sit on the stove."

"I know this part, Ma. You keep the flame low and stir every so often so it doesn't burn," said Babe, finally taking an interest. The smell was irresistible.

Eddie enjoyed cooking with Babe's mother almost as much as he liked boxing. He thought maybe he and Natty could cook together someday. He wanted their kitchen to smell like the Merola's.

Now, Eddie sat with Harry, an overweight man in clothes that had seen better days but with eyes that radiated a fierce intelligence.

"Eddie, before you go off to the Army," Harry began, keeping his voice low so Natty wouldn't hear him, "I want you to have this book to remember me by." Harry handed Eddie a small book with a soft black leather cover thinned from years of handling.

"Thank you sir, but I'll be back after basic training before they send me anywhere for my enlistment term. I'll see you again soon."

The two men, one very young and one nearing fifty, sat across from each other in the small living room. Eddie, in his Bijou Club sweater, sat on the couch while Harry faced him from his arm chair by the window. Harry looked older than his age, especially with part of his face in the shadow cast by the one lamp in the room.

"Of course, we'll see each other again soon, Eddie. I've no doubt of that. But I want you to have something from me. It's a prayer book my father gave me. He brought it with him from the old country. See here: I've inscribed it from me to you," he said as he showed him the inside cover.

Eddie read the inscription written in cursive with black ink "To Eddie, the world holds many mysteries. Explore them, not with fear, but wonder.

Best regards, Harry Leibowitz." The pages were so thin and fragile that Eddie was afraid to turn them.

Eddie felt like crying. He'd never received such a special gift and couldn't believe Mr. Leibowitz would want to give away such a cherished possession to someone he hadn't known very long. He didn't know what to say or do. Not taking the book could cause offense. Taking the book could mean that he might never see Harry again. He wasn't superstitious like his mother but all the same, he felt as if taking the book would somehow hasten Harry's death. He'd never seen his father or Mac cry, so he made sure he didn't.

"What is it, Eddie? You can talk to me. Don't you like my gift?" asked Harry leaning closer to Eddie.

"It's not that, sir. I've never received something so valuable. I don't deserve it. To tell you the truth, I'm afraid to take it. What if it gets damaged or stained?"

Harry took Eddie's hand, "Listen, Eddie. I'm sick. Very sick. Don't tell Natty. I think Rose knows."

Harry had had premonitions that his life was soon to end. He didn't know if he'd ever see this young man again or whether Eddie and Natty would stay together. Yet, he knew that Eddie was a good man who needed to feel he belonged somewhere to someone and he'd surely cherish Harry's father's prayer book.

"What can I do?" asked Eddie, expecting tears to finally fall.

"Nothing. Nothing, Eddie. Just enjoy life."

Both men fell silent as Natty entered holding a tray of coffee and dessert.

"Why are you both so quiet? I thought you had so much to talk about. Honestly, sometimes I think you both forget I'm here!" said Natty good-naturedly. The men abandoned their thoughts to look up and smile at Natty, who stood above them ready to place the tray on a table to which she gestured with her foot. "Please move the table a little closer," she said. Then, she thought, *men always seem lost in their own worlds.*

"Daddy, could you please move the coffee table a little so I can put this tray down? It's getting heavy," she said again as they both continued to look up at her without moving.

"Of course, pobalol," said her father. Eddie looked at both inquiringly.

"It's Daddy's pet name for me. It's supposed to be lollipop backwards," she smiled at her father. I made coffee and I have chocolate chip cookies I made myself! Eddie loves chocolate, don't you Eddie?" she asked teasingly. He smiled back.

"Help yourself, Eddie. I shouldn't have any because I have the sugar sickness but I must try just one since you made them, Natty."

Eddie put the book to the side to show Natty later when they were alone, fearing he would embarrass Harry if he showed it to her in front of him.

"These are delicious, Natty," said Eddie, meaning it this time.

"Yes Natty, you've outdone yourself tonight!" said her father licking the melting chocolate from his hands and laughing. Nothing brought him greater joy than seeing Natty smile.

"Now, I will take myself into the bedroom and read awhile. You don't need me here any longer. Eddie," he said, shaking Eddie's hand with a firm grip, "Stay safe. Keep well. Write when you can."

"Thank you, sir…for everything. We'll see each other again soon. I'm sure."

*****

Natty and Eddie met at the soda shop for a long good-bye. Natty had been busy in school and Eddie had had a lot of farewells to take care of and packing to do. He'd been given a long list of what he could bring and not bring, and where he had to go to get transportation to Camp Hood.

"I'll be back in about two months, after basic training. Don't have too much fun without me," said Eddie, only half kidding.

"I promise not to have any fun while you're away," laughed Natty, sipping her vanilla milkshake. "School's no fun, anyway. I hate math."

"I'm no good at it either. Will you write me?" Eddie sucked the chocolate fudge off his long-handled sundae spoon.

"Every day. You'd better write me. What'll we do when you get back? It'll be September! I'll be back in school. Crummy."

"We'll figure it out. Don't worry. You like to plan ahead, don't you?"

"You'd be surprised," answered Natty with a twinkle in her eye.

The next day, Natty met him at the station, as Eddie was about to board the train on the first leg of his long trip from New York to Texas.

"I'm going to miss you," said Natty quietly, dabbing tears with a cotton handkerchief.

"I'll be back before you know it and have a few weeks leave before I head out again. We'll paint the town!"

"I know but I'm already thinking about when you'll have to leave again," whispered Natty.

"Well, that's pretty silly. That's a few months away," he said laughing but then became serious, grabbing hold of her hands, "I'll miss you too, Nat. Try not to worry and don't go out with anyone else while I'm gone," he finished on a lighter note.

On the train Eddie felt excited. He'd been ready to leave home for years. He decided if he could live with Ma all that time, he could tolerate just about anyone if he kept them at arm's length.

He knew he had a bad temper and held grudges. He'd learned some patience from drawing, and from his father and Natty. Mimi had taught him how to cope with things he couldn't change. Still, he worried he'd be like Ma, who got mad for no reason at all. He was used to using his fists to solve problems, to earn money or to fight off Jew-haters, or guys who liked to fight for the hell of it. There might be real crooks in the Army. He'd try not to use his fists to solve problems. But if he had to be tough, he was ready, confident in his own physical strength and sure he wouldn't have too much trouble in the Army.

******

It was early July and Camp Hood was beastly hot. When Eddie finally got off the last train and onto the bus waiting at the station for the new recruits, he felt like he'd entered hell. New York City was hot in summer, but this wasn't just hot; it took your breath away. He looked out the windows of the bus as he listened to the different accents meld together in one loud cadence. He heard guys who sounded like they'd just walked out of a cowboy western, guys who dropped their "r's," and guys like him who spoke in the only dialect he could decipher.

They said America was a melting pot and the guys on the bus proved it. Eddie heard one new recruit sitting a few seats away, "Ya'll ready for what comes next? We fellas er gonna be as busy as cats on a hot tin roof!" Another guy responded, "What do cats have to do with the Army? D'ya have any idear what weer supposed to be doing heyah?"

Eddie laughed to himself. *I'll have to teach these guys to tawk New Yawk style, the right way for a soldier to tawk.*

The ground outside the window was flat, empty of trees and pale brown. Dust blew up alongside the road as the wheels rolled on. *Where are the tall buildings? For that matter, where are the people? Where are the guys in suits rushing back and forth and the beautiful women walking arm in arm, talking a mile a minute? It looks so dull here. So, along with strange accents, I have to look at this for two months?*

After getting off the bus, they were herded to the middle of a large, flat, asphalt covered square. Eddie was among a motley crew of boys his age dressed in everything from white tee shirts and dungarees to starched white oxford shirts and dress trousers. A man in uniform stood at the top of the square pointing and yelling.

"Let's go. Let's go. Get in line. Hurry up. I aint got all day. Let's go," he said gruffly.

Some sauntered; others ran. Eddie ran.

The night before he'd left home, Mac sat him down for some brotherly advice, "Do exactly what they say, whatever they say. I know you're a tough guy, Eddie, but they're tougher. Don't underestimate them. Follow the rules. The rules are there for a reason. Rules saved my life, more times than I can tell you. And eat what they give you. Ya never know when you'll eat again, so eat it, good or bad and Army food is really bad. Got it?"

Eddie got it. He rushed into line and stood straight, facing the man in uniform. Other guys took their places beside, in front, and in back of him. A guy next to him spoke in a New York accent, "Hey, I'm Freddie, Bronx. How 'bout you?"

"Hey you, keep it down. I didn't say you could talk!" shouted the sergeant in front.

"Brooklyn," whispered Eddie.

The sergeant taught them how to stand at attention and at ease. He drilled them for another hour before marching them into the mess hall. *Mac was right,* thought Eddie as he surveyed the spam and mashed potatoes. *At least the coffee is good.* That night, he had his own bed for the first time, ever.

*****

Eddie got to know some of the other guys from New York and Jersey. He regularly hung out with two of them and was glad to have them as back up when some of the southern guys started a fight. Despite the promises he'd made to himself, he couldn't resist a fight, even when walking away might have been better.

Eddie took a lot of heat for being Jewish. There were other Jews, but very few. The other guys wrongly assumed this skinny Jew was easy meat. Eddie had a secret weapon. If the other guys happened to be too big or too strong, his new buddy Jeb, big and black as night - from Mississippi of all places - stepped in to help him out. Jeb introduced him to the glories of fried catfish and barbeque.

Like Eddie, Jeb was happy to be in the Army, where President Truman had just ended racial segregation. He understood discrimination. His father had been lynched by men in white hoods and no one had ever been held to account. Jeb worried about his mother and younger siblings. But she had told him to go, to find a better life if he could and then come back and get them.

Like Eddie, Jeb had grown up fighting - though not in boxing rings - and had a hair-trigger temper that flared up quickly and burned out just as fast. But while it burned, he was dangerous. Eddie and Jeb made a habit of being arrested by the military police for fighting. They didn't mind that much, since they fought for good reasons, usually because someone had intentionally disrespected them or stolen their gear.

Eddie boxed a few times at Camp Hood and always won, usually in the first or second round. The guys who thought they could box were no match for him. He was so good that they let him out early to box once when he was sent to the guard house for fighting. The guy from the Bronx he'd met on the first day said he'd seen *The Blond Tiger* poster advertising one of Eddie's fights in the window of Dudy's Tavern, the bar Bummy Davis owned until he was murdered. Eddie felt like a celebrity. He remembered winning that fight.

Eddies victories in fights inside and outside of the ring upset some of the "southern crackers" who were always bothering him about being a Jew. They threatened to catch him alone and teach him a lesson. Even *The Blond Tiger* couldn't beat the odds if three or four attacked him at once.

Joe, an Italian guy who was one of his buddies from New York, sidled up to Eddie during afternoon chow one day.

"Hey Joe. How ya doin? Did ya like the corn beef hash as much as I did?" said Eddie, smiling. "It's really a treat when they throw the vegetable and dessert courses on top of it. My girlfriend's mother cooks better than this. That's saying something!"

Joe laughed, "I ain't got much time, Eddie. Listen, we want you to go to the movie tonight in the mess tent."

"What's playing? I was figuring on getting some sleep. You guys go and tell me all about it."

"Eddie, don't ask questions for once. Just go, okay. When you go, sit way in the back next to the projectionist."

"What's this? Some kinda joke? Are you guys gonna do something to get me in trouble? I'm not *that* stupid."

"I'm your friend, right? Do what I say. Not only that, don't you move a muscle during the movie. You stay till the very end. No leaving to get snacks or even piss, you hear?" finished Joe, who was normally jovial and easy going. Eddie decided to take his tone and the grim line of his mouth seriously.

"Okay Joe, whatever you say. I can't wait to see the movie. It'd better be good!" Said Eddie, slapping Joe gently on the back as he turned toward the barrack.

Eddie sat through the movie which wasn't so bad for a western. He thought he'd look pretty good in a cowboy hat. He liked the gangster movies better. The tough guys dressed well. He hardly moved a muscle through the entire show and soon forgot he hadn't wanted to come in the first place.

The next morning the guys who'd been tormenting him missed roll call and chow. Eddie found out later that someone had beaten the "crackers" to a bloody pulp. No one knew who did it but Eddie could guess. He never said a word about it to Joe and Joe kept mum. But when Eddie had any extra cigarettes or chocolate, he made Joe take them.

*****

Eddie learned how to shoot a rifle. When he finally got a weekend pass and wasn't in the guard house for fighting, he went into Killeen with his buddies. He still couldn't believe how different Texas was from New York. It seemed like the Old West from the movies. In Killeen, Eddie and each of his friends posed for pictures looking like cowboys. He decided he really did look good in a cowboy hat. He sent the photo home to Mimi.

Natty and Mimi each received one letter during the months he was away. But he called Natty twice to say he was fine and he missed her.

Dear Mimi,
How are you feeling these days? I'm sorry I'm not there to help you. Thanks for the letter and the pictures. I can't believe how fast Allan and baby Naomi, have grown. I probably won't recognize them when I come home next time. Take more pictures for me, okay? Say hi to Ez.
Love you Sis,
Eddie

The letter to Natty was funny and romantic with verse he lifted from a book of poetry his bunk mate loaned him.

Dear Nat,
I told you I would write. They keep us very busy here digging ditches then filling them again, then repeating the whole thing over and over. We go on long marches with full packs and I'm learning how to shoot. They're going to make me a tanker in Advanced Training, so no need to worry about me. I'll be well protected! Someone found out I can draw so I've been tasked to draw murals all over the post. The latest one was in the Officers' Club. It's a picture of tanks rolling over the hills. Whenever they allow us a spare moment to think, I think of you. I like to think of you roller skating without a care in the world, your skirt swinging and your beautiful smile. When you think of me, please think of Errol Flynn or Clark Gable; they are much more handsome. Pretend I look like one of them.
I don't know when I'll next have time to write but please remember I love you.
What lips my lips have kissed, and where, and why,
I have [not] forgotten, and what arms have lain
Under my head till morning; but the rain
Is full of ghosts tonight, that tap and sigh
Upon the glass and listen for reply.
Yours always,
Eddie

In September, after basic training ended, he went home for a short leave. He and Natty painted the town, just like he'd promised. He finally had some money in his pocket, having saved everything he had left after buying chocolate bars and cigarettes. The Army issued cigarettes to the troops, but there were never enough for him. Everyone in the Army smoked, from the recruits to the sergeants. It was the cool thing to do. Natty didn't like the habit, especially after she'd inhaled once or twice to see what it was like.

Eddie took Natty to the jazz clubs where he and his Bijou Club friends had spent so much time. They went roller skating, one of Natty's favorite pastimes. Eddie was a natural, skating backwards while holding Natty in his arms.

Eddie sang Texan songs to her: *The Yellow Rose of Texas, Muddy Roads, Streets of Laredo* and *Jack a Diamonds*. He changed the girl's name in the songs to Nat.

O Nat, O Nat, it is for your sake alone
That I leave my old parents, my house and my home,
That I leave my old parents, you caused me to roam,
I am a rabble soldier and Dixie is my home.

He only ever sang for her. He had a surprisingly deep, sonorous voice and could hold a tune. He added theatrics to his singing, moving his arms and legs to emphasize the words.

Natty was relieved to see him home. He seemed taller and less skinny. She tried to pinpoint what else was different about him and then realized he was happy. He smiled so much she had to remind herself this was the same person who'd made her laugh before he went into the Army but back then, he'd always had shadows around his eyes. The shadows were a legacy of Gussie, his mother. His eyes had always had a haunted look. Now that he'd been away from her, Eddie seemed to be more carefree and his eyes looked brighter.

Natty knew all about bad mothers. She had one. Her mother loved her, Natty knew, but she devoted almost all her attention to Abby. On the positive side, Rose's neglect of them had brought Natty and her father closer.

While on leave, Eddie visited with Harry who was glad he'd lived long enough to see him again. Eddie thought Harry looked a little thinner and pale. They sat in Natty's house and talked about sports, books, and opera. Natty had become a good baker, so she made him cookies or cake and strong coffee. At Camp Hood, Eddie had received several packages of delicious crumbs that had started out as cookies.

Everyone in the family, except Ma, was happy to see him and caught him up on the latest news about themselves and his friends. Mac and Ez took opportunities to tease him by making him stand at attention and salute whenever they entered the room, but also gave him advice and tips on how to survive military life. Aaron kept to himself.

Natty wanted to show off her improved cooking skills and decided to host a dinner party for Eddie. She didn't tell her mother. She just said she wanted to have a few friends over. She invited her friend, Fagie. Natty's mother, Rose, invited Bernie, a young man she'd met in Cleveland and his cousin, Michael. She didn't tell Natty or Abby until the men arrived at the apartment door.

When Rose and Abby were last in Cleveland, Rose had encouraged the young men to come visit New York and see the sights. Now, they were staying in town with distant relatives. Rose intended to match Bernie with Natty and Michael with Abby. Eddie turning up put her matchmaking plans in jeopardy. Rose liked him but thought Natty could do better. Bernie was destined for the law and Michael for medicine. Her girls would be rich and have everything Rose wished she'd had.

Eddie found the fiasco amusing. He knew how attractive Natty was and that he was not home anymore to date her exclusively, but he knew she was his. Besides, neither of the two nebbishes was her type. Bernie was quiet and serious, already balding and very short. Michael was the opposite, tall and rickety with sallow skin and yellowish sclera. Eddie noticed how flustered Rose was and how embarrassed Natty seemed. After the introductions, he pulled Natty aside.

"Nat, what's the matter? I find this funny. Don't you? What will your mother do now?" Eddie cast a sidelong glance at Harry, who was smiling, apparently enjoying Rose's discomfort.

"Shh, Eddie. Mother will hear you. I can't imagine what she was thinking. She didn't warn me or Abby. I don't think even Daddy knew." They had moved to far a corner of the tiny living room. Everyone else had gone to the kitchen where there was a table set with Rose's best dinnerware, most of it chipped and faded. She'd borrowed a bridge table to tack on the end so the two tables together with their mismatched chairs extended into part of the living room.

"Please everyone, go sit in the living room while we finish getting supper ready," commanded Rose, shooing everyone out of the kitchen.

"Just sit down Eddie and make conversation. Tell a joke or something. I'll help my mother and Fagie in the kitchen," Natty pleaded.

"Let's go into the other room so the women can finish up," said Harry, beckoning the men to find a seat in what was left of the living room. "Bernie, Mike, we're happy you could join us for dinner. Tell me, what do you boys do in Cleveland."

In the kitchen, Natty looked at Fagie who couldn't hold back her urge to laugh. Both girls broke out into loud guffaws until Rose flashed her green eyes at them. Fagie turned to Natty to whisper, "What about poor Eddie?" She giggled. Natty responded, "Don't worry about Eddie, he thinks this is hilarious."

"Mother, there's too many people here. Why are there so many people?" whined Abby as she set the salad on the table. Rose had used money her brother Bob sent her to pay for the relatively lavish dinner of roasted chicken, green bean casserole, and baked potatoes. She'd splurged to buy a chocolate babka for dessert. Every month, Bob sent her money that she hid in her underwear drawer. She knew Harry's pride would be wounded if he knew she got the money from Bob. Harry always said Bob was "a real no-goodnik."

"It'll be fun, Abby. We don't often have company. It'll be good for you. If it gets to be too much, just excuse yourself and go into my bedroom and rest a while," answered Rose.

"Please come now, gentlemen," said Rose, directing the men where they should sit: Bernie next to Natty and Eddie next to Fagie. Abby was seated next to Michael, with Harry at the head of the part of the table that was in the living room. Rose rarely sat down but bustled about serving everyone, starting conversations between guests and giving Natty, Fagie, Eddie, and Harry hard looks to encourage their cooperation.

During dinner, Eddie told bad jokes he'd heard in the Army.
What do you call a kid who enlists in the Army? The INFANTry!
What's a soldier's least favorite month? MARCH!

Everyone laughed but Bernie hardly ever spoke, except to ask someone to pass a dish. Harry tried to engage him in a discussion about the law. Bernie's standard answer was, "I don't know, Sir. I'll have to read up on that."

Michael was more animated but all he could talk about was how much better Cleveland was compared to what he'd seen so far of Brooklyn. Harry, Eddie, Natty, and Fagie took turns holding their napkins to their mouths to stifle their amusement at both guests.

Eddie noted how dry the chicken was and that the vegetables were undercooked. He watched as everyone picked at the food. It was better than Army food and he wanted to be on Rose's good side, so he ate with gusto, drinking a lot of water and more wine than he'd planned, to wash it all down. Thank goodness the babka was from a bakery and the coffee was good.

After dinner, while the women cleared the table, the men went back to the living room to chat about mundane things. Harry and Eddie tag teamed as they tried to get Bernie to talk and Michael to say something positive about anything other than Cleveland. Drying her hands on a dish towel, Natty grabbed Fagie's hand, pulled her into her parents' bedroom and softly closed the door. She knew Eddie had seen them leave out of the corner of his eye. The girls barely noticed Abby sitting on the edge of the marital bed looking out the window.

"Fagie, I can't go out with Bernie. I love Eddie. Would you mind going out with him? Even if it's just once? My mother wants me to marry someone rich, like Bernie. She'll never leave me alone if one of us doesn't go out with him. Okay? Will you do it for me?"

"Yeah, sure. Ask me something hard, why don't you? I like the quiet types. I'll ask him to walk me home now. I guess I won't be seeing much more of you while Eddie's home on leave. Give me a call after he goes back. We'll catch a movie or something."

CHAPTER SIXTEEN

1949

Eddie came home from Texas again to find Mimi desperately ill. She'd been diagnosed with breast cancer and one breast had been removed. The family didn't want to worry him so no one had told him. When he got home, she was getting chemotherapy with something called nitrogen mustard. Thankfully, Ez had temporarily stopped his wandering ways and gambling to take care of her.

Mac had picked Eddie up from the train to give him the news before he got home.

"Prepare yourself, Eddie. It's been bad. She doesn't look well but don't tell her that. The cancer was pretty bad by the time she went to the doctor but it looks like they got it all. The medicine is just to make sure. She'll be so happy to see you. She talks about you all the time. Her 'little Eddie.'"

"Thanks for telling me, Mac. But why didn't anyone call or write? She's my sister. Maybe, I coulda come home for the surgery."

"After a year, you still don't know the Army, Kid? They weren't gonna let you come home. That's only for deaths. Now cheer yourself up before she sees you. If she thinks you're worried, she'll be upset. "

He remembered all the times Mimi had stood between him and their mother, picked him up from school, and admired his artwork. She'd been more of a mother to him than Ma had ever been. He couldn't lose her or bear the thought that she was in pain or suffering. She'd already suffered so much in her short life.

When they arrived at the house, Eddie had rushed in to find Mimi lying on a cot in the living room. Ez and Sam were sitting with her. The children were with their aunts and uncles on Long Island. Ma was in the kitchen cooking. She was helping out by getting Miriam's groceries and preparing meals but displayed no more affection for her daughter than she ever had.

Sam sat with Miriam every evening after work before he ate supper or attended to other tasks. Rugby was doing well due to the postwar construction boom. That, and the sense that the time he and Mimi had was limited, meant he no longer stopped for a drink on the way home. He sat with Miriam until Ez returned from work, while Gussie prepared the meal. Miriam had very little appetite but forced herself to eat what was offered. She knew if she didn't eat, Ma would rant and carry on. Mimi didn't need the aggravation right now. She'd never needed it but just now she knew she couldn't cope with it.

Sam told Miriam stories about the old country.

"Did I ever tell you the story of the heavy snow?" he asked her one evening as he sat beside her bed.

"I don't remember, Pop," answered Miriam, adjusting her position to be more comfortable. She thought she remembered the story but loved hearing her father tell stories. So, she was happy to hear it again.

"Well one winter in Belarus, a man and his son were traveling by sled at night and got lost in a blizzard. Having no other options, they tied the sled to a fencepole, climbed under the sled to have some shelter, and spent the rest of the night shivering there," Sam started to giggle before finishing the story. He sat on the edge of his seat leaning toward Miriam, as if to create suspense.

"What happened, Pop?" asked Miriam to egg him on.

"When the man and his son woke up, they found that the sled wasn't tied to a fence. Guess what it was?"

"I don't know, Pop. What was it?" asked Miriam who'd just remembered the ending but didn't want to spoil her father's story.

"It was the point of the church steeple! Imagine, the snow was so deep and packed so hard after many snowstorms that they'd driven the sled onto the roof of the church. Can you believe it? It's a true story."

Miriam laughed even though it hurt her stitches, "Course it did, Pop. I wish I coulda seen it."

Pop's stories and jokes always made her laugh and helped her forget the cancer that would probably kill her. No one else but Eddie could make her laugh as much.

Eddie plastered a big grin on his face before he faced Mimi.

"The prodigal returns," exclaimed Ez, shaking Eddie's hand. "Great to see ya, Eddie. Welcome home."

"Hey Ez. How ya been? Pop!" said Eddie reaching out to give Sam a hug. "Hello Ma," called Eddie, to his mother in the kitchen. There was no response other than the clanging of pots and pans.

He perched on the bed and gently embraced Mimi. He ignored the bandages across her chest and the pale, mottled skin of her face. She wore a cotton bedjacket that didn't conceal the very large bandage or the drain emerging from under it.

"I'm home Mimi! I made it. What do ya think of that? I'm back to pester you. As Pop always says 'they can shoot ya, but they can't eat ya,' am I right?" Eddie found himself babbling incoherently, more frightened by how his sister looked than anything he'd so far seen in the Army. Pop raised an eyebrow, signaling him to slow down a bit.

"Have you eaten?" yelled Ma from the kitchen. She hadn't seen her youngest child for almost a year. Eddie winked at Mimi and got off the bed to see his mother. He hugged her; she hugged him back with more tenderness than he'd expected. Then she pushed him away and turned back to the sink.

After they ate together, Miriam on a tray laid across the bed, the others sitting in chairs holding the plates on their laps, Miriam motioned for Eddie to bend down so she could whisper to him. Sam and Gussie had gone upstairs. Ez was washing the dishes.

"Eddie, I'm so glad you're home. I've missed you so much. Are you okay? Are you alright?"

Eddie sat on the bed again and moved his head close to hers. "Of course, I'm alright. I'm tough, remember?"

"I'm so sorry you've come home to this. But the doctors say I am doing better. They think I'm cured. I just need to get my energy back. "

"That's wonderful news. You'll be up and around in no time. We'll take walks together. How 'bout that? Remember, you told me I was such a cute baby that everyone stared at us when you used to take me out in the baby carriage? We're both so good looking, they'll be staring again!" he said.

"Eddie, you go and see Natty. She must be waiting for you. Go see her. We'll talk more tomorrow. I'm very tired now anyway. "

"Okay, big sister," he said as he gave her a kiss on the cheek. "See ya tomorrow. Get some rest."

Then, before he went through the door, he whispered "I love you," then louder, "See ya Ez, thanks for supper!"

Eddie felt tears in his eyes as he walked out the front door of the building. He still wore his uniform and couldn't be seen crying in public. He ducked into a nearby bar, sat down on a stool and ordered a beer. He had to recover from seeing Mimi in such bad shape, especially since his next stop after picking up Natty would be to go with her to visit Harry in the hospital.

What's happening? Why are two of the people I care about the most, so sick? I don't know if I can face Harry after seeing Mimi. He hoped the beer would fortify him. Later, he'd explain to Natty that the alcohol on his breath was because everything was coming at him at once: arriving home, seeing how ill Mimi was, and having to face a very ill man who was like another father to him.

Legally, he was too young to drink but the uniform convinced the bartenders to look the other way. Eddie barely acknowledged the men in the bar who offered to buy him drinks and patted him on the back. "Good man!" "Need a job?" they called to him. He thanked them but declined their offers of drinks and jobs or dates with their daughters. He peeled the label off the beer bottle and kept to himself. He didn't know what to do with so many worries. *If only I could deal with one at a time. I might be able to manage it.*

He left some coins on the bar and headed outside. The day was still sunny. He was glad he'd seen his family so he could spend the rest of the day with Natty. He decided to walk to Natty's house although it was a few miles and would shorten the time he had with her. It had been a long time since he'd walked in the sunshine without carrying a rifle and pack.

*****

Eddie told himself to stop thinking about the Army and focus on what was happening now. Before he knocked on Natty's door, he posted a great big smile on his face like he'd done when he went to see Mimi. Suddenly, he felt very tired. He'd barely slept on the trip from Camp Hood. It had been noisy on the trains, and, although that usually didn't bother him, he'd been too excited and anxious about returning home even to get a good nap.

Natty ran down the stairs in the two-family house on Chester Street. Her family was living on the top floor and renting the downstairs to a young couple. She'd left the main door to the house unlocked so whenever Eddie arrived, he could just walk in. She'd been sitting at the window for an hour, waiting to see his characteristic saunter from across the street.

"Eddie!" she shouted, as she ran down the stairs. She wore a white long-sleeved blouse with frills at the neck and a black skirt.

"Nat," he answered, lifting her off the ground. They kissed quickly, then Natty grabbed his hand.

"Come upstairs. I don't want the nosy tenants to bother us," said Natty as she wiped her red lipstick off his lips with her fingers.

"It's great to see you, Nat. I can't believe I'm finally here," said Eddie as Natty led him to the sofa. He gave her a long, wet kiss, then pulled back suddenly.

"But, I'm sorry to hear about your father. What happened?"

Natty sat back against the sofa and tucked her legs under her skirt. She held Eddie's hand.

"Mother says he hemorrhaged," she said quietly, beginning to cry. "I went into the bathroom to brush my teeth before school. I thought he'd spilled coffee grounds in there!" she laughed joylessly. "Mother says that was blood. He was coughing up blood into the toilet and drops splattered everywhere."

"Oh no. How is he now? What's going to happen? Is he any better?"

"No, Mother doesn't tell us much, but she seems very worried. She spends all day at the hospital taking care of him. In fact, I told her we'd go there as soon as you got here. He wants to see you."

"I want to see him, but what should I say? Should we bring anything?"

"Just talk to him. That's what Mother says. You're lucky you can go into his room. I can't. You have to be over eighteen. Abby's there now but I think she'll be home soon. There are a few flowers growing out back. I'll get some for you. Daddy likes flowers. Eddie, I'm so worried. I wish I could see him. What'll I do if he dies?"

"Come on, Nat, calm down. Let's hope he'll get better. Come with me. You can wait in the lobby. After I see him, we'll grab dinner. We have a lot of catching up to do."

They took the trolley and then walked three blocks to the hospital. The light green cinderblock walls were depressing. Eddie wondered why the hospital didn't look more cheerful. He'd been to this one before, when he'd taken Mimi for epinephrine injections for her asthma. Natty sat down in the lobby and began flipping through a magazine.

"I'll give him the flowers," said Eddie.

"And my love," Natty said and kissed his cheek.

Eddie asked a nurse for directions to Harry's room and came upon a ward of men lying in eight beds lined up on each side of the room. Harry's was at the end. Eddie saw the oxygen tent first, then recognized Rose in her crisp white nurse's uniform, tightening the bed sheets around Harry.

Eddie waited a minute before showing himself. It was visiting hour and other visitors stood between him and Harry's bed.

He looks so thin, thought Eddie. *His skin is as white as his sheets. I don't think he's gonna make it.*

He tried to smile and clutching the flowers Natty had picked, he approached the bed in the far corner. He spread his arms wide as if encompassing the whole scene of Harry, the oxygen tent, the bed, and Rose.

"Look who's here," he said, cheerfully.

The transparent oxygen tent covered Harry's bed. He smiled at Eddie and reached outside the tent to shake his hand. Harry's hand was cool and clammy inside Eddie's strong, warm hand. Then, Eddie loosened his grip, slumped into a chair beside the bed, and covered his eyes. He needed a moment to collect himself. It was all too much and he was so tired. He longed to find some way to comfort Harry and keep him from fading away. He wished they could both get some sleep and wake up to find that all was as it should be.

"I'll go get some coffee and let you both catch up," said Rose to the men. "Eddie, can I see you a minute, please?"

Rose walked with him past the rows of beds. "Welcome home," she said without irony. "He's been looking forward to seeing you. I know it's hard but you mustn't look so glum. He needs cheering up. Tell him some funny stories about the Army. Surely, you must have some." With that, she turned on her heel and left. He watched her go, the seams in her white stockings as straight as if she'd taken a ruler to them. He idly wondered how women did it; they had so much to wear and it all had to be just so.

He walked back to Harry and pulled a chair up to the bed. He put the flowers on the bedside table.

"These are from Natty with her love. How are you feeling, Sir?"

"I'm dying, Eddie. I know it. Rose isn't sure whether I know it or not. It's hard for her. She's trying to nurse me, be steady and professional but I can see her gloom," Harry said this in slow bursts, inhaling enough oxygen from the tent to lift it up to say a few words at a time before pulling it around him again.

"I'm sure you'll be fine soon," said Eddie, hands clasped between his knees to keep them steady, unable to look Harry in the eye.

"Listen Eddie, don't kid a kidder. Besides, lying doesn't become you. Let's not waste time talking nonsense, tell me how you're doing? How'd the Army treat you?"

Eddie chuckled, "I suppose as good as can be expected. It's the Army, after all! The food was terrible and green's not my color."

Harry laughed, "Ha! Now, you'll appreciate Rose's cooking. Listen Eddie, there isn't much time before Rose comes back. I need to tell you a few things, but first, I need the bedpan. Can you help me?"

Eddie looked around the bed. He saw an oval metal pan that looked a little like a toilet seat, picked it up and waved it at Harry who nodded. Harry talked him through how to close the privacy screens and help him turn to his side so Eddie could slip the bedpan underneath him. Eddie felt embarrassed for both of them. He hated seeing this man for whom he had so much respect struggling to fit himself onto the cold metal pan, revealing his genitals in the process. Eddie moved to leave the bedside to give Harry privacy.

"No, don't leave, Eddie. Please don't go. Just turn around if you would; face the corner. I'll tell you when I'm done," muttered Harry between coughs. His breath came more shallowly now even as he sat on the bedpan under the oxygen tent.

While Eddie faced the corner, he tried to think of how he could help Harry, a dignified and educated man. He was never aloof or distant but he was out of his element in a family of three needy women and had little to give them. Eddie couldn't bear to watch him die in such embarrassing circumstances.

"You can turn around now, Son. I hate to ask, but I need help cleaning up here. I'm afraid I made a mess of it."

"Sure thing, Sir. You forget, I've been living with a bunch of messy guys for the past year," said Eddie, laughing to ease Harry's embarrassment. "There was one guy who was constantly getting in trouble for making his bed wrong and he never could roll his socks the right way. When he got in trouble, we all got in trouble, so one day when we had a few minutes, I took him aside and showed him how to make his bed and roll his socks. He was a real hick. I don't think he'd made a bed in his entire life! By the end, he was one of my best friends."

Harry was laughing when Rose came back. She laughed with them although she didn't know why they were laughing. Eddie thought it was a good time to leave and let Harry rest.

He said good-bye, then went to the lobby to fetch Natty.

"How is he?" she asked, standing up and walking toward him.

"He's a strong man. Still has his sense of humor. He sent his love."

"Do you think he'll get better enough to come home?"

"I don't know; he says he feels better," Eddie lied. "C'mon, let's get something to eat. I'm starving."

*****

Every day, Eddie went to see Harry and help with his care. Rose took a much-needed break while the two men talked about almost everything, especially Eddie's future plans. That was what Harry wanted to talk about during the first visit but after Eddie had helped him clean up, he was too tired to talk anymore and then Rose came in. During another visit, while he washed Harry, Eddie told him about past boxing bouts and how he'd wiped the floor with his opponents. "I hope to be as good as Bummy Davis," he said.

"Yeah, but look what happened to him," replied Harry. "Eddie, you're a talented artist and you're smart. Focus on your art and going to school. You're liable to end up with hands that are no good and you'll have nothing."

Harry saw Eddie as a Renaissance man, someone who'd be comfortable with art, music, literature, and all kinds of people. He'd tried to groom him for that role since they'd first met. Eddie was bright and inquisitive. He took to the opera after that first visit to see *Carmen* with Natty. He'd not only borrowed the books Harry had suggested but he'd actually read them. Eddie seemed interested in Harry's perspectives on books they'd both read. It was not only for Natty's sake, but for Eddie's own, that Harry intended to use his last breaths to push him in the right direction.

Harry loved looking through the oxygen tent at the caricatures Eddie drew of the doctors who stopped by the room once a day. Even the doctors thought they were funny. Eddie didn't dare make fun of the nurses, although there was plenty to satirize. Rose might have kicked him out of the room which would've been bad for both Harry and Eddie.

Eddie enjoyed the talks and scarcely minded helping Harry with the urinal or the bedpan. Harry always seemed relieved when Eddie showed up and treasured the messages he brought from Natty. After that first day, she waited for Eddie at home. He walked three miles every evening to visit her and often slept on the couch in the living room with Rose and Abby as chaperones. He asked Rose what else he could do to help Harry. He'd tried giving blood, but it was the wrong type. Rose told him to do what he was doing: sit with him, talk with him, and laugh with him.

*****

In the long silences while he struggled to breathe and could no longer recite poetry to Rose or talk to Eddie, Harry thought about his family. He despaired about Abby but guessed that Rose would continue to drag her from doctor to doctor, heedless of anyone's advice. Rose would protect Abby, who perhaps didn't need quite so much protection. He hoped Abby would someday break away from her mother. Abby had never really needed Harry in her life.

Rose, he knew, would find another man before his body was cold. He didn't mind. It was the flirtations she'd had that he despised. He was doing her a favor by dying. As long as she retained her beauty, she would have all she needed and wanted.

Harry knew Natty would be alright. Her natural easy-going personality would see her through most trials and Harry hoped Eddie would get her through the rest. Eddie, on the other hand, had a loving father and siblings but he was mostly on his own. From what Eddie had told him, it sounded like his father doted on the kid but rarely had time for him and they had little in common. Harry knew that after he died, Eddie would have to choose his own direction. The Army was a good start. Unfortunately, Eddie working as an artist would be like Harry's jobs managing stores. Sometimes someone bought something; more often than not, they didn't. An artist's life was going to be one of feast or famine. Still, he knew Eddie would take care of Natty. He wouldn't let her go without.

*****

Harry died an unhappy man. He'd had a bad marriage and a failed career. He'd known his legacy would be his daughters, especially Natty, who was most like him and was sure to remember him with love. His funeral was held in the synagogue he'd attended most weeks. His death hit Eddie hard. He loved his own father but couldn't talk to him about literature or opera. He promised himself that he'd try to be more like Harry. He'd work hard like Pop and take care of his family, but he also wanted to be a man who could talk about books and music.

Natty would mourn her father for the rest of her long life. He remained in her memory as a sixteen-year-old girl would remember her father. He was big and smart and protective but was rarely happy. As she got older, she blamed her mother for making Harry's life a miserable one.

CHAPTER SEVENTEEN

1950

Eddie was in Camp Hood, Texas when he got the telegram saying Pop had dropped dead in the street. He was shocked by the news, although he'd known Pop was not well. Harry's death had brought home to him how fragile both men had been. While he'd been home, he'd made the effort to talk to his father whenever they could both find the time. He asked him if he regretted leaving his family and Russia.

"I wish I could have seen my father again," Pop had answered. "If I'd known I'd never get to see him or talk with him again, I might not have left but I really didn't have a choice. My father made me leave. He saved me. That's what a father is supposed to do for a son. Mac went to war and survived. No thanks to me. Now, you're in the Army. I'm so proud of you both and of Ez and Aaron. But now I know how my father must have felt."

"But you did save us, Pop. You've fed us and clothed us, given us a roof over our heads. You've saved us from Ma when we couldn't take it anymore. You've always made us laugh. I wouldn't be here if it weren't for you!"

Pop laughed, "I suppose I did protect you from your mamma!"

Another time, Eddie asked him if there was anything he regretted about his life. They were the only ones at home. Eddie had made them corned beef sandwiches and coffee. They'd been reading the newspaper.

"Regrets are for people who've never had to work hard to feed a family. Remember this, my boychik, you do what you have to do, when it has to be done. You do the right thing for the right reasons. Then, when you look back, you have nothing to regret. You just work hard and be an honest man. An honest man has no time for regrets."

Now, Eddie thought about the questions he hadn't asked and kicked himself for not making more time for his father before he had. Later in life, he would often wonder what Pop would do in his place.

The Army quickly arranged his transportation. There was to be a memorial service in the house with Mac and Eddie eulogizing. On his arrival home, Eddie arranged to speak to the rabbi at the corner synagogue.

Eddie still in uniform, said. "Thanks for seeing me, Rabbi."

"It's been a long time. I've only seen you a few times since your Bar Mitzvah," replied the Rabbi, who was staring intently at Eddie as they sat opposite each other in his office.

"Rabbi, I've been in the Army long enough now to know it's better to not make excuses, so I won't try. I'm not here for me but for my father. I'm home on leave because he died this week."

"Zayt mir moykhl, I'm so sorry," said the Rabbi assuming the posture of concern and condolence he saved for bad news.

"Thank you, Rabbi. We'd like to have the funeral here. It would mean a lot to my mother."

"When it's her time, I'd be happy to have a funeral here for her. She's a regular member of our congregation. But your father? No. He was not. Never set foot in the place that I can remember, except for weddings and Bar Mitzvahs. No, I won't allow it."

"You won't allow it, Rabbi?" said Eddie, his voice rising. "Isn't that for God to say? What do you mean, you won't allow it?" Eddie rose from the chair and stared down at the bearded man in front of him.

"He should have attended services. What kind of a Jew was he? Raised to be religious, wasn't he? So, your mother said." The Rabbi remained seated, adjusted the yarmulke on the back of his head and straightened his tie. "He might have contributed to our congregation. He chose not to. I'm choosing not to have his funeral here and that's all I'll say about the matter. I'm sorry for your loss though and will say Yizkor for him, if that will comfort you."

Eddie didn't want to have to punch a rabbi, so he held his tongue and left the building. Instead, he punched the outside wall till his knuckles bled.

He squatted next to the synagogue; face turned to the wall. He cried for himself and for Pop. He remembered the last time they were together. They'd stayed up late one night shortly before Eddie left for Texas.

"Pop, please take care of yourself," he'd said, holding his father's hand, sitting in the living room after everyone had gone to sleep.

"I always do," laughed Sam, making light of Eddie's concern.

"Please stop drinking and smoking so much. Pop, I beg you. Please," Eddie had said, looking at his father in the dim light of the table lamp. Sam was fifty-nine years old, but looked eighty due to a life of unhappiness, strong drink, and very hard work.

"You smoke too, Boychik. Do you think I don't know!" was all Pop said, teasingly.

Eddie realized he hadn't made Pop's life any easier. He hadn't taken to the life of a builder. He could've been helping Pop instead of drawing or boxing. *What was I thinking?*

Pop had always encouraged Eddie's art but worried he would ruin his hands or get badly hurt if he continued to box. Like all kids that age, Eddie did it anyway and learned he liked the money and the notoriety he got as *The Blond Tiger*. Although Eddie was twenty, he was really still a kid and resented the Army for taking the last days his father had on earth away from him.

The memorial service at the house was packed with people Eddie had never met, plus the tenants from the old building. The people Sam used to help before, during, and after the Depression by repairing all manner of broken things for free, showed up to pay their respects. Old customers who'd stayed in touch with Sam and newer customers who already liked him, came, until people spilled out of the house, overflowing both the up and downstairs levels. Some even went down into the basement to Eddie's old studio. The studio reminded Eddie that he should honor his father's memory by making the most of his talent.

Eddie hadn't slept more than a couple of hours since he'd received the telegram about Pop. He didn't think he could sleep until he'd had time to think and sit with Natty, who would help him deal with his grief. She attended the memorial service and stayed close to Eddie in case he needed her. She didn't speak, but peeked into Miriam's kitchen now and then to see if she should put more food on the table. Friends and neighbors brought food, all kosher with clean white cloths covering the large plates and platters. She helped Edna put out utensils, dinner plates, and glasses. Gussie remained upstairs bustling about, replacing dishes as fast as she cleared them. Everyone told her to sit and rest but she ignored them.

Gussie had known this would happen. She was angry at Sam for leaving her alone. She always knew it would either be the drink or the work that killed him. During the last few years, they'd barely talked and Sam's attempts at affection had long ceased. She still cooked his meals and washed his clothes.

She remembered how he looked when she first met him at Fannie's house. Sam had just taken the job with Fannie's husband, doing construction. She hadn't thought much of his looks but he'd paid so much attention to her and he knew many of the places she'd known. They'd grown up not far from each other. She wanted to marry someone from home. Besides, he already had a good job and Fannie had told her that he was bound to move up in the company.

So, they'd married and had four children. Sam had been easygoing. He'd let her rant and rave when she needed to and rarely got angry with her. He'd understood why she was angry all the time even if he didn't approve. He was very protective of Eddie, maybe because she was tired of children by the time Eddie was born. Now, Sam was gone. *What will we do without him?* She didn't recall ever telling him she loved him - because she didn't think she did. But he used to tell her he loved her. Maybe if she hadn't ignored him, he would've continued to say it. She'd depended on him. Now, she'd need Mac and Ez to take care of her. *Maybe I'll move out of the building.*

"Ma, please sit down and rest," said Mac. He was the only one of the family who might convince Ma to leave the fussing to someone else, just for today.

"There's too much to do," Ma answered in Yiddish. She wore a long black dress she only took out for funerals. It came from the old country and had been altered many times since. It was stored in an old trunk and smelled like it.

Mac brought his mother into his chest for a hug. He held her there until she scoffed at him, turned away and wiped her eyes with the white apron she wore over her dress.

"Leave me alone. I need to be busy. You can get all these people to leave and then clean up afterward. They're making a big mess."

*****

In July, North Korea invaded South Korea in an attack that surprised everyone. President Truman got the United Nations to intervene and American troops rushed to help stop the Communists. Within weeks, Eddie was on a ship to Pusan. Tanks were needed desperately in Korea, where the North Koreans had big Russian T-34 tanks. The U.S. Army had stopped building Pershing heavy tanks right after the end of World War II and had not developed a replacement for them. The situation was so desperate that the Army was refurbishing Pershing tanks that were being used as monuments and shipping them to Korea. But Eddie would be commanding a lighter Sherman tank, that everyone knew was not an even match for a T-34.

The closest Eddie had ever come to being on a boat was the Staten Island ferry. He was surprised to not get seasick on the ship to Pusan and irritated that because he wasn't sick, he was constantly being put to work. He decided it was best to get lost. He prowled the troop ship every day trying to make himself invisible. He especially liked going into the bowels of the ship and wandering until some sailor spotted him and told him to beat feet.

While he was on the ship, Eddie found a minute to send a short note to Mimi to ask her to convince Ma to invite Natty for dinner and make her feel part of the family. He heard later that Mimi had done her best, but Ma had argued for days before finally agreeing.

Natty had started nursing school in September, about the same time Eddie had shipped out. She was glad she didn't have to pay any tuition since she was destitute. Natty lived in a student residence whose restrictions on dating rivaled the convent. It hardly mattered, since she didn't know when she'd see Eddie again. She was pleased to receive the invitation to dinner. It came from Miriam on lovely cream-colored paper.

Natty traded her shift with one of her roommates for an evening off. She was very excited. Her roommates donated their clothes for an outfit of a red sweater set and black skirt. She borrowed a real pearl necklace and clip on earrings from her classmate Donna. Natty wore her jet-black hair long and added a touch of lipstick. She thought she looked smashing except for her shoes, also borrowed and too small. She once heard that "beauty is pain" so she vowed to silently endure it. Besides, they were black patent leather and very sharp looking. Ez offered to pick her up for which she was very grateful, unsure she could walk all the way to the house in the tiny shoes.

"I hope you won't expect much, Natty. You've met Gussie before. She's not very nice. Please don't take it personally. I don't think she likes anyone except maybe Mac, and sometimes, me. Mac will be there and Mimi and me. You like us, I hope," he laughed.

"Don't worry. I just hope she likes my gift. I've been saving some money from my stipend to buy her these adorable cat and mouse salt and pepper shakers. Do you think she will?" said Natty, carefully unwrapping the plain brown paper to show him the gift.

He replied "They're very nice" but quickly moved on. "Listen, when the boat I was on in the war was torpedoed by a German submarine, I swam in the ocean till I thought I would die. Whenever I hear Gussie yelling, I think of that time. I was alone and scared but it was quiet, too quiet. I make myself think of that quiet. Now, strangely enough, it helps keep me calm. If she yells at you or anyone else, you just do the same. Just think of a place you know that is quiet and keep calm, okay?" He finished with a smile and squeezed her hand for reassurance. When they reached the two-family house, Ez bowed gallantly and held the door for Natty.

"Mimi, we're here. Natty's here," he called into the kitchen from the hallway.

"Why, who's this beautiful Indian princess with you tonight?" laughed Mac, giving Natty a hug. He'd come home early, shaved and showered because he knew the evening meant a lot to Eddie. Tomorrow, he would write and tell him all went well, even if it didn't.

Mimi came through the door; they crowded the small hallway. It seemed that she had recovered from the cancer but was hunched over like an old woman and breathing heavily. She leaned over with her hands on her knees trying to catch her breath. Once she did, she gave Natty a gentle hug. Mimi beckoned for them to go into her apartment and sit down. She and Ez didn't have a dining room but they added place settings to their kitchen table and everyone crowded around.

Gussie emerged from the kitchen carrying the potato kugel platter like it was laden with pure gold instead of a mishmash of potatoes, onions, and eggs. She had cooked upstairs and given Mac the platter to carry down. He'd put it on the kitchen counter in Mimi's apartment so Gussie could bring it to the table and receive the acclaim she expected from her family. She made good kugel so it was not hard to compliment it but it was still best to make a fuss when she placed it on the table.

"Thank you so much for inviting me to dinner, Mrs. Roth," said Natty after everyone had sat down and she got the nod from Miriam to speak to her mother while she was in a relatively good mood.

"I brought these for you," Natty said and smiled as she handed the gift to Gussie who pursed her lips. She unwrapped the cat and mouse salt and pepper shakers, looked at them carefully, and pushed the gift into Natty's hands saying "You think I'm a rat?!"

"Ma!" said Mac sharply. He rose from his seat. Everyone else did too, except Gussie who looked at him and remained in her seat. Taken aback, Natty was silent for a moment, then pushed in her chair and moved away from the table. She went into the kitchen; Miriam followed her. She reached out to her and whispered, "I'm so sorry; she can be so mean."

Natty thought about Ez's story. She realized she couldn't recall a time or place when she'd had complete quiet. Most of her life till that point had been spent sleeping next to her sister in Brownsville or in Cleveland and being awakened every night by Abby's crazy questions. Other times, she stayed with noisy and nosy relatives in Cleveland, or was in school which was always noisy. She loved remembering the times she and her father sat together reading. That was probably the nearest she'd been to complete quiet but she could always hear the tenants in the house or the neighbors through the airshaft.

Mimi tried to comfort Natty in the kitchen, "That's just her, Natty. She's mean, that's all. This is a lovely gift. Where'd you get it? Why, they're just what I've been looking for," she said, chatting as if nothing had happened while fondling the salt and pepper shakers she honestly thought were a bit tacky.

"Do you like them? I do. I thought she would like them. I wanted to bring something. I guess it was all wrong," sniffed Natty. "Please take them if you like them. I want you to have them."

"Lovely. Thank you, Natty. Now, let's go back to the table and eat. Ma may be mean but she makes great potato kugel!" Miriam led Natty back to her seat, thinking of her little brother who clearly hadn't thought this through.

The rest of the meal was uneventful. Natty chose to remain silent but the others chatted cheerfully, ignoring Gussie except to compliment her on the kugel. It was the last time for a long time before Natty would have to see Gussie again. Eddie didn't know the story until many years later, when it made him angry at his mother all over again. By then, she was long gone but not forgotten.

*****

Edna made several trips in from Long Island to look after Ma. Miriam was not well enough to endure her or meet her demands. Her own daughter was three and her son, six. Her children demanded most of her time. Ez paid more attention to Gussie and her needs than to his own family. Taking Gussie to see her family out on Long Island conveniently let him go missing for a couple of hours that he spent with a woman he'd met in Edna's neighborhood.

Edna threw a small surprise birthday party for Gussie during one of these visits. Gussie had never known her birthday because it was bad luck to say the date out loud and no one kept records in Poland when she was born. Edna made up a birthday date. She couldn't say the date out loud for fear of attracting the angel of death, so she wrote the numbers on a slip of paper for Ma to put in her pocketbook. Ma couldn't read but she could hand it to someone if God forbid, she ended up in the hospital.

Gussie derived very little joy from the party. She thought celebrating birthdays was a waste of time and energy. She preferred to spend most of her time cooking, shopping with money her children gave her and could barely spare, and watching soap operas on television. She didn't understand all the dialogue but knew each scenario was largely the same - love matches that started out secretly, became well known, and eventually fell apart with divorce, death, and weddings sprinkled liberally throughout. But everyone else enjoyed the cake Dottie had made, especially the children.

CHAPTER EIGHTEEN

1950-1951

They'd routed the North Koreans out of South Korea and the war was supposed to end by Christmas. That's what General MacArthur had said. The day after Thanksgiving, when every American soldier had eaten real roast turkey with all the traditional side dishes, the Chinese launched a massive surprise attack. Later, the news reported three hundred thousand Communist Chinese had secretly moved into North Korea and were attacking in "human waves."

Eddie and his tank crew found themselves on rough terrain in weather thirty degrees below zero. It was early December and the 2nd Infantry Division was cut off by the Chinese and forced to flee south. Chinese, hiding in the hills near Kunu-Ri, ambushed them in the worst American defeat since the early days of World War II.

Eddie saw trucks blocking the road that had been shot to pieces by enemy machine guns. As his tank pushed the trucks off the road, he realized they were crammed full with American soldiers, both the dead and wounded. His battalion's job was to open the pass to let the 2nd Division's survivors escape from the trap. He watched from the turret of his tank as panicked GIs came running toward him, yelling shrill warnings that hordes of Chinese were close on their heels. There was massive chaos. Blood and body parts were strewn about the road. Sometimes, his tank carried wounded on the back deck where the heat from the engine would keep them from freezing to death. Other times, exhausted and mentally spent soldiers who were not wounded climbed aboard the tank as it slowly moved along, cramming themselves on to every available space. He had to force some of them off because the tank would be useless in combat – which seemed endless.

Sometimes, Eddie and his crew slept under the tank in a hole dug in the dirt. But when they didn't have time to dig and knew that lying down in the snow and slush would be a death sentence, three men would lean together in a triangle, wrap their arms around each other's shoulders, and sleep standing up. Impossible as it seemed, this worked pretty well. Eddie learned to change his socks frequently, pinning an extra pair inside his shirt to dry them out.

The Chinese usually attacked at night from the mountains. One night, a bazooka hit Eddie's tank and set it on fire. He and the other crew members jumped out and used the tank for cover, firing until the shells inside the turret started exploding. Eddie later remembered he and his crew riding out on the surviving tanks while other men waded across a frozen stream.

As the tank commander, Eddie spent most of his time with his head sticking out of the turret using binoculars to scan for enemy tanks and soldiers. He wore a converted, leather football helmet which gave scant protection against bullets and shrapnel. He was well aware of his vulnerability, but knew that maximizing his visual capability would help save them all. Eddie was in a reconnaissance platoon, so stealth was essential. They could hear the Russian tanks the North Koreans and Chinese were using before they saw them. Unlike American tanks, their wheels and treads had no rubber covering, and the bare metal rubbing on bare metal caused an earsplitting shriek. More than once, his Sherman tank had knocked on an enemy tank whose deafened crew never heard them sneaking up from behind.

The radio and the Army's *Stars and Stripes* newspaper, which amazingly continued to reach the front during the great retreat, kept Eddie up-to-date on what was happening outside of his view. In January, 1951, the Communists took Seoul, South Korea's capital, for a second time. That conceited glory hound Douglas MacArthur, who spent most of his time in Tokyo and never visited the troops in the field, was warning that he could not stop the Chinese offensive without attacking China, itself - possibly with nuclear weapons. It looked like World War III was right around the corner and MacArthur was anxious to get it started.

Yet, for all of MacArthur's gloomy predictions, things were improving at the front. General Walton Walker, the man who was really commanding the allied forces in Korea, had died in a jeep accident near the end of December. General Matthew Ridgeway, known by the soldiers as "tin-tits" since he always wore a pair of grenades on his web gear, took over the dispirited 8th Army and soon breathed new life into it. He proved MacArthur was wrong by halting the retreat and it turned out that the dreaded Chinese were, at least for the moment, incapable of advancing any further.

Eddie liked Ridgeway, who had made a point of visiting every unit in Korea to buck up the troops' morale and promised that they'd soon have the enemy on the run and take back the ground that had been lost. When Ridgeway visited Eddie's unit, his presence buoyed all of them and he listened earnestly to their gripes about the conditions in which they had to live and fight. Eddie even got to shake the General's hand. It was quite a change from MacArthur, whom they all hated for taking credit for victories while he sat comfortably in Japan.

They all got to see Ridgeway's trademark grenades close up. They said the General always wore them because he was a paratrooper in World War II and knew that he could wind up in combat anytime he jumped behind enemy lines. To prevent the grenades from going off by accident, he taped the handles. Eddie heard a soldier with a southern drawl yell out from the crowd, "Sir, I don't think those grenades will do ya much good with tape on em."

Everyone laughed, including Ridgeway. But the company commander was embarrassed and angry. After the General left, Eddie heard that the poor guy got a dressing down you could hear a mile away.

Ridgeway led them back north to retake Seoul and then push on towards the 38th Parallel that marked the border between North and South Korea. Although they were winning again, the fighting was hard. Luck ran out for Eddie's tank when an antitank shell penetrated the armor and started a fire that quickly spread to the fuel and ammunition. Eddie, with his head and shoulders sticking out of the turret as always, climbed out before the explosion that killed his four crewmates.

They'd been like brothers to him and had learned to read each other's thoughts, working in unison like a single machine. Their deaths devastated Eddie and he reeled in grief and disbelief, heedless of the incoming enemy fire. One of the platoon's infantry scouts ran to him and pulled him to cover. Later, Eddie could only think about how he shouldn't have survived. *Who am I? Nothing. Bubkes. My own mother can't stand me.*

He was shaken. He'd lost his crew and many of the guys who'd hung onto his tank or had run alongside trying to climb aboard, were dead. Eddie had frost bite and there was shrapnel buried in his back and his legs. After he'd been treated for his injuries, Eddie was sent to Japan to rest. He didn't spend much time resting but went bar hopping and got into a couple of fights, wading, practically at random, into brawls between groups of drunken servicemen. He had a grand time and even managed to purchase real jade earrings and a bracelet for Natty.

While he was in Tokyo, MacArthur finally went too far and Truman sacked the bastard. The President had decided, sensibly Eddie thought, to seek a ceasefire and negotiate an end to the fighting with the front line pretty much on South Korea's prewar border. But MacArthur had gone public with a statement threatening to destroy Red China itself. He also wrote a letter to a Republican congressman declaring "there is no substitute for victory" and the man read it on the floor of the House. There was a big brouhaha back at home where everyone seemed to be denouncing Truman and applauding MacArthur, but were any of those loudmouths going to volunteer to come over to Korea and personally drive the Chinese back to the Yalu – and beyond? It was easy to talk about fighting until victory was achieved when you were safe, warm and well-fed back in the U.S.

When he got back to his unit, he found a letter from Natty. He'd had little time to think of her; that world seemed far away and from another lifetime.

Guess what? Norm and Gloria are thinking of getting married! Can you believe it? You remember Gloria, Arnie's sister? I think they'll be good together. Fagie and Bernie are still dating. I wouldn't be surprised if they tied the knot someday, too. I'll never forget that dinner when my mother tried to set me up with him! I only asked Fagie to go out with him to please my mother. Who would have guessed they'd hit it off?

School is good. I'm glad I'm usually so busy I can't think of anything else, but I always think of you, especially when I finally get ready for sleep. I'm so worried about you. Please write.

I love you,

Natty

P. S. Are you using the cigarette lighter I gave you? It should remind you of me no matter where you are.

Eddie sat on his bunk and wrote back.

Dear Nat,
Thanks for the letter. I'm sorry I haven't written. You've probably read in the papers about what's been happening over here. But don't worry. I'm fine. I got a little frostbite in my ankles but that's healing well. I thought NY winters were cold! They're warm compared to here.
I just got back from Japan. They sent me to Tokyo for a rest. I loved it. I hope I can take you there, someday. I bought a surprise for you, too. The food was great.
Well, I have to go. I'll write to Norm and Arnie when I get a chance. Don't worry about me. Say hello to your mom and my folks if you see them.
I miss and love you,
Eddie

A few days later, he wrote to Norm and Arnie who were also still serving. He gave them advice.

Norm, why are you thinking of marrying Gloria? She's not right for you. She'll always want more than you can give her. I'm telling you. It'll be a mistake.
Arnie, you know Gloria and Norm are all wrong together. She's a great gal but they're so different. You know it won't work. Anything you can do?

The guys wrote back but didn't say anything about Norm's impending engagement. The letters were brief. They were safe and relatively well. That was all that mattered. Babe and Eppy wrote to try to keep Eddie's spirits up. Babe's hair had grown back, blond and thick. He'd become quite handsome, but he was told he was still unfit for service. Eppy was in and out of prison for a variety of crimes. Eddie secretly resented his safety.

Mimi had also written saying nothing about her asthma or her fear of the cancer returning. Instead, she dwelt on her childrens' exploits, and the nieces and nephews. She was increasingly unhappy with Ez, who was rarely home. Ma visited with her pots and pans and made a point of harassing her on a daily basis.

Mac wrote Eddie about how to survive in combat. He reminded him to stay out of the guard house and to take his anger and fear out on the enemy or in the boxing ring. But the advice wasn't heeded or necessary. Eddie had found himself in the guard house more than once, usually for legitimate reasons. The Army was still antisemitic and anti-black. He was always defending his buddies like Big John, another tank commander in Eddie's battalion, who returned the favor when the Jew haters decided to have a little fun.

When they were bored, the soldiers fought each other. When they weren't fighting, they were complaining. They griped about the filth, the food, the mud when it was warm and the ice when it was cold - and the officers' incompetence and the stupidity of war. Eddie was promoted to corporal but with each stay in the guard house, he lost stripes until he earned them back again in combat.

A few weeks after Eddie returned to Korea, the Chinese launched a big counterattack and tried to take Seoul yet again. When a South Korean division routed off to the east somewhere, the whole UN front had to fall back practically to the outskirts of the capital, but they stopped the enemy attack there and Chinese casualties were incredibly high. Eddie's unit, the 79th Tank Battalion, also had painful losses. Big John was killed when a shell hit his tank turret and sent shrapnel into his brain. Shortly after, a shell bounced off Eddie's tank killing a soldier sheltering alongside it. The explosion also blew one of the officers into the air to land like one of Eddie's boxing opponents, hard on the ground. Mortar rounds hit other men, killing a few and severely wounding others. The confusion allowed some enemy soldiers to rush the tanks but most were shot before they could inflict further damage.

Years later, instead of talking about the horrors of war, he liked to tell everyone about the letter a guy in his outfit in Korea had sent to the Women's Christian Temperance Union after they lobbied successfully to stop the soldiers' beer rations. They didn't think good American soldiers fighting godless Communists should be drinking beer. The soldiers gave up their beer and made moonshine out of potatoes instead. Eddie said the letter sent to the WCTU went something like this:

Dear Kind Ladies of the WCTU,
I am writing on behalf of my fellow soldiers to thank you for stopping our beer ration. It surely wasn't good for us. The moonshine we make now is much better and we can get much drunker, thanks to you.
Sincerely yours,
The Men of the 79th Tank Battalion

CHAPTER NINETEEN
1951

"Don't go there, Eddie. Stay away. Don't go there," said a voice that sounded like Pop's. Eddie was on guard duty, walking the perimeter. It was late at night and icy cold. He carried his rifle against his shoulder. It was miserable duty and Eddie was afraid.

"Don't go there," said the voice again. He could swear it was Pop's voice but he didn't believe in ghosts. He was dead tired and thought he was probably hallucinating. After arguing with himself about fantasy and reality, he decided to listen to the voice. He walked the opposite way. Soon, he heard gunfire from where he'd been headed and silently thanked Pop for warning him.

He never forgot the incident. It stayed with him throughout the rest of the war and the remainder of his life. It was not the first, nor the last time he'd face death and escape, but it taught him to follow his instincts.

*****

Ceasefire negotiations were underway in Korea. They sent Eddie home in the spring on a short leave before sending him to Camp Irwin, California to train other tankers. He had a hard time adjusting to being home without his old comrades. Natty found him affectionate but serious. She missed his easy laugh and how happy he'd seemed when he'd been home after basic training.

Mac, Ez, and Aaron recognized the look in his eyes as someone who'd seen combat. It was a look Eddie recognized in years to come on the faces of other veterans he saw on the streets of New York. His buddies sat with him over a few beers waiting patiently for him to talk sitting companionably with him when he didn't. He looked thin and drawn like he hadn't slept in years. He slept more than anything else while on leave, taking time in between to see Natty and Mimi. He had no interest in seeing Ma, who made no effort to spend time with him. He slept on the two chairs in the living room where he'd spent his nights as a kid. He didn't care. It was better than sleeping standing up in a foxhole or under a tank.

Eddie roughhoused with Mimi and Ez's two children, Naomi and Allan. They climbed all over him while Mimi pushed him to eat.

"Don't hurt him," said Natty to the children as she watched them wrestle with Eddie on the floor.

"They can't hurt me, Nat. I'm invincible," he said as he raised his arms, clenching his fists in a mock show of strength. His muscles bulged above his skinny arms.

Natty and Mimi laughed. "Okay, that's enough. Let's let Uncle Eddie have a chance to rest and eat something," commanded Miriam.

"Thanks, Mimi, but I think I'll grab a smoke first. I'll go outside for a bit." Natty followed him out while Mimi settled the children with glasses of milk.

Natty kissed him as soon as they were outside. He kissed her back, long and passionately, and then lit a cigarette using the silver lighter Natty had had engraved before he entered the Army.

"See, I always carry it in my left breast pocket." He held the lighter in his hand so she couldn't see the dent in the silver casing. He quickly put the lighter away, trying not to think of how it had saved his life when a piece of shrapnel, heading for his heart, had hit the lighter instead.

He smoked quietly, savoring the way the cigarette calmed him. The twitch in his left eye that had appeared at Kunu-Ri started acting up while he was playing with the children. He'd needed to hide it before Mimi and Natty began to fuss over him.

"How are you, really?" asked Natty, her arm around his waist as they sat on a bench in the front yard. It was a beautiful day, too beautiful for there to be blood and misery elsewhere in the world. People seemed to be going about their business as if this was a parallel universe, totally disconnected from Eddie's world. He thought of Korea as real and "home" as unreal. *How can the sun be shining so brightly while children play and women smile?*

"I'm fine, Nat. Really," he answered, flicking the cigarette ashes onto the sidewalk and squashing them with his shoe.

"Tell me about you. How's school? How are Rose and Abby?'

Natty had permission to spend the day with Eddie but had to return for the hospital night shift. Her roommates had once again dressed her for this visit with Eddie because Natty couldn't afford her own clothes. She had parted her black hair and fastened one side with a barrette. She wore no make-up except a little red on her lips to match her red blouse. It had barber pole stripes and Gibson girl sleeves. The black knife pleat skirt was her own. It emphasized her generous hips.

"I'm not doing well in one class, but Mrs. Shafer let me repeat an exam so I'm passing now. I begged her and am so glad she agreed. I do well in the clinical portions. I love the patients but anything involving math or science is still really hard."

"What about those doctors? I bet they ask you out a lot."

Natty laughed. "Oh, they ask everyone out. I don't go, of course. My heart's been in Korea with a skinny guy with curly hair."

Eddie tossed the remains of the cigarette; they kissed again and went back inside. The short leave was not long enough to readjust to the outside world. Eddie felt lost, only just beginning to find his feet again when it was time to go California. He figured the Army didn't want you getting too comfortable at home.

He felt just as tired as when he'd left Korea. He didn't think he'd ever be able to make up for the sleep he needed. He'd been well fed by Natty, Mimi, and Edna. Mac, Ez, and Aaron had tried to help him come back to himself. They wondered if he'd ever be the same again as they tried in vain to explain to the women that his behavior was expected. When Eddie suddenly snapped at Edna during a brief visit out on Long Island, Mac had explained it wasn't personal. Eddie went outside to have a smoke and pull himself together but he didn't apologize when he went back in. Later, after Eddie had returned to the city with Mimi and Ez, Mac apologized to her for him.

*****

Eddie liked California. It was certainly prettier than Camp Hood or Korea. He enjoyed tank training, especially when they hosted a British "armored regiment" which didn't have space to train back in England. But he rarely told others what real battles were like. He still hadn't recovered and doubted he ever would. The nightmares came every night but he'd awaken to find he was safe and stateside. He still got into fights in California. He was a sergeant now and was supposed to set an example, but had to work out his tension somehow. Drinking and fighting generally did the trick - for a while anyway.

Sometimes he and a couple of buddies went into Los Angeles in an old jalopy they'd pitched in to buy. They had a great time hanging out at the bars and listening to music. It wasn't New York but at least there was night life.

CHAPTER TWENTY

1952

Early in the year, Eddie and his buddies were ordered back to Korea. Before they left, they took the jalopy for one last ride to L.A. They left the car on a road in the hills. Inside were the keys, the ownership papers, and a note Eddie had written in his calligraphic handwriting:

Enjoy

They caught a couple of buses back to camp and shipped out a few days later.

In Korea, Eddie had a new tank crew, mostly battle-hardened soldiers. Enzo came from a New York Italian family like Babe Merola's, close knit and loving. He said he dreamed of his mother's cooking every night. That and thoughts of his girlfriend kept him going. Kevin was second generation Irish from Chicago. He grew up poor and lost his mother when he was a kid but he still had three brothers and his father. Two of his brothers were in the other services; his dad was a World War II veteran, highly decorated. Kevin said his father was proud of them, even the brother who'd been allowed to stay home and was working hard to help keep the family hardware business afloat.

Carlos and Jeff were both from Texas. They had drawling contests while their buddies from the East decided who was the least understandable. Then they became the judges when Eddie and Tony put on their strongest New

York accents. Carlos and Jeff didn't know each other when they were drafted but had become very close, having shared similar childhoods of ranches, horses, cows, and rural life, which the rest of the crew had only experienced through books and movies. Eddie and Tony teased them about being hicks. Eddie asked Mimi to send him the photo he'd sent her from Camp Hood when he'd posed as a cowboy in chaps and a vest, a cigarette hanging from his lower lip. He told Carlos and Jeff that was how a "real" cowboy should look.

The front line was pretty static and had been for almost a year. Neither side was launching major offensives while they waited for the endless peace talks in Panmunjom to produce a ceasefire. Since the UN command had decided they'd advance no further, the only way to keep pressure on the Communists and convince them to finally end the fighting was to kill Chinese and North Koreans. Eddie's new unit played a key role, driving out into no-man's-land – which was over a mile wide in many places – and firing into enemy positions at close range. It was like a complex dance. His recon platoon's jeep-mounted scouts drove out into no-man's-land and planted flags showing where the tanks could shoot from, then quickly reverse down behind a hill or low rise where the enemy couldn't see them. The tanks fired a few rounds from each position, reversed down, drove up into another position, fired a few more rounds, and then did it all over again until they ran out of ammo. Although the platoon only had five tanks, they captured a Chinese officer who insisted that an entire battalion of American tanks had attacked his unit.

******

Eddie tried not to get as close to this tank crew since he was too afraid of losing them. By now, he moved and acted as if in a trance, except when in the turret of the tank. The fight had gone out of him. He still stuck up for his buddies, fighting off other guys who were drunk or mean. But his enthusiasm for combat had faded away. He was still sent to the guard house on occasion and got bumped back down to private but he didn't care. He only cared about surviving and going home. Many years later, as an old man, facing one cancer after another, he accepted the imminence of death as long overdue. He waited for it, almost inviting it into his life to pay for his having lived, while his Army buddies had died before their lives had truly begun.

The next miracle that saved Eddie's life happened after a terrible fight with no tank to protect him. He'd been walking in a trench, when a Chinese infiltrator turned the corner and hit him in the jaw with his rifle butt. The enemy soldier must have thought he killed him. Several times, Chinese troops ran back and forth over Eddie's unconscious body. He lost a few teeth and couldn't chew on that side for months afterward. He was promoted back to Corporal again.

One day, several months into the year, Eddie was told to report to company headquarters "Right away." He jogged to HQ then walked inside. He stood at attention and spoke to the sergeant behind the desk.

"Corporal Roth, reporting," he said.

"Yeah Roth. Okay. I'll tell the captain you're here. Have a seat," said the sergeant, pointing to a chair by the desk. Eddie removed his service cap and looked around but was reluctant to be found sitting when the captain walked in.

"You're not supposed to be here Corporal Roth," said the captain without preamble. "Have a seat."

Eddie stood at attention and saluted before sitting down. He wasn't quite sure he'd heard what the captain had said. "I was told to report to HQ, sir."

"Right. You're not supposed to be here…in Korea. What d'ya think a that?" said the captain sitting behind the desk. The sergeant stood next to him, shuffling papers.

"Excuse me, sir, but I'm not sure I heard you right," said Eddie.

"You heard me right, Roth. You did your time in Korea during your last deployment. The Army made a mistake. Imagine that?" he said with a half-smile.

"You're going home," said the sergeant. "I've got your papers right here."

Eddie was dazed, as he rose from the chair and stood at attention again, facing the captain behind the desk.

"Congratulations, Roth. Sergeant Jacks will take care of you. Lots of papers to be signed. You'll be shipping out next week, Corporal. Good luck." Eddie moved his arm to salute but the captain reached out and grasped Eddie's hand in a firm handshake. Then he went back to his inner office.

The sergeant gave him a purple heart in a box. Eddie didn't think much of it because he thought, *everyone gets a purple heart.* When he got home, he put it in a shoe box. Years later, when he discovered his mother had thrown it away, he punched a hole in the wall.

*****

Eddie mustered out in New York with two buddies. When an Army psychiatrist said that he was going to require them to come in regularly for psychiatric treatment, they dangled him out of the fourth-story window by his heels until he agreed they were all perfectly sane. Then they'd wandered over to the East Side of Manhattan and wound up in a bar that was a virtual shrine to Douglas MacArthur, with photos and mementos of the 'great man' displayed on all the walls. Since the three veterans were still in uniform, their money was no good, but things turned sour when they began mocking 'Dugout Doug' and they'd had to beat a hasty retreat.

That was the last time Eddie backed out of a fight for a long time. He'd returned to New York a changed man. He'd "seen the elephant" and survived. He didn't think he deserved to survive. He was angry and emotional. He punched guys passing on the sidewalk if he thought they were looking directly at him. Old friends started to cross the street when they saw him.

He wanted to resume a normal life as soon as possible. That meant getting a job where he could hone his artistic skills and keep on boxing until he could make enough money to formally propose to Natty. *The Blond Tiger* started taking professional fights again and won almost all of them by channeling the anger he'd brought back from Korea. Eddie learned that it was very therapeutic to beat some guy up in the ring and found himself less inclined to punch random passersby after a match.

Eddie went to the Art Students League in New York for night classes. He figured he'd eventually open his own art studio. He went to work for the prominent graphic artists, Schwab and Winkelman, to learn the ropes of advertising art. Part of his job was to run out every day to a drug store and get Mr. Schwab two gallons of vanilla ice cream. On the weekend, Emil Schwab liked to bicycle long distances; he made up for the lost calories with ice cream. He was slim and handsome with square black framed glasses he constantly pushed up on his nose. His girlfriend, a former Miss New Jersey, visited him in his studio once or twice a week. Eddie thought her a vacuous beauty, but tall and well-rounded in the right places with sandy blond hair and green eyes.

Sometimes Mr. Winkelman, an older man, happily married, treated Eddie to lunch at the automat near the studio. One or the other partner liked to take clients to lunch where they could sit, drink martinis, and talk business long into the afternoon. They both seemed to like Eddie. But they never took him to a fancy restaurant and probably thought they would be wasting their money on him. The automat was fine with Eddie. The food was great and the prices low. He was thrilled to have this job, even if it meant being an errand boy while he learned the trade.

Eddie's friend Eppy, now out of jail, was eager to see him again. He had a proposition. His friend Nicky, was a mob guy but a "straight shooter," according to Eppy. Praise from Eppy, about a mobster friend was like praise from Al Capone for John Dillinger.

"Eddie, Nicky might buy your contract. He'd make sure you got fights and was well paid," explained Eppy one evening outside Eddie's house.

"I'm not going to throw any fights, Eppy, if that's what he expects," said Eddie, leaning against the lamp post, smoking.

"I know, you're an honest guy but do ya need the money or not? Just talk to him. Ne-go-ti-ate," said Eppy, dragging out the word to emphasize it. He motioned to Eddie to give him a cigarette. Eddie lit Eppy's cigarette using the lighter with the dent in it.

"Ok, I'll talk to him but I'm not promising anything."

They met at the automat near Schwab and Winkelman's. It was Eddie's lunch break and he was hungry. That made him testy. He'd grown up with enough Italians, most of whom he liked, like Babe Merola and his family, to know the general etiquette. He, Eppy, and Nicky sat at a table at the back. Eddie ate a chicken salad sandwich and drank a soda while Eppy watched him nervously, hesitant to eat his fried fish until the meeting had reached a satisfactory conclusion.

"So, you're the kike Eppy won't stop talking about. He tells me you box… pretty good, too. Is that right…that you're good?" Asked Nicky, a tall, fat man, a lit cigar hanging from his lower lip. Eddie noted the bulge on one side of his coat; *Probably a gun,* he thought.

Nicky sat with a cup of coffee and a Danish. Eddie looked askance at Eppy. Kike? Eddie's typical response when someone said that was to punch them in the face – though he was smart enough to know that might not be such a good idea in this case. Eppy smiled, a signal that he should just ignore it this time.

"Eddie Roth, nice to meet a friend of Eppy's," said Eddie, shaking Nicky's hand vigorously, holding on long after customary handshaking was supposed to end. He felt strongly that you could tell a lot about a guy from his handshake. Eddie examined the guy in front of him. Nicky looked to be in his late thirties with slicked back black hair and a slim mustache. He'd taken off his hat and placed it on the table. Before he sat down, he'd unbuttoned his charcoal pinstriped suit jacket, unbuttoned his coat and draped it around his shoulders. Eddie could see the pocket watch dangling from a chain hanging from Nicky's vest. Eddie laughed to himself, thinking, *Just like in the movies.*

Nicky kept his voice low. "I asked if you was a good fighter. Well? I'm a busy man."

"He's a great fighter, Nicky. He never loses. For such a skinny guy, he's really powerful," put in Eppy. Nicky gave Eppy a dirty look, then looked at Eddie, expecting an answer.

"Yes, I'm good, better than most. I learned at the PAL. I had a great coach."

"Yeah, okay. When's your next fight, Kid?" said Nicky, checking the time on his pocket watch.

Eddie had brought along a copy of the poster announcing *The Blond Tiger* was to fight *The Viking* the following week. He handed it to Nicky who grabbed it and left the automat without another word. Eddie finished his sandwich as Eppy started to wolf his down, smacking his lips with spittle flying.

"Hey, Eddie, I think he likes you!"

"Yeah, how could you tell?"

"He took the poster, didn't he? You gotta win this fight. Ya think ya can win it, Eddie?"

"That's a dumb question, Eppy. Course I'll win. You said yourself I always win," Eddie cleaned up his tray and stood up. "Thanks for setting up the meeting, Eppy. I gotta go back to work. See ya at the fight."

After work, Eddie went to see Babe. He wasn't too comfortable with the idea of the mob having his contract but he also wanted to keep boxing and the wise guys ran the game. He was adamant that he wouldn't throw a fight. He hoped to talk to Babe and Mr. Merola about it. Maybe they could advise him. Maybe Mr. Merola knew someone in the neighborhood who could check Nicky out, see how "straight up" he really was.

Babe's large family lived in a two-family house, some upstairs, some downstairs. Babe's father had his own dry-cleaning business. He opened another one after the first store had exploded leaving Babe hairless. He was a large man with a ready laugh and a strong Italian accent. The family always seemed content with sisters and brothers running up and downstairs all the time making cheerful noises. Babe's mother was cooking all the time. Incredible smells emanated from her kitchen that was always steamy with heat from the stove.

Babe looked good with hair. He answered the door and gave Eddie a suffocating hug. When they pulled back, Eddie could see Babe had eyebrows and a blond crewcut. Babe was starting to look normal again after several years of looking like a ping pong ball. "Hey, you're lookin pretty good! I bet you've got a bunch of girls after you now," said Eddie.

It was late. Eddie could smell what had been the family's supper several hours earlier. His stomach growled. He hadn't eaten since the chicken salad sandwich.

"Eddie, Eddie, come in, come in. How ya been? Ya hungry? Mama left some sausages. Want some? She's gone to bed now but Pop's still up."

As if on cue, Mr. Merola entered the hallway. He wore a terrycloth bathrobe that had seen better days. The hallway felt cold and dark. Babe led Eddie into the kitchen where it was still warm from the cooking.

"How you been, son?" asked Mr. Merola in his heavy accent while shaking Eddie's hand in both of his, then kissing him on each cheek.

Eddie was overwhelmed with the welcome from these two men. He felt tears forming, but blinked them away. Before he could speak, Babe plunked a steaming plate of Italian sausage and pasta with gravy on the table. Both men bade him eat while they continued to question him. They didn't seem to mind that his mouth was too full to answer and seemed content to know he was there and he was eating. Babe brought him a glass of red wine.

Finally, Eddie said, "Holy mackerel, I've missed you both and your mom's cooking! There's nothing to compare. Forget about me, how are all of you?"

The three men chatted about the neighborhood and what Eddie had missed while he was away. Eventually, he came around to the purpose of his visit.

"It's great to see you. I'll stop by again when everyone is awake so I can see your mom and the gang. I came by tonight though, because everyone else would be asleep. I need to ask some advice," he began after gently wiping his mouth with the cloth napkin, folding it slowly to give him time to gather his thoughts, and placing it next to his plate. He explained the situation to the two of them.

"I'm not sure what to do. I can't talk to anyone else about this. What d'ya think, Mr. Merola? Any way you might check this Nicky guy out for me?"

Mr. Merola chuckled, "Well you know Eddie, just cause I'm Italian don't mean I know every Italian in New Yawk!"

"I know, I guess it was a stupid question."

"You didn't let me finish. I may not know every Italian in New Yawk but I know someone who does. He knows a lotta Italians," responded Mr. Merola while placing his finger on the side of his nose and pushing it to the left. "He's an old friend from my village. He knows all the wise guys. I'll see what I can do. Meantime, stall with this guy."

"Thanks a lot Mr. Merola. I really appreciate it."

"Now, I'm off to bed. You fellas, don't stay up too late. Eddie, there's the couch for tonight. Make yourself comfortable." He shook Eddie's hand again and gave it a squeeze.

"Eddie, ya gotta be careful," said Babe after his father left the room. "They mean business. Once you're in with them, it's hard to get out."

"Yeah, that's what scares me, Babe. Hey, I'll let you get some sleep. It's late. I promised I'd stop in to see Natty. She's waiting up for me. I'll give you a call. Maybe we can double date…now that you've got hair on your head!" Eddie laughed and slapped Babe on the shoulder. "Great to see you pal." He walked down the cold, dark hall to the front door. Babe slapped him back and closed the door behind him.

******

Eddie was still having trouble adjusting to being home from war. His temper was unpredictable and he still slugged people for looking askance at him. He remembered everything Harry had tried to tell him about quitting boxing and getting an education instead. But despite his job at Schwab and Winkelman's, he didn't have enough money without boxing to consider moving out of his mother's apartment or getting married.

The Art Students League didn't cost a whole lot, but it ate into his wallet enough to notice.

Babe came by one Saturday when Eddie was home. They sat in the back yard, sipping beer.

"My dad says it's okay," started Babe after they'd caught up on their other news.

"To box? Was he able to check out this guy, Nicky?"

"Yup, he's on the level. He's mobbed up but you can't get fights without being mobbed up," said Babe pulling out a cigarette for Eddie and one for himself.

"So how can he be on the level if he's mobbed up?" asked Eddie taking a cigarette and lighting them both.

"Well, let's just say he's more honest than most of those guys. That's what my dad says, anyway. So, what d'ya think? Are you gonna do it?"

"Yeah, I gotta do it. I need the money. Thank your dad for me, will ya? Let's go in and see what there is to eat."

Soon, Nicky was getting Eddie more fights and he didn't have to throw any of them. He started palling around with Nicky, who turned out not to be a bad guy at all. He took Eddie to restaurants he couldn't afford and bought fancy gifts for Natty. Eddie won most of his fights and the purses were substantial. He didn't tell Natty he was boxing, but, even as a trainee nurse, she could see the signs clearly enough.

CHAPTER TWENTY-ONE
1953

Natty graduated from nursing school in April. Eddie went to the ceremony and sat with Natty's mother, Rose, and Mimi. The young women, dressed in their white uniforms, carried lit candles in tribute to Florence Nightingale, "the lady with the lamp." The school's director pinned each student with a pin depicting the school's emblem and alma mater. Eddie was proud.

They went back to Mimi's apartment to celebrate. Ez was not there but no one pointed out his absence. Mimi made an elaborate dinner and made sure Ma was visiting the family out on Long Island. Natty could tell how much Mimi had tired herself but was trying not to let it show. Mimi slouched when she walked. The strenuous effort to breathe had taken its toll. Yet, she loved Natty and knew she would be handing Eddie over to her before too long. She was eager to celebrate Natty's special day.

Rose too, was proud of her daughter who had followed in her own footsteps. A love for nursing had brought them closer in the years Natty was in school. Rose was no longer hiding from the fact that Natty's sister, Abby, was very mentally ill. Abby had married Ira, an insurance salesman, who resented Rose's continued involvement in Abby's life. Rose realized that Natty had succeeded despite her own neglect.

Rose had remarried, as Harry had predicted, though he would not have imagined that she'd pick his own cousin Herman. Rose and Herman now lived in a beautiful apartment and the poverty she had known with Harry was a thing of the past. She had developed a liking for Eddie thanks to his devotion to Harry as he lay dying. She enjoyed hearing Eddie tell funny stories about the Army and his work for Schwab and Winkelman. But Rose was an excellent nurse and had seen her share of psychiatric patients. She could tell Eddie had returned unsettled from the war. There was a persistent tenseness about him. His smile was forced, even when telling his humorous anecdotes. Eddie also had a twitch in his left eye and frequently drummed his fingers on the table as if he had to get up and go. It was a restlessness Rose had seen in Abby and the patients she had cared for over the years.

Natty noticed it too. She knew Eddie was not how he had been before the war but thought she could help him and was determined to begin devoting her life to doing that. She was also tired of waiting for Eddie to ask her to marry him. After all, she knew he loved her and they spent all their free time together. Eddie always met her at the hospital entrance and walked Natty home when she came off duty at midnight. It had been five long years. They had fewer money worries. Natty could get a good job making better money than the five dollars a day Rose had brought home years ago.

One day, Natty had had enough and ran out of the hospital during her lunch break. She took a streetcar to Eddie's house. People stared at the beautiful, black haired, young woman in the white nurse's uniform and cap running down the sidewalk. Breathless, with hair flying, she opened the door and ran into Mimi's apartment. She knew Eddie was babysitting Mimi's young children.

"Nat, what are you doing here? Are you alright? What's happened?" asked Eddie, who was just giving his niece and nephew their lunch.

Natty leaned against the door for a minute so she could catch her breath. She stood up, straightened her collar and smoothed her hair with her clean, carefully trimmed fingernails, smacked her lipsticked lips and said "Eddie!"

"What is it Nat? Are you alright?"

Natty faced him, eye to eye. She was almost the same height. Eddie was not a tall man. The two young children stared up at them.

"Eddie!" she said again. "Are you going to marry me or not? Cause if not, I'm leaving," Natty turned, ran out the door of the two-family house and into the street. She walked to the streetcar that would take her back to the hospital. Eddie ran after her, leaving the children on their own.

He grabbed her and kissed her hard on the mouth. Then he held her tightly, silently. Natty pulled herself away from his embrace. "You know, you're crazy as hell!"

"I know. I know," he said.

Eddie got down on the sidewalk, on one knee, grabbed Natty's hand, looked up into her unsmiling face, and said "Nat, will you marry me?" Businessmen, mothers pushing baby carriages, cabbies having a smoke on the curb while waiting for their next fare, and passengers looking out the windows of their taxis, carried on around them.

Finally, Natty smiled, "Yes, Eddie, I will. Now, get up off the sidewalk. Everyone is staring at us."

Before she boarded the streetcar, after a last embrace, Natty said, "November. We'll get married in November."

"Yes Nat. Whatever you say."

"Now run home and look after those children!" commanded Natty from the window of the trolley.

Rose and Herman hosted the engagement party, held in a cozy Italian restaurant Babe suggested. Natty wore a white cocktail length dress with a wide red belt and red shoes. Eddie wore his first new suit, charcoal gray with a black tie. They were all smiles as they ate from an elaborate buffet and drank champagne till late in the evening.

Eddie missed Sam as much as Natty missed Harry. They felt their fathers hovering about the restaurant, smelling the delicious food, laughing with each other about the happiness of their children, united in ghostly pleasure that things had turned out well.

*****

Eddie and Natty married on the first of November in the synagogue on the corner. He was reluctant to give the Rabbi the satisfaction after his refusal to have Pop's funeral there, but Gussie won out. Eddie figured he had to pick his battles with Ma. Fagie, Bernie, and Natty's nursing school roommates attended along with Babe, Norm, and Arnie, Eddie's Bijou Club pals. Eppy was back in jail, but sent his congratulations. Some of Eddie's Irish and

Italian friends from the old neighborhood came. Rose's brothers came from Cleveland and Eddie's family from Brooklyn and out on Long Island.

Herman paid for the wedding and walked Natty down the aisle. She wore an ankle length white satin dress with a V-neck. Her veil fell to the small of her back where Eddie had his arm around her in the photograph that captured the newlyweds. Eddie wore a black suit with a boutonniere of flowers that matched Natty's small bouquet of pink carnations and baby's breath. Her satin shoes with the medium heels were a little too big, but they matched the dress, giving it just the right touch of elegance.

Gussie attended the wedding but wore a smirk that occasionally melted into an infinitesimal smile. The smile was because she was pleased with herself. She quickly reined it in lest anyone think she was happy or enjoying herself. She'd come from the shtetl and raised a family. She felt her pride in what she'd accomplished was justified. But Eddie, Eddie had never been good enough to compensate for the bother he'd caused her and had never made any effort to please her. She certainly wasn't pleased with his choice of a wife or a profession. *Why'd he choose this big boned woman who came from nothing and has nothing? An artist. Eddie? He'll be scratching in the dirt for food the rest of his life. He should've gone to work at the department store like I told him. Eh, but he never cared for anything I said. Only ever listened to Sam. What did Sam know? Nothing, except how to build things.*

Eddie and Natty honeymooned in Washington, DC. Both were impressed with the Lincoln and Washington monuments. They walked along the reflecting pool and Pennsylvania Avenue. They giggled about their family members and how grateful they were to finally be alone and away from all of them.

They found a one room apartment behind the furnace in the basement of a one-story brick house. They salvaged discarded lamps, tables and chairs. The only thing new was a double bed they bought with the money they'd been given as wedding gifts. The bed frame was mahogany with a canopied arch over the top. Natty was very proud of it.

Soon after they settled in, Natty left the hospital to work for an internist, Dr. Applebaum, who was kind to her and always dressed magnificently unlike his secretary, Van, who looked pinch faced, like the actress Agnes Moorehead, and acted like Gussie.

Van, was also unkempt and dirty. She never washed her hands and frequently interfered with medical care by giving patients advice. Natty often stepped in to reproach her. Natty left the practice when she became too frustrated with Van and went to another hospital, near to where she grew up on Chester Street in Brownsville. There, Natty usually worked the evening or night shifts. When she was old, Natty reminisced about the staff gatherings in the hospital cafeteria for evening or late-night meals. The food was great. She especially liked the homemade roast beef with mashed potatoes and fresh green beans followed by homemade ice cream and hot coffee. The doctors and nurses teased and flirted. She loved telling her family and friends how she ate and joked with the famous Hungarian doctor, Bela Schick, who'd developed a vaccine against Diphtheria and George Papanicolaou, the Greek inventor of the Pap smear. To her, they'd been like Gods but they didn't act that way. Sitting with them taught her not to be intimidated by doctors who were just as human as nurses, no matter what they thought of themselves.

CHAPTER TWENTY-TWO

1954

Ez started sending work Eddie's way from the Lion Match Company. Eddie thanked Schwab and Winkelman for their tutelage and mentorship, and went to work designing match book covers. Soon, he was able to pay for a three-room apartment. Now, they had a bedroom, small kitchen, living room, and their own bathroom. He began to save money for his own art studio.

Eddie took the subway to the Lion Match Company and typically met Ez for a quick automat lunch. He didn't like what he was hearing about Mimi's deteriorating health. He and Natty tried to visit on weekends but Natty's mother liked to see them regularly, in Brooklyn. On occasion, they took the Long Island Railroad out to visit Mac, Dottie, Edna, and Aaron in Merrick and stayed for the day. Mac taught Eddie to barbeque. He had become an expert, turning the coals at just the right time and concocting various sauces. Edna and Dottie made all the side dishes, like cucumber salad with cucumbers sliced so thin you could see through them. Natty always brought something sweet and Eddie brought the beer.

The trips out on Long Island were a nice break from busy city life. Sometimes, Miriam was up to the ride. Ez had a car, so if she felt reasonably well, he drove her, Gussie, and the children. Gussie complained the entire way. Mimi made sure to sit up front so Ma could sit with the children in the back seat. Ma still insisted on bringing food and pots and pans that everyone had to carry on their laps once the trunk was full.

In the summer, the car was hot. Although Ez held his cigarette out the window, Miriam still coughed frequently and kept her window rolled down to catch the rare breeze. She tried to ignore her mother's admonitions that Mimi shouldn't have come, she was too sick. Mimi thought, *It doesn't matter anymore where I am. I just as soon have trouble breathing in the countryside than in the city.* Miriam wanted to see her brother and Edna and Dottie. The cousins loved running around together while the adults sat in the yard and talked about old times. Aaron hardly spoke. He nodded often but always seemed to be thinking of something or somewhere else.

One Sunday, as they rode the train home from a visit, Eddie thought about the previous week. Natty was looking out the window. Sometimes, she'd look at the other people on the train car and comment on their clothes.

"She shouldn't wear that hat with that dress. It's the wrong color. It's really the wrong color for her complexion. She'd do better with pastels" or "Look at that elderly man. He's dressed like it was the 1890s! Very dashing though. Maybe you should dress like that," she teased.

Eddie always nodded or laughed with her, resisting the urge to look at the person in question. Right now, he was thinking of his taxi ride downtown last week, when a bullet came through one window right next to where he was sitting and out the other, breaking both. The driver stopped the car and ran out before Eddie knew what was happening. His combat instincts kicked in and he ducked for cover. He didn't emerge from the cab until he had his trembling hands and legs under control, and he'd patted down his body for wounds and blood.

He hadn't told Natty what happened and didn't plan to. She worried about him working downtown. He also didn't tell her about the time he'd walked out of the Lion Match Company after delivering his sketches and was slammed up against the wall of the building by two uniformed policemen. Eddie was wearing a cheap suit but he was always very careful about his appearance. In the Army, he'd learned to dress with meticulous care. The suit was cheap but he wore a clean, starched handkerchief in his left breast pocket and his tie was straight and stylishly gray with maroon stripes, over a starched white oxford shirt.

One of the cops stuck a gun into Eddie's back.

"You're coming with us," said the cop with the gun.

"Where? Why? What's going on?" asked Eddie as he felt his wrists pulled behind his back and handcuffed.

"Shut up and get in the car," said the cop standing next to Eddie, blocking any possible getaway.

"What's this all about?" said Eddie again as they jammed him into the back of the police car. The handcuffs chafed his wrists. He started to think about what he might have done. *Do they know about my contract with Nicky? What about my friend Eppy? Can they arrest you for being friends with wise guys? Did I forget to do something I was supposed to do?*

The ride to the police station was erratic as the car wove in and out of Manhattan traffic. The cops refused to answer his questions and Eddie started to panic. They finally reached the station; the cop with the gun pulled Eddie roughly out of the car and pushed him into the building. They took him to an interview room and left him there, handcuffed and confused.

Soon, a man in plain clothes entered the room.

"I'm Detective Hines. What do you have to say for yourself, Nathan? Did you really think you'd get away with killing a cop? You'll probably get the chair this time."

"Detective Hines," said Eddie trying to summon the calmness he'd learned in combat. It was never good to panic; you couldn't think clearly.

"Sir, my name is Edward Roth. I work for the Lion Match Company. I'm a Korean War veteran. You've got the wrong guy."

"Where you'd think up that one? Just picked another Jew name, huh? Nice try, Nathan. You got some ID? If you ain't Nathan, we can clear this up right quick."

Eddie didn't have a driver's licenses because he'd refused to drive since he left the Army. Luckily, he had his card from the Art Students League and an old, battered card from when he belonged to the Police Athletic League. He gave them to the detective, who left him sitting handcuffed in the interview room with a cop standing in the corner watching over him. They left him there for nearly a half an hour, but when the detective returned, he was all smiles and apologies.

"Sorry about that, Pal. You look just like this guy we've been after. Here's his picture. Ever see him?"

Eddie, with his artist's eye, noticed a passing resemblance- curly, dirty blond hair, brown eyes, slight build.

"No sir, I haven't. I'll be sure to report it, if I do. Now, can I get outta here? I was on my way to see a client."

"Yeah sure," said Hines, removing the handcuffs, then attempting to straighten Eddie's tie and his pocket handkerchief.

"Thanks, but I can dress myself. I need a ride back uptown," said Eddie not waiting for an answer. He stood up straight like someone who was innocent and knew it, instead of like a guy at the mercy of men with guns. Eddie laughed to himself thinking about the incident - another close call. But he'd been pretty shaken up at the time.

*****

Toward the end of the year, Natty became pregnant with their first child. She was so ill with morning sickness that she couldn't work. The obstetrician Rose recommended made a house call to give her an anti-emetic so she could hold down food. Gussie made frequent visits to criticize Natty's housekeeping and her maternity clothes but only dared to come when Eddie wasn't home.

CHAPTER TWENTY-THREE

1955

Daniel was born in July, fat and robust with Natty's dark eyes and hair. He reminded them of Natty's father, Harry. She and Eddie were overjoyed. They kept him in a drawer as a crib, but he soon outgrew it. Mac passed on the wooden cradle Sam had made so long ago before Eddie was born. Gussie had given it to Mac before Dottie delivered their first child. Gussie insisted on tying a red ribbon on the cradle and enforcing the other old-world traditions she'd used with her own children. As soon Eddie returned home from work, he'd tear it off and throw it away. Gussie retaliated by throwing Eddie's high school art and gymnastics medals in the garbage, making sure to tell Natty about it on her next visit.

Daniel was an easygoing child who was constantly hungry. He loved looking at books. Both parents recognized how smart he was but what he had in intelligence, he lacked in physicality. He was slow to walk and preferred to sit and play or look at his books to running or climbing.

Natty stayed home to take care of the baby. They wouldn't let Gussie babysit despite her protestations, but Miriam came when she had enough energy and her children were in school. Nothing stopped Gussie from giving advice. She told them how to change Danny's diapers, when and how to feed him, and to let him cry his lungs out.

Eddie found an office he could afford to start his own studio. He called it "Penpoint Studios" and designed its logo of a palette, pen, and paintbrush. He began to develop contacts and visit companies that might be interested in having him produce advertisements for them. He leveraged his experience with Schwab and Winkelman and the Lion Match Company to get other work. He was an excellent calligrapher, a skill that was already becoming rare.

Soon, he had enough business to take on a partner, Bob Patterson, as a salesman. Bob was a tall, thin WASP from New Jersey with a wife who was a Presbyterian pastor and a young son and daughter. He invested in the business because he knew Miriam's husband, Ez, who vouched for Eddie's talent and potential.

Nicky also spoke to people who might know people who could use Eddie's services. But when Nicky said a friend of his wanted to use Eddie's studio to hold poker games one night a week, Eddie said no.

"Eddie, they say they'll only be here after you've all gone home. It's only one night a week. I promise you'll like what you find on your desk in the morning," said Nicky rubbing his fingers together to indicate a lot of money.

"I don't know, Nicky. Once you do something for those guys, you're kinda stuck. Am I right? What do you think I should do? I have a wife and kid at home now. I don't want any trouble."

"I tell you what? Yeah Eddie, I agree with you. I was told to make you the offer. So, I made you the offer. As your friend, I think you should respectfully decline, know what I mean?"

"Ok, but what the hell do we tell the guy?"

"I'll tell him you gotta stay and work late sometimes and don't always know when you'll be done. They'll buy that. They don't wanna take the chance of anyone else being around. Okay?"

"Okay, Nicky. You know best. I just hope he buys it."

"Oh, he will, pal. You can count on me. Although, I think you could use the money!"

They were sitting at their favorite – Chock-Full O' Nuts - eating the famous raisin bread sandwiches with cream cheese and walnuts and drinking coffee. The place was crowded with lunchtime customers, mostly businessmen, cabbies in need of a quick bite, and shoppers who needed a nosh between stores.

"Thanks for taking care of that for me, Nicky," said Eddie after a sip of coffee. "I need to ask you about something else that's been on my mind since I came back from Korea."

"Yeah, okay. What's troubling you, my friend? How can old Nicky help?"

"I need to get outta my boxing contract. I need more time to find clients and to take care of my family. I've really got no time," said Eddie, first with trepidation about what Nicky might say but soon gathering strength from the arguments he'd been having with himself for months.

"Hmm, that's not so easy, my friend. You're dealing with people who don't like to be told no. They've been making money off you a while now and want to keep that up. You just started your own studio. Do you have enough dough to buy out the contract?"

"No, I probably won't for years, if ever."

"Let me think on this a bit, Eddie. Get yourself another raisin bread sandwich on me and finish your coffee. I'm going outside for a smoke. You have one too, while I'm thinking." He gave Eddie twenty-five cents.

Eddie did as he was told; he signaled the waitress behind the counter, asked for a top up and a sandwich and sat back down to light his cigarette. He thought about what might happen. He might still need to box later, if another kid came along or if the business didn't take off. It was true he was very busy but the real reason was that while this connection had served him well, it might sour if it continued. He couldn't take a chance on having his corporate clients find out he had a connection with Nicky or any of his wise guy friends. He'd have trouble getting or keeping legitimate business. He'd still meet Nicky and his other shady friends once in a while for drinks or a quick game of pool but that was where he had to draw the line. Nicky was smart. He probably saw through Eddie's little speech but would never admit it.

"Okay," said Nicky returning to sit beside Eddie at the counter, the remaining half of a cigar hanging from his lower lip. "This is what we're gonna do," said Nicky, switching the cigar from one side of his mouth to the other.

"I'm gonna pay off your contract. Hold on, Hold on. I aint finished yet," said Nicky when Eddie tried to interrupt. "I'm gonna pay off your contract, but you're gonna do a different kinda work for us now."

Whoa, thought Eddie. *What's this now? This could be worse than having a boxing contract with these guys.*

Reading his mind, Nicky answered Eddie's thoughts, "Don't get excited. I mean with art work. You're gonna paint walls and murals in our restaurants and anywhere else we need art. It'll be like doing business with anybody else. We'll hire your studio to paint, only we don't pay you. No strings attached. Okay?"

"Yeah, I can do that, Nicky. No strings, huh? Great. It's a deal. You tell me when I've done enough painting to pay off the contract and we'll be square."

So, Eddie spent time in Little Italy painting murals of the Italian countryside, sometimes with the faces of 'made' guys on the shepherds and farmers in the scene. He also learning how to make eggplant parmigiana and stuffed shells from expert chefs who let him watch them in the restaurant kitchens. He started what would become a family tradition of making Italian dinners every Sunday. He thought of Babe Merola and his family who'd welcomed him most Sundays when he was growing up and needed to get away from his mother.

As he sketched and painted, Eddie watched the crowded streets and the religious processions as Italians carrying banners made their way along the streets. Sometimes, he stopped at a vendor to grab a bite or an Italian ice in a paper cone. In the summer, he watched kids cool off in water gushing from open fire hydrants into the street.

Eddie liked being in Little Italy. The food was great. But he had to fit in painting around his other work and home life. Sometimes, he became a little nervous, like when Nicky gave him a picture of a guy he wanted painted into a mural then asked him later to go back and paint that guy out.

CHAPTER TWENTY-FOUR

1958

A second child was born, a girl they named Rachel, but later nicknamed Yenta because she nagged and hardly ever stopped talking and giggling. She was not an easy baby like her brother had been. She was whiny and fussy. Born with vision problems, her early years included frequent trips to the eye doctor and two eye surgeries. Natty laughingly complained to Eddie that by the age of two, Rachel was arguing about what she would wear. She liked to fill shopping bags with her toys and take them in the crib with her. She was a small human bundle among the paper bags that towered over her.

Eddie loved being a father but wished he had more time to spend with the children. Although he no longer had a contract with Nicky, he'd gone back to boxing at nights to make some extra money. He didn't tell Natty. He didn't tell anyone that he was terrified before every bout. He'd pace back and forth asking himself why he was always allowing other guys to hit him. He was scared to death right up until he got into the ring and started punching. Then the old combat instincts kicked in.

Some of Eddie's clients paid him on time, others didn't. Usually the bigger the client, the less likely they were to pay when the bill was due. He needed to box to make up the difference. Nicky put him in touch with a washed up wanna-be wiseguy named Nunzio who helped Eddie collect what was owed. Nunzio was fat, slovenly, and intentionally obnoxious. Like Nicky, he always had a big smelly cigar hanging out of his mouth. Unlike Nicky, who was fastidious in all other ways, Nunzio wore the remnants of his lunch on his shirt and tie. Eddie called Nunzio when he was desperate to be paid.

Nunzio presented himself in the lobby or waiting room of whatever company was delinquent in payments and always asked to see the boss. When he was met with excuses, he always replied, "That's okay. I'll just sit here until he can make time to see me." He was very polite; he just sat there looking threatening, and puffing his smelly cigar, making inappropriate noises now and then, and walking around the lobby or waiting room to make sure everyone could see him. It didn't take long before he was called in to see the boss who promptly gave Nunzio a check in the amount owed. He placed the check in the inside pocket of his suit and walked out smiling broadly. None of the family then or later ever met Nunzio. Most suspected he was a fiction but Eddie stood by the story.

*****

Eddie couldn't explain why, but every night, when he came home from the studio or from boxing, he changed into pajamas and climbed right into bed. It wasn't because of the boxing. He rarely had bad bruises because he invariably won his fights before his opponent could do much harm but his nose had gradually become squishy. The cartilage was gone. He couldn't remember how many times it had been broken but that was in the past. Natty had noticed the changes in his nose but thought that was all behind him. She could tell he was very tired. He said he had heart palpitations.

"I'm fine at work but I don't feel well at the end of the day," he told her when she began questioning him. "My heart starts racing as soon as I get on the subway."

"What is it, Ed? Are you unhappy about coming home?" asked Natty sitting beside him on the bed.

"I love our home and family and I love you, but I'm just so tired," he answered as he got under the covers and turned away.

Natty asked Mimi for help. "He gets into bed every evening when he gets home. I ask what's wrong but he says he doesn't know, that he's just very tired," said Natty as they sat at Mimi's kitchen table eating a sour cream coffee cake. Natty thought she might attempt the recipe but add chocolate chips and walnuts for Eddie. The coffee was rich and hot. Both women took it black.

"Eddie's always been a sensitive person, Natty. Maybe the work is too hard or he's worried about money. I don't know," she held Natty's hand across the table. It was a Saturday morning. Both husbands were working. The idea of resting on the Sabbath was long gone.

"Please don't tell anyone," said Mimi changing the subject, "I'm seeing a therapist. It's the asthma and my worry the cancer will come back. Ez is hardly here and I've got the children…."

"Oh Mimi, I'm sorry. You've so much to deal with and here I am telling you my troubles. Forget I said anything," she stood up and grabbed her pocketbook.

"Please, Natty, sit down. We're sisters now and who knows Eddie better than me? I'm glad you came. I think we can help him. I'll ask my therapist to recommend someone to speak to Eddie."

"Do you think Eddie will agree? He's so proud."

"I'll ask him to make a home visit," said Mimi giggling, "Eddie will have no choice."

Eddie was unsuspecting. As usual, he came home from work, changed into pajamas, and slipped under the bed covers. Natty brought a light-haired, middle-aged man in a neat brown suit into their bedroom.

"Ed, this is Dr. Silverman. He's a psychiatrist."

"A psychiatrist? I'm not crazy. What are you thinking, Nat, bringing a shrink here?" he asked angrily, sitting up and moving to the edge of the bed. "What's this about? No offence Doctor, but please leave so I can get some rest."

"Your wife and sister are concerned. It's not normal to get into bed every evening after work, especially for a young man with a wife and two young children." Dr. Silverman nodded at Natty, signaling for her to leave the room.

"Why don't you tell me what's bothering you?" said the doctor with a quiet voice and bright blue eyes. He gently touched Eddie's arm as he talked. Eddie surrendered and lay back on the bed. Dr. Silverman pulled up a chair.

"I don't know. Can you tell me?" asked Eddie, resigned to talking with the doctor. "My heart races all the time. I always feel tired no matter how much sleep I get. In Korea, I went without sleep for days and never felt as bad as this."

Doctor Silverman looked in Eddie's eyes with a penlight he brought out of his suit jacket pocket. He listened to Eddie's heart and lungs with his stethoscope and palpated his thin belly.

"Listen, Eddie," he said when he'd finished. "There's nothing wrong with you other than stress. I know your sister, Miriam, who told me a bit about you. You fought in a war, you were wounded, and saw men die. You came home, got married, started a business, and now you have two young children. I hear your life wasn't so easy before the war." Eddie opened his mouth to refute all this.

Doctor Silverman continued, "You need to get out of bed and stay out until it's time to go to sleep at night. Tend to your family and your business but find a way to relax in a normal way. I hear you like opera and jazz. Maybe listen to music?"

"I like to cook. I've been learning from the chefs in some of the restaurants near my studio."

"That's wonderful. I'm sure your wife would love a break. You can pound the meat to tenderize it. Pound out your stress on something that needs it. I can smell smoke on your breath. That's not good for you. Try to stop it, if you can," finished Silverman as he rose from the bed.

"Now, get up, change your clothes and go play with your children," he commanded before reaching for his pocket watch, checking the time, and leaving the bedroom. Natty thanked him as he rushed out the door, waving away her offer of the few dollars they had on hand.

It took a long time, but Eddie taught himself how to cope with the grief and anger he still felt after growing up with Gussie, losing his father and Harry, and surviving the war. He had terrible dreams, especially about losing his crew when their tank exploded. At night, he thrashed and yelled. Eddie always reached out, ready to punch someone when he was awakened from these nightmares. Natty learned to stand beside the bed and nudge him gently.

CHAPTER TWENTY-FIVE

1962

They bought a house in Brooklyn that Mac found for them. It was spacious, with a screened in front porch and a large, flourishing peach tree in the small backyard. There was a driveway but they didn't own a car. Eddie took the subway to work. They closed in the front porch so they could use it as a sun room year-round and built an open porch in the backyard. They picked peaches off the tree every summer. The milk man left large glass bottles of milk in the metal box on the back porch by the kitchen door. Natty walked with the children and her shopping cart to the fruit and vegetable stalls, the bakery, and to the butcher and fish market on King's Highway.

The neighbors on one side were an older couple who were friendly with Natty and Eddie. On the other side lived a family of two parents, two boys and a girl. Natty soon recognized the mother was a drunkard. When Natty and Eddie entertained, the woman frequently left the party to return with peppermint on her breath. The husband called Natty to attend his wife whenever she fell down from drinking too much. Their children liked to visit Natty and Eddie and play with Danny and Rachel. Many years later, when Natty and Eddie prepared to move their family to Westchester County, the oldest boy begged them to take him along. Natty had to refuse, but it was something she never forgot.

Miriam came to visit one Saturday afternoon not long after Natty and Eddie had completed the renovations on their new house. Mimi was dressed in a black cocktail dress a la Audrey Hepburn. It had three-quarter length lace sleeves that matched the lace bodice. She wore black strap shoes and a faux fur stole. Natty was happy to see her but surprised by the evening outfit. Miriam had come by bus and Natty wondered what the other riders thought about Mimi's clothes.

Since it was a lovely day, they brought her out to the back porch. Eddie made them some drinks. Mimi's asthma had worsened over the years, and she looked nervous and unwell as she sat on a lawn chair with nylon straps woven around a metal frame. She sat on the edge of the chair although the metal bar pressed against the back of her thighs. Natty and Eddie sat near her so the three formed a circle. Danny was playing in the yard and Rachel was sleeping in the stroller.

Mimi seemed eager to speak but Eddie didn't notice; he was so excited about her visit.

"Mimi, it's so wonderful to see you. How do you like the house since we've done some fixing up? It still needs some work but we love it. I'll give you a tour after you finish your drink," he said rapidly, smiling his wide toothy smile.

He still had occasional jaw pain from the rifle butt to his mouth in Korea but the dental work he'd had recently helped. Mimi ignored his comments and questions. She just looked at him, then at Natty and smiled as she glanced at Danny playing happily in the yard.

"The cancer's back," she said suddenly. "It's in my bones now. I just came from the doctor's office."

Eddie was stunned into silence. Natty quickly stepped into her nurse persona, asking, "Are you sure? Have you had a second opinion? Where did you go? What tests did they do? I can refer you to a doctor I know. Why didn't you tell us sooner?" *No wonder she's dressed up,* thought Natty.

Eddie interrupted her, rose from his teetering lawn chair and reached out to his sister. She rose to hug him. He kissed her cheek and smoothed her hair, much thinner since her first bout with cancer.

"Mimi. It can't be true. How can this be true? I don't believe it."

"Look," said Mimi, gently pushing Eddie away. She grabbed a hand from each of them. "Look, you both have to believe it. Yes Natty, I got a second opinion. I've had all the tests. Yes, Eddie, it's true. I didn't tell either of you sooner because I didn't know for sure and I didn't want to ruin this happy time for you. Please, no more questions about the diagnosis. I know it's terrible news and a lot to take in. I just came to tell you. Now, I need to get back to Naomi; she's waiting at home."

"You know we'll do whatever you need. We can help with Naomi and Allan, whatever you want," said Eddie. Natty squeezed Miriam's hand and nodded in agreement. Naomi was fifteen and still in high school. Allan was attending Brooklyn College.

"I know. I know. I will need you and so will the children." Lowering her voice, she added, "Ez has been having an affair. Another piece of news I just found out, although for years I've suspected he was seeing other women. This one's the wife of someone he works with at Lion and lives in New Jersey."

"I'll kill him," said Eddie in a gruff voice, clenching his fists. "Where is he, Mimi? Tell me where he is and I'll kill him."

"Calm down," said Mimi with a quick look at Natty for support. They both knew Eddie's temper could be volatile and impulsive. "You can't kill him. The kids are going to need him when I'm not around. I'm sorry to leave you with so much bad news. Daniel, come give your old aunt a kiss, sweetheart."

Mimi, Eddie, and Natty hugged each other tightly as Danny made his way up the three cement stairs that led from the yard to the porch, holding tightly to the wrought iron railing,

"Don't leave yet, Mimi. Please. Couldn't you stay a little while longer?" said Natty.

"Ah, such a sweet boy. I'm not going to see you or your little sister grow up," said Mimi, with tears in her eyes as she reached down to give Danny a hug and a kiss. At seven years old, he was a chubby boy, too big for her to pick up. Danny laughed as she tickled his belly.

"I've got to go."

"I'm going to ride back with you on the bus. No argument," said Eddie, running inside to grab a light jacket and his wallet.

"Natty, I'd like you to look at my breast quickly before we go. Do you mind?"

"Of course not. Danny, come inside with Aunt Mimi and Mommy," she said picking up Rachel and leading Danny into the house through the kitchen door. Natty sent Danny and Rachel, who'd awakened, to their rooms to play. Mimi and Natty went into the large bathroom off the kitchen.

"Unbutton this for me, will you?" asked Mimi turning her back to Natty. After her dress was unbuttoned enough so she could gently pull down the bodice of the dress and the top of her slip and bra, she turned to sit on the toilet to face Natty.

"Oh," said Natty involuntarily. She was taken by surprise to see the necrotic, dimpled skin of Miriam's left breast. Miriam had put some wadded-up tissues inside her bra to catch bloody drainage seeping from her nipple.

"I know it looks bad," Mimi said, holding Natty's wrist as she palpated the breast with her fingers.

Looking up at Natty, Mimi said, "I know I'm going to die. I just need a bit more time with the children. I need to arrange things. Ez hasn't been a good father. He's never around," she finished, as she stood up and turned so Natty could rebutton her dress.

Natty composed herself. "I'm sorry Mimi but it does look bad. We're here and will help. Edna and Mac will help too. Why don't you stay with us for a while? I can take care of you. It's almost summer. Naomi goes to sleep away camp anyway and Allan will be busy with his friends." The two women hugged as Eddie called from the kitchen.

*****

Miriam's condition continued to worsen. She'd been seeing her psychotherapist regularly and had told him about her fears of dying and her despair about Ez and his love affairs. She worried he wouldn't be around for the children. On a Friday morning, not long after she visited Natty and Eddie, she went to see her therapist for the last time. After this, she didn't know if she would ever again rise from her bed. She dressed up to see him but without the joy that dressing up had brought her in recent years. When she was younger, she didn't care about clothes but she'd learned their power to disguise illness and unhappiness.

She walked into the therapist's waiting room and reminded the receptionist who she was. Before she could sit down, the psychiatrist called her into his office. She didn't sit in the chair he offered. Instead, she stood in front of his desk, looked him in the eye and said,

"Thanks for your help but I no longer need you. I'm dying. I won't live much longer and won't waste any more of your time." She turned and left the office and the waiting room while the therapist stood dumbfounded. He didn't follow her to try to bring her back. He knew she was right just by looking at her.

*****

Eddie brought Mimi to their house so Natty could take care of her. They put her in a rented hospital bed in the front room, so Miriam could get the brightness and warmth of the sun. Ez finally realized they were nearing the end of Miriam's ordeal and he needed to stay close.

She stayed in Natty and Eddie's sunroom for two weeks before she had to be admitted to the hospital. The pain had become very bad and the drainage from the breast unmanageable. She was still alert when they took her there by ambulance. Natty went along to see Miriam settled and made as comfortable as possible.

Natty had been dressing Mimi's breast, thinking all the while that Miriam had waited too long to return to the oncologist. She might have had another surgery and perhaps prevented this painful decline. Perhaps, she thought, Miriam was so unhappy that she wanted to die.

A week later, on Mother's Day, Eddie, Natty, Allan, and Naomi went to the hospital by subway. They brought Mimi flowers. She smiled wanly when she saw her children. Natty had told the nurses they would be coming on Mother's Day so they could prepare her. The nurses had brushed her hair and applied rouge to her cheeks and lips.

Mimi broke into a wide smile when her handsome, olive-skinned son with dark brown hair bent down to kiss her. He'd grown a moustache that suited him. Naomi, fair skinned and petite, with short brown hair and a dazzling smile gave her mother a gentle hug. Today, the smiles were forced. On the subway, Natty had explained that showing their grief would only make things worse for their mother. They had to think of her first and their own grief later.

Natty and Eddie stood back from the bed so the kids could get as close as possible to Mimi.

"I'll be coming home soon," she said, sitting up in bed against two pillows. Mimi looked awful, a shadow of her former stocky self. Only her voice and laugh seemed familiar.

"I can't wait," said Naomi, positioning herself on the bed to get closer.

"Mom, Uncle Ed said I can work part-time for him this summer. I'll be a messenger," added Allan, holding his mother's hand.

"That's great, but I thought you wanted to take summer classes at the college."

"I can do that, too. I'll finish school a semester early and am applying to Indiana for grad school."

"Mom, when do you think you'll be home? What is 'soon'?" asked Naomi, eager to refocus the conversation from Allan to her mother.

"It's all up to the doctors. In a few days, I hope. Thank you both for the lovely flowers."

Natty watched the small family gathering and felt angry that Ez wasn't there. She decided she'd have a talk with him. Allan and Naomi were trying hard not to show their emotions. Allan avoided looking at his mother. Naomi's eyes filled with tears. It was time to leave.

*****

Natty and Eddie continued to visit. Eddie took an hour off here and there from his burgeoning business and Natty left the children with her mother. She watched as the flowers Allan and Naomi had brought gradually died. It was as if Mimi and the flowers were dying together, bit by bit. Natty came to hate fresh flowers because they reminded her of Miriam and her premature, ghastly death.

One day, Natty left the children with her mother and went into the city with Eddie. She had prearranged to have lunch with Ez. She discouraged Eddie from joining them. Ez would feel threatened even though Eddie was younger by more than a decade. Mimi had been like a mother to Eddie. He might not be able to control his temper.

Natty met Ez in the lobby of the Lion Match Company. Together, they strolled to the restaurant. It reminded Ez of when he and Edna had met for lunch years before. It was the day Edna met Aaron. So many years had passed. Now Edna was a balabusta, a good housewife with two children! Ez knew what Natty would say over lunch. She'd ask him why he hadn't come to the hospital on Mother's Day and why he hadn't given Mimi the attention she deserved. Natty would try to psychoanalyze him, like Freud himself, gently at first but soon, more forcefully, then tell him what he should do. Natty was no longer the young student nurse, easily upset when Gussie didn't like her dinner gift of salt and pepper shakers. She'd become a force to be reckoned with. She liked solving other people's problems and would try to solve his.

"What's going on with you, Ez?" asked Natty as soon as they had sat down and ordered drinks - a martini for Ez, coffee for Natty.

"You know, what's going on. I have a wife who's dying and two scared kids."

"But where are you? Mimi and the kids need you around. Last time she had surgery, you stayed with her. Now, it seems you're hardly there. What's gotten into you?" Natty buttered a roll and took a large bite.

"I'm frightened, is the truth, Nat. She's always in pain and I can't do anything. I've never been able to do anything. I can't save her. It's too late anyhow."

"What do you mean too late?" asked Natty, leaning across the table and lowering her voice. "You can't save her from dying but you can save her life!"

"That makes no sense. How can I save her life as she is dying?" Ez hadn't touched his roll but swallowed the martini in a couple of gulps. The food arrived. He ignored it and the waiter.

"I mean you can make her feel her life was worth living before she dies. She never got to go to college but she raised two wonderful children. She was a good wife to you even if you weren't a good husband - gallivanting all over creation," Natty sounded disgusted. She became silent and focused on eating her manicotti.

Ez was silent but signaled to the waiter to get him another drink. He finished that and then spoke, "I can do that. It's the least I can do for her."

"Stop feeling sorry for yourself. It's Mimi that needs the attention and your children. We'll help you but I hope you'll be there for them. The food here is very good, by the way."

Natty had a way of making her displeasure known in no uncertain terms and then changing the subject quickly as if nothing had happened. She did this now as she asked for the dessert menu and ordered a slice of buttercream cake.

*****

In June, Miriam was discharged and moved into the new apartment Ez had finally rented. Eddie and Natty prepared it for Miriam's arrival. The rented hospital bed that had been in their front room, was now in the apartment's living room. Ez picked Mimi up in a cab. He and the cab driver carried her into the back seat where she lay during the twenty-minute trip while Ez sat up front with the driver, smoking out the window. He'd intended to speak to Mimi and tell her what Natty wanted him to say but he could never bring himself to do it. He could barely look at her, an invalid who appeared twice her actual age.

Soon, a motley assortment of medicine bottles and syringes sat on every flat surface in the apartment bedroom. Ez was a terrible housekeeper, although he could cook, but Mimi barely ate or drank. He listened carefully when Eddie and Natty taught him how to help Miriam with the bed pan and change the linens. Natty conferred with Mimi's doctor and advised Ez regarding the pain medications.

Natty visited as often as she could to tidy the apartment and look after Mimi. Ez took Natty's arrival as his cue to take some time for himself. Mimi silently wondered what that meant. When she wasn't sleeping, she looked out the window and contemplated the trees. Except for her children, she thought that her life had been wasted and said as much to Eddie the next time he visited.

"What was it for, Eddie? To have a nasty mother and an unfaithful husband? To be ill with asthma my whole life and then get cancer? I never got to go to college. I could hardly take care of my poor children, being so ill all the time," she paused to catch her breath and wince from the pain.

"Do you need more pain medicine, Mimi? I think it's time," asked Eddie anxiously. He was sitting in a chair as close to the bed as he could get.

"No, I can stand it a few minutes more. I want to talk to you, Eddie. I'm so proud of you. I love Natty, and the children are so sweet and so good. Look what you've done with your life! Other than Naomi and Allan, you've been what's kept me going, Eddie, seeing you grow up and survive the war, Thank God."

"I couldn't have done anything without you. Please don't say such things about yourself or your life. What might have happened to me without you, Mimi? Ma was determined to destroy whatever good things I had. Look at Pop! He destroyed himself because of her. The same thing would've happened to me without you. It kills me to hear you say these things about yourself."

"I'm glad you think so, Eddie. From the moment you were born, I decided you were my baby. I wouldn't let Ma hurt you like she did me. Still, I couldn't protect you all the time and I'm sorry about that."

"Please, no more of that, Mimi! You made me who I am. And Naomi and Allan will turn out great because of you. You may not have gone to college but you know more than anyone I know who's been there. Please let me give you something for the pain so you can rest. I'll sit right here while you sleep."

*****

Mimi had encouraged Naomi to go to summer camp like always and for Allan to take summer classes while working part-time for Eddie. She felt the children needed a sense of normalcy. Allan couldn't bear to sleep in the new apartment that smelled of sickness and was a constant reminder his mother was dying. Instead, he went back to the old building to stay with his grandmother, who fussed over him.

Grandma had always been good to him and her other grandchildren, skipping the generation that had needed her the most. She and Allan had coffee together every day when he got home from the library. She had nothing good to say about anyone except Mac and Ez. After a while, Allan developed severe facial acne due to the stress and Gussie's ranting about his mother's faults wasn't helping. With what little money they had, Aunt Natty and Uncle Eddie paid for him to see a dermatologist. He started going to study at their house after school or work and drew comfort from his young niece and nephew.

Edna visited Mimi with her children. Dottie came, too. The grown-up children seemed to cheer Miriam. Edna helped Mimi recall old times when they'd lived together and the fun they'd had despite working so hard, Miriam at the secretarial pool and Edna tailoring.

"Remember when you tried making coq au vin and the chicken ended up so dry, we couldn't eat it? Then you forgot to put sugar in the pumpkin pie!" laughed Edna sitting on the bed.

Miriam laughed weakly," What about when you sewed the zipper on that dress and the lady came to try it on and it was backwards? That was worse. She yelled so loud, I thought Ma would hear her and find out you were taking in sewing."

"Luckily, she wasn't home. That was funny. At least that lady gave me another chance. She actually gave me a little extra for putting in the zipper twice. I couldn't believe it. And she told her friends I was a good seamstress. She was a mensch!"

Aaron visited and did what he could to help. He had always liked Miriam, especially her intelligence and sense of humor. She never pushed him to talk about his wartime experiences, not since those first few months after he'd returned home. He was comfortable in his silence when around Mimi, unlike when he was around Gussie or Dottie. He knew Mac and Ez understood his reluctance to talk but they were less understanding when it was just the three of them sitting around at a barbeque or a family dinner party. They seemed to think he should let it all out with guys who'd been there, too. They didn't know it all came out in his nightmares. Edna had taken to sleeping in the guest room. It was better for both of them that way.

Dottie fussed and dusted and cooked, trying to entice an appetite from Mimi. She told jokes and pretended all was as it always was, and that Mimi wasn't dying in the living room. When Mimi pretended she was sleeping, she thought about how each member of her family was handling her illness.

She liked that Dottie pretended all was well. It made her feel like she wasn't always the center of attention and, for a little while, she didn't think about death. Mac played the role of patriarch, keeping a stiff upper lip, making sure she was never alone and had everything she needed. Edna and Eddie made her laugh and helped her remember the rare good times. She could talk to Natty about anything, and she would listen and not tell her she wasn't going to die. Aaron's silence was welcome when she was tired out by all the fussing and laughing and talking. She had no further use for Ez and no need to try to make their relationship work or pretend it had ever worked.

She didn't want to see Ma, so Mac occupied their mother by helping her find a realtor to sell her house. Gussie didn't like strangers, interested in buying the house, traipsing through looking at her things. Mac found her an apartment in the same neighborhood. As much as she had mostly ignored her neighbors all these years, she was familiar with the streets and the shops. She'd never liked anything new.

She did not like living alone. Off the boat, she'd lived with her sister, Fannie and her husband. Then, she'd married Sam. Since he died, she'd had Mimi and Ez downstairs and Eddie when he was home. She was used to people being around even if she didn't like them. She wondered what it would be like to live alone but she wasn't afraid or reluctant. *I've always done whatever anyone asked of me. I've given all of myself to my family.* Now, she could do what she wanted and make all the decisions. Of course, she'd still need Mac and Ez's help now and then.

Meanwhile, Naomi wrote letters to everyone from her summer camp in the Catskills and Allan spent more time at Natty and Eddie's house. He offered to watch the children when he wasn't studying or working. He visited his mother every day but it was too painful to sit there for hours and watch her wither away. She understood and never coaxed him to stay longer.

Natty wrote Naomi back trying to sound cheerful and avoiding any mention of her mother's rapid decline.

Dear Naomi,
Sounds like you're enjoying swimming and canoeing. I love the ocean but I can't swim. Maybe you'll teach me how when you come home. It's very hot here. I let the children play in the sprinkler to help them cool off. Have you made some friends?
Love,
Aunt Nat

One afternoon, Natty phoned the camp director to say they would be driving there to pick up Naomi and take her home. Ez had called Eddie early that morning.

"I think you'd better come over, Eddie. Bring Natty, if you can," said Ez, sounding uncharacteristically frantic. "I'm not sure Mimi's breathing. I held a mirror to her mouth. I don't see anything. Ask Natty what I should do."

"We'll be right over. Call her doctor."

Natty brought the children over to stay with their elderly neighbors. She and Eddie arrived before the doctor called back. Natty checked Mimi's carotid pulse; there was nothing. The skin was mottled and cooling. It was clear Mimi was gone.

Natty looked at both men standing anxiously on either side of the bed. "She's gone. We need to call the police," she said and turned to Eddie to hold him. He collapsed in her arms. Ez stood still, looking down at the wife he'd taken for granted, who never did get to go to college, who'd never divorced him despite suspecting his peccadillos. He touched her cheek. Then, he picked up the phone.

"I'll go get Allan. Natty, please stay with Ez," said Eddie, struggling to control himself. He needed time alone but soon they would have to call Mac and get him to drive them to Naomi's camp.

Natty made Ez a cup of coffee and sat him at the table in the kitchen. She called Mac, who said he, Edna and Dottie would come straightaway. Then, she called Rose to see if she could pick up the children from the neighbors' and watch them until Natty got home. Finally, she called Naomi's camp. The director was not to tell her the news, only that her family was coming to see her.

The police and coroner arrived. The coroner examined Mimi, signed the death certificate, and left. Natty was finally allowed to wash the body. She brought a bowl of warm water, a towel, and washcloth into the room where Mimi lay. Slowly, she began to wash her sister-in-law and good friend, gradually stripping the bed jacket and nightgown away from her body. Natty used warm water because it was soothing and felt more like she was bathing Mimi than preparing her for the funeral home.

"I'll miss you. No one was like you, Mimi. No one will ever be like you," said Natty, tears pouring down her face as she slowly stroked Mimi's arms and legs with the warm cloth. "I'm so sorry you had such a hard life," she whispered, removing the bandages Mimi no longer needed. "I wish I could have made it better."

"Don't worry. Ed and I will take care of Allan and Naomi. We'll help with whatever they need. I heard Allan say he wants to get a PhD in history. Did he tell you?" she continued, gently washing the surgical scars. "I think he'll make a wonderful professor. He's brilliant. But you know that. Naomi is a beauty and so smart, like her brother."

She wiped her tears away with her arm as she dried Mimi's body with a towel and began to wash her face, having left it for last, unlike the correct procedure for bathing a living patient. You always washed the face first. It was the cleanest part of the body. She looked into Mimi's brown eyes, then closed them. She brushed her short hair, the little that had grown back since the chemotherapy treatments. Finally, she dressed her sister-in-law in a fresh nightgown and straightened the bedclothes. She turned to see Ez standing in the doorway, unsure of how long he'd been there.

"You were always so good to her. She really loved you," he said softly. Natty pulled a chair next to the bed.

"Why don't you sit with her for a while. The family will be here soon."

"I think she stopped loving me a long time ago," Ez continued, as he moved toward the chair, stumbling as he sat down. "I don't know why I did what I did. I was such a fool."

Natty stood by the bed and listened. Ez needed to talk and she figured she was the only one in the family who might listen without interruption.

"She'd always been sick. Even before the cancer. I wanted to go to clubs and parties. She never had the energy. Then, the war and the kids," he trailed off. Natty started to leave the room when Ez bent over in the chair and began to sob. She put her arms around his shoulders.

"I know it was selfish but what was I supposed to do? Sit home every night?'

Just then, Eddie arrived with Allan, who ran into the room.

"Mom, Mom," cried Allan rushing to hug his mother. Natty and Eddie left the bedroom.

"Mac, Edna, and Dottie are on their way," said Natty, getting Eddie a cup of coffee. They sat at the kitchen table. "How are you, Ed?"

"Thanks, Nat. I can't think about me. I'm worried about Allan and Naomi. I told Ma. She wanted to come but I told her she'd only be in the way. She listened, for once."

When Mac, Edna, and Dottie arrived, they all went into the bedroom to pay their respects.

"Ez, Allan, shall I call a rabbi?" asked Eddie. "We'll need to call the funeral home. Ez, do you want the one on Front Street?"

"The coroner said he would contact the funeral home. I told him to use the one on Front Street. So, that's all set. They'll be here in about an hour," put in Natty.

Ez rose from the chair and signaled to Eddie that they should go out into the apartment hallway.

"Thanks, Eddie. Mimi told me she spoke to the funeral home and told her what she wanted. I couldn't believe she could be so calm about it. She wanted the rabbi from the synagogue in the old neighborhood. I can call him. It'll give me something to do. Will you and Natty go get Naomi?"

They went back into the apartment. "Mac, can you drive us to the Catskills to pick up Naomi?"

"I'm staying here," said Allan.

"We'll stay with them," said Dottie speaking for herself and Edna. "We'll call Aaron. He's on a business trip. He'll want to get home as soon as possible."

The family grieved for Miriam. Gussie, who had never been affectionate or motherly to her daughter, cried the longest and hardest. Mac had taken her to visit his sister when she was in the hospital. Ma had simply sat beside the bed without speaking. Toward the very end, when Miriam was already unconscious and lying in bed in the apartment, Ez permitted Gussie to sit by his wife and hold her hand. She cried but didn't speak. Mac thought maybe somewhere in her heart she had loved Miriam. He hoped that was so. Eddie had argued that Mimi wouldn't have wanted Ma there, but Ma had always been nice to Ez and he felt sorry for her losing her eldest daughter.

*****

Mac prepared to move Ma into her new apartment. Natty, Edna, and Dottie packed things up and the men moved the boxes and furniture. There was nothing of Sam's left. Gussie had thrown away his clothes, his old radio, and the few mementoes he'd brought from Russia. Eddie was angry. It was one thing to throw his things away but to throw away Pop's things without offering them to his children! He'd never thought he could dislike Ma more than before but there seemed to be no end to what she could do to anger him.

Edna and Dottie shared Naomi. Dottie had girls a little older than her and Edna's daughter was almost the same age. Her son was in college but he had little in common with Allan, who preferred staying with Natty and Eddie. Ez brought women to the apartment and barely saw his children.

Like Miriam, Aaron had been seeing a therapist for a long time. He still couldn't talk about what he did during the war and had been briefly institutionalized with nervous breakdowns more than once. Edna was sympathetic as his hospital stays became more frequent. He was devoted to his family and found it hard to see his children start leaving home. He did not feel close to his brothers-in-law, had no friends outside the neighbors Edna cultivated, and he often felt alone. The family didn't know about the hospitalizations. Edna told them and their children he had influenza or pneumonia or another illness that required special care. He always came home seeming a little less like himself, but Edna wondered if she'd ever really known him.

CHAPTER TWENTY-SIX
1967

Eddie and Natty visited the family out on Long Island, bringing Danny and Rachel who enjoyed being with their older cousins. Edna and Dottie always spoiled them with homemade cakes and cookies that rivaled those Natty made. Eddie and Natty envied the lovely green lawns and neighborhood playgrounds and liked the small town feel of the neighborhood. They were ready for life in the suburbs but Long Island had become more crowded and too expensive. They decided to look in Westchester County.

Eddie sent Natty to look for houses. She took the train while the children were in school. A realtor showed her several different houses in villages along the Metro-North Hudson Railroad Line. She fell in love with an old Tudor style house in Croton-on-Hudson, about forty-five minutes north of the city and brought Eddie to see it. He too loved the house. It sat at the top of a street that rose to a hill. It was called "Old Post Road" because it had been the mail route when mail had been delivered on horseback in the colonial days. Their new next-door neighbor on one side was quite old and claimed that when she was younger, she'd seen the famous writer, Ernest Hemingway, ride by her house.

The new house required some renovation. They wanted to turn the garage into a playroom for the children and build a new garage.

The price of the house and renovations was a little more than they could afford, so Eddie returned to boxing without telling Natty. Despite Nunzio's assistance, he still wasn't paid on time or at all by some clients. By now, he had three other artists working for him at his studio in Manhattan's business district. He had a reputation for integrity, unlike many of the Madison Avenue men of the time. He still painted murals now and then for Nicky and his friends in their restaurants, but he ran his business honestly.

Bob Patterson, his partner, told Eddie about a potential client who offered a lucrative opportunity to advertise for a company selling pornography. Eddie turned it down, flat. He soon learned Bob was having an extramarital affair with the client's wife. Worse yet, his son was espousing Nazi ideals. Eddie didn't need Bob anymore since the studio was attracting most of its clients by word of mouth. But he wasn't quite ready to get rid of him.

Eddie cared about his employees, two men and one woman. They were kids, by his lights, recently out of art school, eager to show what they could do. Before long, they were seeking his opinions about politics and life, and listened, even though he was "in the establishment." He even liked Nixon, so much so, that he'd worked for his 1960 presidential campaign. They respected him for taking them on and being a patient teacher, so they listened, if not without amusement.

Eddie had stopped talking to his family. Shortly before the move to Westchester, Rachel had a second eye surgery to correct a condition she'd had since birth. The first one had left her with little improvement. She still saw two images of her mother due to her 'lazy' left eye.

The day of the surgery was Purim, a festive Jewish holiday. Eddie and Natty left Danny with Rose and brought Rachel to the hospital. They were worried about the surgery and about paying the surgeon, Dr. Romaine, who was in late middle age with white hair and bushy white eyebrows. Rachel loved to stroke them when Natty took her to Manhattan to see him. He looked like pictures she had seen of Santa Claus. Dr. Romaine was kind and told Eddie, "Pay me later, or never, just so long as your child can see. That's all that matters."

Eddie and Natty gave her kisses before Rachel was taken into the operating room, looking quite tiny lying on the adult-sized stretcher. Rachel smiled, unaware of exactly what awaited her. The surgery took three hours. Natty and Eddie took turns pacing, sitting, and going to the cafeteria for coffee.

"Where are they?" asked Eddie, about an hour after Rachel had been wheeled away.

"I don't know. We told them the date and time. I'm surprised no one is here," responded Natty.

Just then, Allan rushed in, "I'm sorry I'm late. I just got out of class. How is she? Is it over yet?"

"She's still in surgery," said Eddie embracing his nephew. "Where's everyone else? You're the only one here, except for my friend Nicky, who had to go make a phone call."

In fact, Nicky had told Eddie the week before, "Don't you worry about your little goil. I got everyone in the parish praying for her…or else!" Eddie was never sure if he was kidding. Nicky had brought a doll to the hospital. He told Eddie it was to be given to Rachel as soon as she was awake. The doll was bigger than she was and it was a long time before she could play with it.

Eddie sat tensely with his hands clutched between his legs. He gritted his teeth and imagined what he'd say to his family. *Why didn't you come? This is my child! She's almost blind and having surgery! Will she ever see? Why aren't you here to sit with us?*

Later, when he confronted Mac about not coming to the hospital, his brother answered, "It was Purim. We were having a party!" Eddie punched Mac in the face and went home. Eddie vowed to never speak to his family again although would miss his brother, especially.

When Edna called, he asked her the same question; her response was almost the same, as if they'd planned it together. Then, Ma called to see how Rachel was. Natty answered but Eddie refused to take her call.

CHAPTER TWENTY-SEVEN

1968

Victor was born on Armistice Day. He was ten years younger than Rachel who, not unlike Miriam with Eddie, decided he was her baby. Unlike Gussie, Natty was an attentive and affectionate mother but Eddie's business was not doing that well, so she had to return to work full-time. Natty had been out of nursing so long, the only job open to her was at the veteran's hospital nearby. She brought in an elderly woman to take care of Victor.

Natty worked in the geriatric-psychiatric unit managing one other nurse and three aides. One of her patients had been an officer in the Spanish-American War. Every morning, after a meticulous grooming regimen, he offered his arm to Natty and asked her to help him "review the troops" – the old veterans slumped in their wheelchairs. She enjoyed the patients, most of whom had what was later called Post Traumatic Stress Disorder. But the staff was comprised of people who would have preferred to work elsewhere and didn't like taking orders. They carried heavy rings of keys to lock and unlock parts of the unit. One day, she went to her car and the tires had been slashed. Another time, she was slapped with a ring of keys. It wasn't the patients causing the trouble; it was the staff. She and Eddie needed the money, so she decided to endure it.

Natty was overwhelmed by the adjustment full-time employment made in their lifestyle. She and Eddie were still products of the 1950s marriage, when the wife was expected to do the chores and have dinner on the table. She raced home after work, shed her uniform, and took a bath before hugging her children or preparing dinner. While it was cooking, she lay on the sofa and listened to their stories. After she fed them, they piled in the car to collect Ed from the train station, unless he got a ride.

To make sure the children had time with their father, Natty brought Rachel into their bedroom every morning as Eddie prepared for work. He'd finished showering and shaving and had put on his tee shirt and dress pants. He sipped the coffee and munched on the English muffin with strawberry jam Natty brought up on a small tray. Meanwhile, Rachel sat in their big mahogany rocking chair and chatted happily about nonsense while Eddie continued to dress, putting on his dress shirt, suspenders, and his long black socks. Rachel loved watching him tie his tie. The complexity of the over and under and up and down fascinated her. Then, Eddie grabbed his suit jacket and briefcase and went downstairs to meet a friend, who'd drive them both to the station.

*****

Edna died that year. She was forty-three, the same age Mimi had been at her death. She'd had headaches for years but didn't think anything of them, especially since Ma had told her she and Yetta – Edna's grandmother – sometimes had bad headaches. Mimi hadn't had them but she'd had enough problems already. The headaches were always in the back of Edna's head and seemed to get worse when she felt tired or anxious, like when Aaron and then Eddie had been away at war. They also got worse when Mimi got sick and Aaron was in and out of the hospital for depression. Aspirin helped but never quite relieved all the pain.

When the headaches came, she went into her bedroom and lay in the dark with a cool, damp cloth on her head. She couldn't always do that. Her children were grown but she saw them daily. She still sewed for her long-term clients and took care of the house and yard. She'd learned to take the headaches for granted. They were a part of her just like her red hair and her still beautiful legs.

One day, Edna was home alone, sewing a dress for a neighbor, when she noticed tiny spots on the dress. I don't remember there being spots on this dress, she thought. She blinked a few times and then the spots started to float. She felt dizzy and kept sticking her finger with the needle instead of sticking the dress. She got up to get a glass of water. It's hot today. I'll open a window. She staggered to the window, then fell to the floor with throbbing pain piercing her skull like a corkscrew.

Edna lay on the rug, conscious but in severe pain that got worse whenever she tried to open her eyes. The sunlight in the room sent daggers under her eyelids. She reeled sideways and spewed vomit across the room. Then she saw nothing.

Aaron came home from work at five o'clock to find her unconscious on the floor. The smell of vomit lingered along with bits and pieces of Edna's breakfast scattered all over the furniture and the drapes.

He turned her on her back and tried to open her eyes, "Edna, what happened? Wake up!" He gently slapped her face. Her skin was warm; her pulse was present but weak. He grabbed the phone to call an ambulance. Then, he called Mac.

"Ya gotta come. Something's happened to Edna. I just got home. We gotta get her to the hospital, now!"

Mac drove with Dottie in the front passenger seat, repeating "Oh my God. What happened? I talked to her on the phone this morning." Aaron sat in the back cradling Edna's head in his lap. Her legs were curled on the seat. The emergency room was full but for once, the usually silent Aaron raised his voice to no one in particular, "Something's happened to my wife. Hurry, hurry."

Mac went up to a nurse at the desk and yelled in his loudest Marine voice, "We don't know how long she's been like this. Hurry!"

Edna was taken on a stretcher to a small room. They weren't allowed to follow. A nurse as old as Natty's mother, Rose, pulled Aaron toward the nurses' desk.

"Are you this woman's husband," she asked as she sat down behind the desk and motioned for Aaron to sit in front of it. He nodded.

"What's your wife's name?"

"Edna Cohen, can I go in with her?"

"I'm sorry, sir. Not right now."

Aaron glanced at Mac and Dottie who sat in chairs lining the wall. Mac glanced back as if ready to jump from his seat at a word.

"What seems to be the problem?" asked the officious nurse as she made notes on a form.

Aaron was too shaken to speak. "Come now, Mr. Cohen. I know this is a difficult situation but we cannot help your wife if you don't tell us what happened."

Aaron glanced at Mac again and turned back to the nurse. "I just got home and found her on the floor. She wouldn't wake up. There was vomit everywhere," he said slowly and quietly.

"I see. Anything else? Had she complained of being sick before this happened?"

"Not that I remember. Wait, she has had headaches for a long time. She mentioned they were getting worse."

"Okay then, you sit down by your friends there and wait. I'll go see the doctor." Then, "Don't worry, Mr. Cohen. We'll take good care of your wife," she patted his hand and helped him stand up.

The tests showed Edna had inoperable brain cancer. She regained consciousness but was too ill to go home. Despite Demerol and Morphine to treat the pain, the headaches were relentless. The narcotics made her sleepy but it was too painful to be without them.

Aaron sat with her day after day, skipping work altogether. Their children went to the hospital to be with them. Mac and Dottie shuttled back and forth. Mac had to work but Dottie made a point of coming every day during visiting hours. She made Aaron and the children take breaks.

"We should go see her, Ed," said Natty after hanging up from Dottie's call. "She's your sister."

"Where was she when Rachel was having eye surgery?"

"She was wrong. They were all wrong, but Edna's dying, Ed. Let's go see her before she dies. The least we can do is comfort Aaron."

"Edna and I were never close. Mac and my mother are bound to be there. I don't want to see them. You go if you want to. I'm not."

"I won't go without you," Natty answered, regretting her words then and ever after. When she looked back on that time, she wished she'd kept in touch with Eddie's family, for the sake of her own children.

A few days into her hospital stay, Edna awoke for a short period at night after everyone had left and the nurses were busy at the nurses' station. She didn't feel sleepy but she didn't feel in any pain, either. She thought about dying. There was no escaping it. She'd heard everyone talking when she was half asleep and they thought she couldn't hear them.

She wasn't ready to accept death the way Mimi had. But she knew she couldn't stand the headaches or sleep the rest of her life while her family hovered around her bed talking about whom she had been and who she might have become. She wished someone would kill her. The next day, she asked Aaron if he would.

He simply shook his head and left the room.

*****

A few days later, Edna died in her sleep. She was alone again and it was midnight when the nurse discovered her gone, so that's what she wrote in the chart and told the doctor when she called him to come and officially pronounce the death. The night nurses bathed Edna and called the family. Mac and Dottie brought Gussie and Aaron to the hospital. Edna's children went to the hospital on their own. Mac called Ez and Eddie.

Ez wasn't home but Eddie answered, "Edna's dead. I thought you'd want to know," said Mac.

"Thanks for telling me," Eddie answered and hung up the phone.

Mac rejoined everyone and said Kaddish, the Jewish prayer for the dead. After that, Aaron left for home while the others stayed a while longer. Aaron returned to an empty house. The next morning, his children went to see him to discuss the funeral arrangements and found him hanging by a rope in the garage.

*****

Eddie didn't go to either funeral. He quietly mourned Edna and Aaron. He'd never gotten to know Aaron well because he'd been a hard man to get to know. Eddie didn't have anything against their children and barely knew them. He thought he'd try to make contact and help them in any way he could. Maybe it had been a mistake to shun his family for so long. He'd always found it hard to forgive; perhaps he'd gotten that from his mother. She'd never forgiven him for being born. She'd never forgiven Pop for becoming an American or Mimi and Edna for not listening to her advice. *Natty said I should forget about what happened after Rachel's surgery but I just can't. It was like a slap in the face. I feel like I've never really been part of the family except to Pop and Mimi. Since they've been gone, it's as if they ignore me. But Mac? I thought Mac and I were close.*

CHAPTER TWENTY-EIGHT
1970

Life was generally good in Croton-on-Hudson, even if Eddie's business waxed and waned and he wasn't always paid. As products of the Great Depression, Natty and Eddie never spoke to their children about money, when they had it or when they didn't. They were inclined to expect the worst, appreciate what they had, and protect their children from bad news.

Eddie was finally ready to fire Bob Patterson because he wasn't bringing in any new clients or doing anything to keep the old ones. Eddie did all that himself. Plus, Patterson was still cheating on his wife and still giving his Nazi son room and board. Eddie rehearsed how he'd tell Bob it was time for him to move on. He'd try to focus on the early days of the business and thank Bob for believing in him when he'd really needed it. Then, he'd offer Bob a nice severance package. That was the least he could do. He was saved the trouble when he walked into the studio one day, before the staff arrived, and found Bob dead, his head on his desk, dead, it turned out, of a heart attack.

*****

Eddie took some of his clients to lunch, a technique he'd learned from his old bosses, Schwab and Winkelman. The money spent on lunch and two or three martinis each, was usually well worth the work those clients gave him. He'd go back to his office after these lunches, pleased with his efforts and hopeful they'd bear fruit. He'd work a few more hours and head to one of his favorite gin mills before catching the train home. Eddie could always feel the stress flowing out of him as the evening drinks took hold. He remembered Pop going to bars to get away from Ma. *I'm a chip off the old block, I guess,* he thought. He knew it wasn't healthful to drink so much and he was starting to put on weight, but alcohol seemed expected and was often necessary to get the client to relax and listen to Eddie's pitch. When followed by a great meal, Eddie couldn't lose and rarely did.

As ever, the richer or more prominent Eddie's clients were, the less likely they were to pay on time. But they regularly took him out to fancy restaurants and introduced him to famous people. Since it was New York, he sometimes encountered celebrities all on his own.

One day, he stopped at a bar he liked while a film crew was setting up. A famous movie star sat down a couple of stools away from him.

"Hey, you make more money than I do," Eddie said looking over at the actor. "Why don't you buy us both a drink?"

"Buy yourself a drink," was the ungracious response.

Eddie frequently had lunch with Omar Bradley, a former five-star general and hero from the second World War. Bradley was president of the Bulova watch company for which Eddie regularly did advertising. As an enlisted man, Eddie never liked officers. In Korea, when they asked if he'd like to attend officer training school, he declined. In his view, the officers never worked as hard as the enlisted men. He'd resented them for it.

Still, he loved talking to Bradley about the Army and World War II, and they agreed that MacArthur had been a grandstanding loose cannon. Eddie had become a history buff as well as a gourmand and an opera fan. He wished he could introduce Mac to the General. Boy, would he be impressed.

From time to time, Eddie still met up with some wise guys, who were old friends, like Nicky. He also had friends on the other side. One evening, as Eddie paid his bar bill and was grabbing his coat, a friend of his, a police detective, sidled up to him.

"Listen Eddie," he whispered, "you've gotta stop palling around with some of your buddies." As he said this, he put his finger to his nose and pushed it to the left.

"Hey Mike. What do you mean? Want a drink? On me."

"Listen Eddie, I'm here as your friend but also as a cop. Look at these," Mike pulled some polaroid photographs out of his suit jacket pocket and handed them to Eddie under the bar. Mike waved away the bar tender when he signaled to ask if he wanted a drink. The bar tender walked away with a scowl. Eddie and Mike were the only men at the bar. It was early yet.

The photos showed Eddie going in and out of mafia owned restaurants in Brooklyn and Little Italy. "We call you 'Eddie Crewcut' down at the station."

"Listen Eddie," he said again. "You're a good guy, a businessman, and a family man. You can't be seen with these guys anymore. It'll ruin you. We'll have to take you in. My advice: Stay away from them." Mike put the pictures back in his suit jacket pocket and left the bar without another word.

Eddie took the hint and cut all ties with his wise guy friends, some of whom he'd grown up with. He occasionally caught up with Babe, Arnie, and Norm, but he'd heard Eppy had been executed at Sing Sing prison. He didn't know what for but was sad to hear that's how his old friend had ended up.

He focused on his family and his business. Alcohol became even more important in helping him deal with the stress. He'd graduated to three martini lunches which weren't' really for his clients anymore – they sustained him through the day. When he got home at night, he'd have a beer or two with his dinner. Danny and Rachel sat at the table with Eddie and Natty while Eddie ate. They'd all catch up on what they were doing. It gave Eddie a chance to spend time with his older children.

*****

Eddie learned of Nicky's death from the newspaper. He'd been murdered in upstate New York. It was sad, but Nicky had once told him, "You play with bad guys, you end up six feet under."

He remembered the last time he'd seen him. He had gone to one of Nicky's restaurants to finish a large mural. Nicky had recently opened the place and wanted Eddie to paint a large wall with a man and a woman in a gondola with the moon in the darkening sky above them.

It was early Saturday morning, before the lunch crowd came in. Eddie finished the mural in a room not yet opened to the public. He'd been working every Saturday morning for weeks and he was glad to have finally finished. His compensation was watching the chef prepare the meals and eating a big one, on the house, before he left. On this final Saturday, he went up to Nicky to tell him he was leaving when two wise guys came in. Eddie didn't know them. They looked at the finished mural.

"It's the sun," one guy said pointing to the round object in the painted sky behind the gondola.

"No, it's the moon," said the other guy.

"It's the sun," said the first guy pointing a gun at his companion.

"Okay, it's the sun."

Eddie beat a quick exit with barely a wave to Nicky. That was the last time he went to the restaurant and the last time he saw his friend.

Fortunately, life had changed for the better for Eddie's other old friends. Babe Merola finally got married and took over his father's dry-cleaning business. Norman married Arnie Siegel's sister Gloria, but the marriage went sour after she gave birth to three children in quick succession. Eddie resisted the urge to say "I told you so." Fagie, Natty's friend who went out with Bernie from Cleveland to do Natty a favor, had ended up marrying the guy.

Eddie met businessmen on the train to and from Croton-on-Hudson who became new friends. Natty joined The League of Women Voters and the Zoning Board. She also made friends with the parents of her children's friends. They'd frequently sit in Natty's kitchen in the afternoon drinking coffee and eating something Natty had baked, until the kids came home. The family acquired a large German Shepherd Danny ironically named Rommel, after the German WWII general. The three kids wrestled with Rommel on the floor of their parents' bedroom. Rommel was always gentle, as if he knew this was all a game and he was the star player. But everyone else in town feared him. He was large and dragged Rachel around when she took him for walks. "Who's walking who?" the neighbors asked.

Rommel was a good watch dog. One evening, when Eddie was not home, two men Natty didn't recognize came to the house and knocked on the front door. They wouldn't give their names. Natty thought they looked menacing. She held the dog by his collar and let him bark through the screen door. The men turned away quickly and never returned. Eddie claimed he had no idea who they were or why they had come.

*****

Eddie missed Mac. Natty begged him to consider getting in touch with him, for the sake of the children, if not his own.

"The children need to know their cousins and I'd like to see Mac and Dottie again," argued Natty.

"Allan and Naomi still keep in touch. They're the only ones worth seeing. We don't see anyone on your side of the family. I think we're better off this way."

Allan had lived with Natty and Eddie off and on until he went to the Midwest for his doctorate and then moved to Brazil when he couldn't find a professorship teaching in the U.S.. Naomi left Brooklyn College after a year and moved to California to attend school there. By then, Eddie and Natty had banished Rose from ever visiting them again. She'd interfered in their marriage just as she had with Natty's sister Abby and her husband. Eddie said if they were to stay married, she had to stop visiting.

As soon as he was old enough, Danny started working as a messenger for the studio in the summer. He ran around Manhattan and into Brooklyn delivering contracts and art work. He loved the job and his father paid him well. He learned about the city and how to navigate it despite the noise and the constant flow of people. He loved hearing the taxis honk at one another and watch the traffic snarl as he walked in between cars to cross the street.

Sometimes, Eddie took him out to lunch with his clients, many of whom had become good friends. They often socialized on weekends at the house in Croton. Eddie barbequed in the back yard and served the cucumber salad Dottie had taught him to make many years before. Eddie painstakingly sliced the cucumbers as thin as paper. Natty made orzo salad with mint leaves and German potato salad. Dessert was always homemade and delicious.

In the winter, Eddie and Natty entertained their neighbors or Eddie's clients, serving spaghetti with homemade 'gravy', salad, and chocolate cake or melt-in-your-mouth cookies and ice cream. Liquor flowed and some of the guests got carried away. But no one became offensive. They just laughed a lot and talked about old times- as if they had been any better.

Danny observed closely when he went to lunch with his father and his clients. He realized how knowledgeable his father was about paper and printing and all the parts of the business that happened after the art work was completed. As he watched the men, always men, drink their martinis and gimlets during the meal, later relaxing with Galiano wine, Danny caught on to what a good salesman his father was.

Eddie had little problem acquiring clients but when they didn't pay their bills, he worried about how he'd pay himself and his staff. He didn't share his worries with Natty or his friends. He didn't think that was manly. Sometimes, he thought about the wise guys he'd known and how lucky he'd been to escape what had amounted to a Jewish ghetto and avoid a criminal life.

One day when walking with Danny down a New York City Street, a man rushed up to Eddie and gave him a big hug. Eddie proudly introduced his son to the man who was dressed in a black trench coat. The men exchanged a few words and went on their way. After the man passed them by, Danny asked,

"Who was that man, Dad?"

"That man, Danny, was Jimmy the Nose!"

"Yeah? Who the heck is Jimmy the Nose?"

"Well, I'll tell ya Dan, your old man has had some shady acquaintances in his day. I'll tell ya all about it sometime, but not in the middle of the street. Ya never know who might hear," Eddie winked.

Danny remembered thinking this was a bit over the top, an exaggerated response to a chance meeting. His father loved to tell stories, each of which changed slightly each time he told it, depending on who was listening. Danny wondered how much was true.

CHAPTER TWENTY-NINE
1973

Danny continued working as a messenger for PenPoint Studios until the summer he left for West Point. Eddie suppressed his dislike of officers when his son announced he wanted to apply there. Instead, he supported his son wholeheartedly. He mentioned it to General Bradley at lunch one day. He offered to pull strings to get Danny a spot.

"My son wants to go to your alma mater," announced Eddie as they sipped their martinis. They were sitting at Luchow's on East 14th Street.

"That's great, Ed. When does he graduate high school? Is he applying now?" asked the General, dressed in a brown suit, white oxford shirt with West Point cufflinks, and brown tie.

"He graduates in June. He wants to go this summer. The guidance counselor is helping him with the application now." Eddie used his soup spoon to anchor his fork as he wound his spaghetti around it.

"It's Fall. Sounds about right, although things were very different in my day. I'll tell you what I'll do, Ed. I'm going give your son my nomination. I have one, you know. Because I'm a former five-star."

"Well, thanks, General. But Dan already has a congressional nomination,"

Eddie signaled the waiter to bring the bill.

"What? I could've given him a nomination off the bat! Why didn't you tell me sooner, Ed? Didn't you know I could nominate someone directly to the Academy?" asked Bradley, putting down his napkin, angrily.

"He wanted to see if he could get a nomination on his own. I promised I wouldn't ask you about it, General."

Well, I have to say," started Bradley, calming a bit, "I admire the kid. I imagine he'll do well in the Army. He took the initiative." Then, he laughed and let Eddie pay the bill.

That evening, Eddie asked Danny to sit down with him in the kitchen while he ate dinner. Eddie always ate after the family on weekdays. He didn't get home until eight o'clock. Natty preferred to feed the kids and herself at five. Tonight, it was Spanish rice with a hamburger and some fresh green beans.

"I saw General Bradley today. He got a bit upset when I told him you already had a nomination. But, in the end, he seemed proud of you for not taking the easy way," said Eddie between bites, washing them down with a cold beer.

"What do you mean?" asked Natty, sitting with them at the wooden kitchen table her father, Harry, had brought home from his furniture store many years before. Rachel was in the playroom they'd made from a garage, watching TV. Victor was already in bed, upstairs in the room he shared with his brother.

"General Bradley is a retired five star general. He can automatically nominate someone to the Academy," Eddie explained.

"Really? Why didn't we do that? How wonderful to have a nomination from a famous general!"

"Mom, if I'm going to go to the Academy and into the Army, I have to be able to make it on my own. I don't want other people pulling strings for me," said Danny, eating the second helping of homemade chocolate pudding Natty put in front of him. "You get it, Dad, right?"

"Of course, I do," Eddie answered proudly.

Eddie was thrilled when Danny was accepted into the class of 1977. They brought him to the Academy on a hot June day. Rachel and Victor waved good-bye when Danny walked through the sally port and into the barracks. Eddie shuddered to think what his son would have to endure. It wasn't combat, but the Academy surely was no picnic. Danny was an easygoing kid, like his mother. Eddie wasn't sure how he'd adjust.

Once Danny was allowed to have visitors, Eddie, Natty, Rachel, and Victor traveled to West Point on weekends bringing picnic lunches for Danny and his friends. They boarded a ferry, with all their baskets and bags, and headed out to Constitution Island, a short distance away in the middle of the Hudson River. There, they laid the food out on picnic tables and spread blankets on the long grass.

Natty cooked and baked all week for these picnics. She made fried chicken or Italian sausages with onions and peppers. There was always an abundance of summer salads and desserts. She dressed in sleeveless summer pantsuits and floppy hats to protect her perfectly unlined complexion.

Rachel, now in high school, attended West Point's "hops," Saturday night dances held for the cadets and girls who traveled there from all over to pursue boyfriends who were clean cut and destined to have secure military careers after graduation. There were five girls in each hotel room so ten young women shared one bathroom as they put on their makeup and got ready for the dances.

Rachel loved every minute. All the cadets were young men, on the brink of greatness. Every single one seemed handsome and physically fit. Live bands played popular music and always ended the night with a slow dance. Then each cadet grabbed the girl they were dancing with, helped her with her coat and pocketbook, and they ran back to the hotel where he kissed her good night before running back to the barracks before the one AM curfew.

*****

Eddie looked after several cadets, friends of Danny and the children of friends across the country, who lived too far away to visit more than once or twice a year. People they didn't know were advised to contact Eddie and Natty, who lived just eighteen miles from the Academy and seemed to love feeding and hosting the young men. The house became a place the cadets could count on for great food, much laughter, a nice driveway where they could wash their cars, and surrogate parents.

Eddie embraced the boys as honorary sons. He encouraged them to stick it out and not give up, no matter how hard the military training and the courses became. He mentored one former cadet to become a successful salesman after he left the Army and helped another to become a Renaissance man after Eddie taught him to appreciate the finer things in life.

He also advised other young men who came upon the family by accident or design. He convinced more than one set of parents to let their sons study art, because Eddie saw their potential and told them not to waste it. He saw the potential in each boy just as his father, Harry, his high school art teacher, and Schwab and Winkelman had seen it in him.

After Danny graduated and married, Eddie continued to mentor the new young second lieutenants as they progressed through the ranks. While Natty fed them as much as any self-respecting Jewish mother could, Eddie fed their minds, introducing them to literature, music, good food, and art.

CHAPTER THIRTY

1976

Eddie also took pleasure from his own children. One evening, he, Natty, Victor, and Rachel had a grapefruit peel fight. They ducked behind the kitchen chairs and crawled under the table. It was messy and fun. They thought they'd never laughed so much.

He told his children, "School is your job" and explained how important it was to go to college. He shared with them his love of dark chocolate and mayonnaise - "but never together." Eddie never let them know about his concerns about money and never let his children go without winter coats or other necessities.

In the summer, on weekends, he liked to lie on a lawn chair in the back yard and sun himself. He'd listen to classical music or Johnny Cash, and sip a martini as he absorbed the healing sun. He never used sunscreen that anyone could recall. The ruddy color of his face made him look and feel happy. Then, he'd arrange charcoal in the barbeque grill so neatly and precisely that his children laughed at him behind his back. He grilled steaks, chops, and chicken, enough for a platoon. The family, plus whomever happened to be visiting, sat outside at a picnic table under the weeping willow tree and devoured the meal. Afterward, Victor regaled everyone with his banjo, playing songs like *The Wabash Cannonball* and *The City of New Orleans*.

Rachel's wedding reception was held in the backyard on a day in late June. She married a cadet in Danny's class. The ceremony took place at the Old Cadet Chapel on Academy grounds, but the reception was at home where she and her family had spent so many happy hours. Natty and Eddie made all the food that Eddie's friends from the restaurant kitchens in Manhattan served to the delighted guests.

CHAPTER THIRTY-ONE

1984

Eddie started coaching boxers to earn money because he was having trouble making ends meet in the art studio. He couldn't always pay himself. He worked hard to bring in new clients and to get the old ones to pay up. Every Friday morning, he gave Natty one hundred dollars to spend for the week. He'd done so for years, but it was no longer enough.

"I need more," said Natty one Friday morning, "Victor needs school supplies and he eats like a horse!"

"He's like me, isn't he, Nat? Skinny but strong. I'm glad he likes playing baseball. Maybe, I can take him to a game."

Have you asked him what he'd like to do when he graduates? Maybe, he'll go to the Academy, too!" said Natty, excitedly. She was worried about money; the Academy was free and prestigious.

"We'll have a good talk soon. I'll see if I can get some tickets for this weekend or next. I have a client with connections."

Natty quit the veteran's hospital and worked as a school nurse. It was less exhausting and left her more time for Victor, and hosting cadets and neighbors. With Victor still in high school, Natty and Eddie took in another child. Abby's teenaged daughter Claudia, was fifteen and had been living with her father. Her mother was in and out of psychiatric institutions and couldn't care for her. Her father didn't know what to do with a teenaged girl. Both of her parents agreed Claudia would be better off with Natty and Eddie.

Claudia, a beautiful, black-haired waif, was a good companion for Victor. He helped her navigate the small village high school and alerted her to which teachers wouldn't notice if you wrote recipes on the pages you handed in, instead of the actual assignment and about the kind math teacher who gave you credit for spelling your own name right. He laughed when he told her to watch out for Mrs. Smith.

"She's the English teacher. Shorter than you. She likes to hold one of the desks over her head and lecture everyone about listening in class. One time," said Victor, warming to his topic, "We all climbed on the roof outside the window of the classroom and waited there. She looked around for us when she came in. Then, she heard us laughing. Man, was she mad. We all had a good laugh, though. Oh, she loves *The Rime of the Ancient Mariner*. Everyone has to memorize and act out parts of it. Did Danny already tell you?"

Water, water, everywhere,
And all the boards did shrink;
Water, water, everywhere,
Nor any drop to drink.

Claudia laughed. Victor was a wonderful mimic.

*****

The family absorbed Claudia into it as one of their own and she startled them with her intelligence and street smarts. Eddie was warm and tender with Claudia, since she reminded him of himself when he was young and was spurned by his mother. Claudia's parents loved her enough to give her to Eddie and Natty to finish raising, because they knew they couldn't do it well. Eddie remembered being loved by his father and Mimi. He'd been close to Mac and Ez when he was young. But the lack of his mother's love and attention had given him a thick skin. He saw that same quality in Claudia. He hoped she'd retain a little of it to help bear life's disappointments but also that those hard edges would soften and free her from the depression that occasionally still plagued him.

Eddie called Victor "champ" and made him kippers and eggs on Super Bowl Sundays. When Victor wore a kilt for a role in the chorus of the high school's production of *Brigadoon*, Eddie said, "and here is my son, in a dress." But he was proud. He was not the typical dad of the play catch, mow the lawn or fix things variety. Instead, he took Victor to baseball games to see the Yankees, Victor's favorite team, even though Eddie preferred the Mets.

Eddie taught Victor that a hard glare or a silly face could change the tone of any situation and that you should never avoid using a bad pun. It made people laugh and loosen up. From Eddie, Victor learned that sunglasses are always "cool," and the words "bird" and "curb" are often mispronounced as "boid" and "coib," especially if you're from Brooklyn. When Victor got older, Eddie told him that facial hair is always fun for children and if your angry voice is scary enough, you need never spank them.

At home, Eddie played jazz or classical music on the stereo while he made veal parmigiana, paella or Italian gravy. He tucked a dishtowel into his belt and named the pieces of meat he aimed to tenderize after folks he didn't like. Then he pounded them with a mallet till they were almost transparent. It helped him vent his frustrations with clients who wouldn't pay.

As Victor and Claudia got older, Eddie took them to Italian restaurants for lunch while their friends ate at fast food joints. During the summer, he took them to the city with him. They rode the stuffy, cigarette smelling train of commuters with newspapers practically stuck to their faces. Eddie always read the comics first, showing Victor and Claudia which were well drawn and which were not. He insisted on walking the twelve blocks to his Manhattan studio despite Victor's grumbling.

Eddie said, "A city is meant to be walked through."

They took the elevator to the penthouse studio; it smelled of art markers, paper stock, dried ink, and rubber cement. There was always a thin layer of eraser dust on the floor. While Eddie worked – often kicked back in a chair, feet propped on the desk or hunched over typing with two index fingers - Victor and Claudia took turns answering the phones, "PenPoint Studio. How can I help you?" Between calls, they'd talk to the other artists or draw stick figures with the numerous colorful pens and pencils or look through the enormous, illustrated advertising books.

CHAPTER THIRTY-TWO

1986

Natty wanted Victor to go to West Point, just like his brother had, but he wanted to become a musician. He'd been playing banjo since he was eleven, had taught himself guitar, and thought he was good enough to become a rock star.

"You can do that later," said Natty. "What kind of a career is that, anyway? You're smart. You can do anything."

Eddie agreed, "Victor, it's very hard to make it as a musician. I see a lot of out-of-work-actors and musicians working as waiters. Try the Army. If you don't like it, you can leave after your commitment is done. You'll have your whole life ahead of you."

When Eddie looked back on his time in the Army, he realized what it had meant to his life. *I got away from my mother and met people who were also running away,* he thought. *We stuck together and some of us survived. I grew up and I learned I could die.* He knew other war veterans who'd decided to do whatever they wanted. They ran around with other women, cheated in their business dealings, and neglected their families in pursuit of their own dreams. Eddie didn't think he asked for much. He wanted a good marriage, decent children, and honest friends. He never forgot the comfort of being warm and dry and safe.

"You can learn a lot in the Army," he told Victor. "It won't be wasted time."

Victor went to West Point after serving in the Army as an enlisted man for two years. So began a whole new round of picnics and barbeques, and cadets sleeping on the living room floor and washing their cars in the driveway on weekends. Eddie wrote long, supportive letters encouraging Victor to keep on course. He was especially excited when Victor received a grade of "A" in boxing his freshman year.

Victor suddenly became religious, attending services every Friday night at the synagogue on campus. He went because Eddie and Natty drove there to see him and because the Sabbath Oneg buffet of bagels and lox filled his empty belly.

Victor thought of his father as a combination of Humphrey Bogart, The Godfather, and Groucho Marx. He could be very tough and very funny. Dad had a story for every possible situation in life. He always arrived dressed as the suave, debonair man-about-town. He wore a suit jacket with a pocket square handkerchief. He waxed the moustache he'd cultivated so it curved upwards on its own. The moustache took attention away from the nose that had long since caved in from boxing. It also framed his smile, the same one Natty fell for when they first met at the Valentine's Day party so many years before.

Claudia was in school in the city to become a teacher. She rode the train back and forth to attend classes while living at home in Croton. Both Natty and Eddie advised her to play down her beauty while traveling, to avoid unwanted attention. Claudia had beautiful long, jet black hair and Rose's green eyes. Her skin was fair and flawless. She wore faded jeans, a sweatshirt and a baseball cap on the train and changed her clothes once she reached school. But unlike Danny, Rachel or Victor, she'd grown up street smart. She'd spent a lot of time on her own as a kid and knew how and from whom to protect herself.

Claudia loved Uncle Ed and Aunt Natalie. She remembered being sent home from school one day because she had been skipping classes and had been scolded by the principal. The principal had called to tell Natty what had happened.

She confronted Claudia when she walked in the door.

"Skipping classes, Claudia? Why? Where are you going? What are you doing?" asked Natty in her characteristically straightforward manner.

"I don't like school. It's boring," answered Claudia, beginning to cry. They were sitting in the living room on Natty's prized black love seat with the orange accent pillows.

"You have the chance to learn here. If you're having trouble, we can find someone to help you. But you must attend school. Ed and I have a reputation in this community. Our children attend school and do what they're told," Natty's raised voice startled Claudia. So far, Aunt Natalie hadn't yelled at her. This was new. It made Claudia cry harder.

Natty put an arm around the young girl and hugged her. "I'm sorry I'm making you cry. I just want you to have everything you should have. I shouldn't have yelled at you. I'm sorry."

Claudia looked at her and said, "I'm not crying because you yelled at me. I'm crying because you care enough to yell at me."

Later, when Eddie came home and the children were busy with homework, she told him the story. "I understand how she feels," he said. "I used to wish my mother would care enough about what I was doing to say something, even if it meant yelling at me. She yelled often enough, but I knew it was not because she cared. It was because I was an inconvenience."

*****

The computer sounded the death knell for Eddie's business. He and his studio artists had done everything by hand. He'd become known for his calligraphy. Now, computers allowed 'artists' to do the same work in much less time and only a skilled one could really tell the difference. Eddie redoubled his efforts. Clients he'd had for years stayed with him but it was hard to get new ones. But, he still welcomed young artists who came to New York to find work.

Richard came from England and found Eddie through a complex network of contacts. Eddie hired him for the summer and gave him a place to sleep in the sun room in the Croton house. Naomi came to visit from California and they fell head over heels for each other. She stayed with her cousins out on Long Island and visited Croton often that summer. In the evening, she, Richard, and Eddie liked to sit outside the house in the front yard on the old nylon lawn chairs they had brought with them from the back porch in Brooklyn.

Naomi and Eddie reminisced about her childhood and the old days in Brooklyn before Natty and Eddie moved to their own house. They avoided mentioning Miriam and Ez. Neither Naomi nor Allan was close to their father. Allan had achieved his dream of earning a doctorate but soon after, married another student and fled to Brazil. He'd hoped to escape all the unhappiness he'd known, especially the loss of his mother. He sent letters or called every six months or so.

Eddie told Naomi and Richard stories they didn't know or that Naomi was happy to hear again. A second martini or beer usually loosened Eddie's tongue. He told Naomi some of his problems with Gussie and complained that he, unlike his siblings, never had roller skates or a bed of his own. Naomi mentioned the recent wedding they all had attended out on Long Island. One of the cousins had married and Natty and Eddie had been invited.

Natty had convinced Eddie to go. It had been many years since he'd severed ties with his family. It was time to reconnect. Natty wanted them to know how much Eddie had accomplished and how much they'd achieved together. She wanted her children to know their cousins as adults and have relationships with them. Naomi recalled the scene when Eddie, always well-dressed, approached his elderly mother to say hello.

"Who's this handsome looking man?" said Gussie in her still strong Yiddish accent. She turned her attention from another conversation to look Eddie over. He was wearing a well-tailored suit and had a neatly folded white pocket square in his left outside pocket; his shoes reflected the afternoon sun. Natty was not standing with him. She was occupied talking with Dottie and Mac and blatantly kvelling or crowing about her family's accomplishments.

"It's me, Ma," replied Eddie. He could barely speak.

"Eddie?" she asked skeptically. "No, not skinny Eddie who never cared about his mother?" she said while noting the still full head of blond hair with only a little bit of gray, the handlebar moustache, pinstripe suit, and small beer belly.

Eddie turned away from her and walked toward Natty. She could tell by the look on his face that the meeting had not gone well. She smiled sympathetically, grabbed his arm, and steered him away from the crowd of relatives.

"Let's go home," he said.

*****

PenPoint Studios began a slow, inexorable slide into bankruptcy. Eddie hid his fears for the business from Natty and the children, but his employees knew the art world was changing and that he was not changing with it. They loved him for all he'd done for them, giving them jobs when they were just starting out, teaching them, and mentoring them about both art and life and encouraging them when one or the other became too much. But, outside of work, they began to cultivate their computer skills to be ready when the inevitable end arrived.

CHAPTER THIRTY-THREE
1991

Victor had graduated from West Point and Claudia from college with a teaching degree. He was headed to his first assignment in Massachusetts. She, to her first elementary school classroom. Danny and Rachel and their families lived not far from each other on Fort Leavenworth, Kansas. They'd meet for dinner or at the officer's club pool. Their children enjoyed playing and attending school together. It was a rare opportunity for two related military families to live on the same post.

Eddie and Natty visited every two to three months. Natty taught her grandchildren to bake and Eddie read to them before bed. It was an idyllic time. He showed the children how to stick their fingers in their cheeks to make a popping sound and to blow into beer bottles to make music. They liked to play with his moustache, proving the truth of what he'd told Victor about children and facial hair, was true. Eddie frequently cooked for everyone. He made the old favorites but also new recipes that usually got the thumbs up, except when they didn't, which was rare.

Eddie liked being on an Army post again. He liked the atmosphere of close community and traditional values, especially since he didn't have to dig ditches or sit in the guard house. Sometimes the USO came to the post.

The entertainment was lighthearted and kid-friendly. The children especially liked the rodeos because of the animals and clowns.

The visits to his children helped with Eddie's melancholia as the business slowly spiraled downward. He was paying credit card bills with other credit cards and was stuffing unpaid bills into his desk drawer. He didn't know what to do. Clients weren't paying him when or how much they owed. He was still wining and dining clients at expensive restaurants hoping the meals would pay off in business. He tried not to think of what could happen and knew if he did, he wouldn't be able to keep going.

CHAPTER THIRTY-FOUR
1997

One morning, Eddie went to his Manhattan studio and found it padlocked with a notice from the Internal Revenue Service stuck to the door. It said *Closed Until Further Notice* in boldly printed letters. He was stunned and confused.

He rode the subway, unsure where he was going. He couldn't think. He was in a panic, not knowing what he could do or if there was anything left to do. He couldn't pay his taxes because he couldn't pay his bills. He couldn't pay his bills, because his clients didn't pay him. He couldn't get more clients because of the damned computers. He knew he couldn't get on the train back to Croton, because he couldn't yet face all the men he'd ridden it with day after day, year after year. Most had become friends, good friends. Several were frequent guests at the house for Saturday night parties or Sunday dinners.

He knew their secrets. Several of the men would sit in the bar car on the way home and get drunk enough to talk about things they shouldn't. Eddie heard about love affairs that shocked him. Sometimes, he'd see one of the regulars sit down in a seat next to a woman they didn't know. They'd get off the train together. Eddie knew the wives and wasn't surprised when the marriages failed.

He wasn't up to the friendly chatter of the men that evening. It was such a contrast from the morning ride when they all rode silently, reading their newspapers or pretending to, as they contemplated the stressful day ahead of them. Riding the train home was like a party. He was not in a partying mood that day.

So, he spent some of the day riding the subway uptown and downtown till he could calm himself enough to catch the train home from Grand Central Station. He'd been riding for hours before he realized he hadn't eaten all day. He figured he'd get off at the next stop and grab a quick bite. He looked like any successful businessman on his way to meet a client.

Eddie was well-dressed in a starched white Oxford shirt and a blue tie with tiny West Point emblems all over it that Danny had bought for him for Father's Day. His suit was navy blue and his black shoes were shined to strict Army standards. Natty was a genius at dressing herself and the kids cheaply in what appeared to be fine and stylish clothes. She'd learned how to do this when she was very young and had developed an interest in fashion from her grandma's magazines. She had a natural flair for putting the right things together. But Eddie bought his own suits off the rack and had them tailored.

Eddie stood hanging onto a pole in the very crowded subway car. People jostled him this way and that. Like a seasoned New Yorker, Eddie looked anywhere that wasn't into the face of a fellow traveler. He didn't read the advertisements on the walls above the passenger seats. Only tourists did that.

He noticed a large Black man wearing frayed jeans, a dirty sweatshirt, and sunglasses, standing nearby and staring intently at him. The guy looked like Eddie's old tanker friend Big John. But reminiscing only added to his misery. Big John had always looked friendly except when he and Eddie were fighting someone. This guy had a sinister look on his face. He didn't have the look of a tourist. Eddie decided to move to another car. As he made his way, he noticed the man following him. Eddie surreptitiously patted his inside suit pocket to make sure his wallet was there. He knew he could still throw a good punch, but this guy looked like a tank wouldn't knock him down.

Finally, the subway stopped at the station. Eddie hurried off. The man followed him, whispering to Eddie's back:

"Walk quickly. Don't stop until we're out of the station."

Eddie walked quickly, keenly aware of the man following him. They both hurried up the stairs and out onto the street. Before Eddie could run off, the man gently grabbed the back of his suit collar and stopped him. Eddie turned around as he struggled to break free.

"Sir," said the man in a normal tone. "Sir, I'm a cop. There were two men on the subway who had been following you since the time you got on. They were out to rob you. I wanted to make sure you got off okay."

Eddie looked up at him in surprise.

"Yeah, these guys like to pick on older businessmen they think won't fight back. But I think they were probably wrong about you. You move pretty fast for an old guy!" he said laughing.

Eddie calmed himself, "Thanks. I don't think I could've outrun them, but my fists are still in pretty good shape! Can I buy you a cup of coffee or something? "

"No sir. My job today is to ride the subways. I've got to get back to it. Take care of yourself, sir. So long," said Eddie's savior.

Eddie had to stop somewhere, get a drink, and sit and think, somewhere no one knew him. He found a small restaurant near the station and ordered a beer and a corned beef sandwich. He tried to be philosophical. His career in business may have been ruined, but his life had been saved. He added this near-miss to all the times in Korea when he'd almost died, and the time someone shot a bullet through his taxi's window, and the time his detective friend warned him about his wise guy friends. Almost everyone he'd known from those days was dead. As terrible as this day was, maybe he was lucky. Maybe, he'd come through this, too.

He finished the beer and the sandwich, and felt restored enough to go home. He decided to head home to seek refuge in bed, just as he had decades earlier when the stress of returning from war, a new marriage, a new baby, and a new business had overwhelmed him.

He would walk to Grand Central Station, which wasn't that far away, and the fresh air might help his mood. It wasn't his usual train to Croton, so he didn't have to face his friends.

Eddie took a cab home from the Croton station and crawled into the canopied double bed he and Natty purchased shortly after they'd married. He felt strangely comforted by it. He was still wearing his shirt and trousers. He remembered when, so many years before, the psychiatrist practically dragged him from his bed in the tiny apartment back in Brooklyn. He'd rarely indulged himself in sorrow since. Instead, he'd cooked or read and listened to the opera on the radio, and drank martinis sitting by the fire in winter and outside in the sun in summer. When he pounded the meat he planned to cook, he felt like he was getting revenge on the people who'd wronged him.

Natty was out when he got home. When she came in the kitchen door and put her grocery bags on the counter, she heard movement upstairs. Afraid, she grabbed the dog who'd been outside tied to the run in the yard, and walked upstairs with him. She saw Eddie lying on the bed, curled up on his side. Rommel went over to him and licked his hand that was hanging off the bed.

"What is it, Ed? Don't you feel well?" Natty asked, sitting on the edge of the bed and placing the back of her hand on his forehead and cheeks. "You don't seem to have any temp." Natty pulled down his lower eyelids and then felt his pulse.

"I'm not sick, Nat," Eddie said as he gently pushed her from him. He'd felt comforted by her cool hands. He sat up in the bed. Natty stuffed extra pillows behind him.

"They locked me out, Nat," he said weakly. "I couldn't get into the studio."

"Who locked you out? What do you mean? I don't understand what you're saying."

Eddie looked away from her toward the window. "The IRS. The IRS locked me out."

"What? Why would they do that? How can they do such a thing? You mean you haven't been in the studio? Where have you been?" Natty rose from the bed now to stand beside it.

Eddie was silent; then he groaned, "It's a long story. It's a big mistake. I don't know what to do, Nat," he said as tears began to roll down his face. He cried like he hadn't cried since he was young.

*****

The day after he found his studio padlocked, Eddie roused himself and set to work making phone calls. He returned calls from his employees to tell them what had happened and reassured them that he would pay them until they found other work or the studio reopened. He called friends- a lawyer and an accountant. Meanwhile, Natty called other friends and asked them for loans and got her old veteran's hospital job back. Natty's fear galvanized her to act. But Eddie's fear sent him back to bed.

Natty convinced him to see a psychiatrist at the veteran's hospital. Eddie was reluctant to go, remembering with horror how he and his buddies, just returning from Korea, had dangled the army psychiatrist out of the window. At the time, Eddie laughed at the psychiatrist's fear. He laughed because anyone who called them crazy must have been crazy themselves. As the years passed, when he allowed himself to think of the days and months after his return from Korea, he felt great remorse and anger at himself for his stupidity. He had been unable to see what everyone else could see. You didn't have to be a shrink. Early in their marriage, the psychiatrist who'd visited him at home had been helpful. He made him get out of bed and do what he had to do. This time, he expected much the same but it wouldn't bring his business back or solve their financial problems.

Perhaps a few sessions will help me face what's happened, he thought. He felt like he was fighting another war. The worst casualty was his self-respect.

CHAPTER THIRTY-FIVE
1998

Eddie thought he'd never recover after filing for bankruptcy. Bob Patterson's wife called and asked for money, claiming she was entitled based on what her husband had contributed to the business. Eddie refused, saying, "I'm sorry. He never contributed much and there's nothing left anyway." Natty still had enough energy to work, so her salary, combined with an annuity their accountant had created, allowed Eddie and Natty to live in relative comfort. But they'd have to sell the cherished house in Croton to pay their debts. They learned who their true friends were when some refused to loan them money.

They'd let some relationships go, unable to face friends they'd been close with for years and had money, but couldn't part with it to help them in a crisis. Eddie's old friends Norm, Arnie, and Babe came through, however. Only Norm had real money. He worked behind the scenes in television. But the others gave what they had, emptying their pockets for their old Bijou Club pal. Another close friend and neighbor, and Danny's in laws, were generous. Danny went in military uniform to state and federal agencies to plea for assistance for his father. None was forthcoming. Natty and Eddie made sure to pay everyone back with the money from the sale of the house.

Eddie became sick with colon cancer, that the doctor said might have been triggered by the stress caused by the loss of his business. He lay in bed in his pajamas as the realtor- saving the master bedroom for last- brought prospective buyers into his sanctuary.

His children rallied around him as he awaited surgery. Rachel, now a nurse like her mother and grandmother, asked him how he could seem so complacent about a cancer diagnosis and major surgery. He thought about his tank crew who died in their twenties and his old friend Big John who'd all lost their lives in the Korean War. He thought about Mimi and Edna who'd lost their battles with cancer and his father, Sam, and Natty's father, Harry who also died before their time.

Eddie answered Rachel's question, simply, "I'm alive and they aren't. I shouldn't be. All of this has been borrowed time."

Eddie recovered from his surgery in Virginia, where Danny and his family were stationed. Danny arranged the move so his parents could live in a refinished basement in his large house. He'd made sure it had a fireplace, so Eddie could sit by it and read while listening to opera on the stereo. The kitchen was small but when he felt up to it, Eddie made pasta and gravy or other Italian, Spanish, Mexican or Asian dishes he'd learned to make in the restaurant kitchens of New York. He told old war stories and stories from his childhood to anyone who'd listen. But he never talked about the blood or death or trauma of war. His war stories were amusing and intended to entertain.

One day, when Rachel visited and asked him how she should handle her own memories, because time was going by so fast; he told her, "Don't look back. Enjoy the present and look to the future. Don't look back." It wasn't the answer she expected.

*****

When he felt well again, Eddie and Natty moved into a one bedroom, one bathroom apartment in Croton so they could live where everything was familiar and enjoy the friends that remained. Still, they both managed to create wonderful meals in the tiny, turn around kitchen and host their growing family.

Eddie drew caricatures for the amusement of his children, grandchildren, and all their surrogate adult children. He drew caricatures of nurses and pictures of red and white blood cells on overhead projector slides for Rachel who was teaching nursing students, Disney characters for all the children, and anniversary and birthday cards for Natty and the family. The director of the Croton Historical Society asked him to make a coloring book of the village's historical sites. He donated his time to help the Society raise money but he thought he could've paid them for making him feel useful again.

He and Natty continued to travel. Shortly after the move, they went to visit Victor, who'd completed his five-year Army commitment and was living in Toronto with a girlfriend while trying to get a record contract. It had been very cold. But they'd had a good visit. Victor showed them around the city. When it was time to leave to return to New York, Eddie realized his son was without a winter coat. Victor had been wearing layers of sweatshirts and a woolen hat.

As he and Natty started to go through customs, Eddie took off his coat and said, "Here, Vic. You shouldn't be cold. I don't want you to be cold." Victor took the coat and never forgot the moment or the look on his father's face that said, *Go and enjoy your life. Be warm and happy.* Natty remembered when Eddie bought her first winter coat. She was fifteen.

When he wasn't telling stories to amuse his family and friends, Eddie thought about how far he'd come. His mother hadn't wanted him, but he'd built a life despite or in spite of her. Yet, he knew he was a bit like her and Sam. She might have had an excuse for her temper coming from poverty, alone to the States, and marrying a man who was only occasionally financially successful. But he still couldn't forgive her. In the end, he'd decided she was simply a mean person. He was glad he had inherited Pop's sense of humor and will to survive but he'd also inherited a predilection for alcohol. There were times with clients when he'd had to drink but there had been other times, he'd known he was drinking to excess and couldn't excuse himself.

His successes lay in his survival, his marriage, and his children. He'd made it out of a poor neighborhood and into the Army, and had somehow survived its horrors to start his own business and open an art studio. He'd loved and advised not only his own children but other people's children to live happy, productive lives. He'd learned to enjoy life through his marriage, children and a vast number of friends but also by reading and from music- Harry's legacy that Eddie had passed on. He remembered when Harry had given him his old prayer book. The inscription had read "To Eddie, the world holds many mysteries. Explore them, not with fear, but wonder. Best regards, Harry Leibowitz."

Eddie felt he had experienced fear, maybe more than most people, but he had tried to follow Harry's advice and explore with wonder. He and Natty had traveled, tasted fine food, and seen great works of art and sculpture. They'd seen some of the sights they'd read about and enjoyed the company of good friends.

Eddie survived cancer, more than once. When it was his turn to die, he'd die knowing that he'd tried to make up for all the people he'd known who'd died too soon and with the certainty that his mother had always been wrong about him.

****

On a visit to Rachel and her family, Eddie began to feel pain in his back. They were dining with a doctor and his wife, people Rachel knew from work. They'd been having a lovely dinner, most of it cooked by Eddie. Natty had prepared an angel food cake for dessert. It had chocolate whipped cream in the middle and on top. The children had finished the main course and had been excused until it was time for dessert.

"Why are you making that face?" asked Natty.

"What face? Am I making a face?" grinned Eddie. "Ow!" he said suddenly, as he reached behind his back.

"Everything okay?" asked Rachel clearing the table.

"I'm not sure," said her father.

"Here, let me take a look," said the doctor, standing up from the table. Eddie stood, too.

"Why don't you both go into the bathroom?" said Natty.

Once in the bathroom, the doctor pulled up Eddie's shirt and looked at his back.

"You've got something coming out of your back. Here's another one," he said.

"What do you mean, something coming out of my back? Am I bleeding?"

"I'm afraid so. Could this be shrapnel?" asked the doctor, a former military man himself, but one who'd never seen combat.

"It's almost fifty years late, if it is!" said Eddie turning around to try to see his back in the bathroom mirror.

"I have my bag in the car. Let me go get it." Natty and Rachel were concerned when they saw the doctor leave the house.

"What's going on?" asked Natty, following him out the door. "Is he alright?"

"Believe it or not, I think he's got some shrapnel coming out of his back."

"Shrapnel? I don't believe it. What are you going to do?" she said following him back into the house.

"What's wrong, Mom?" asked Rachel. "Is Dad okay?"

Natty ignored her and followed the doctor into the tiny bathroom. Soon there was a line of worried family outside the door.

"Sorry, but I need some room," said the doctor as he opened his black bag and pulled out some forceps. He wiped them with alcohol from his bag and surveyed Eddie's back.

"Ed, are you alright?" called Natty.

"I'm fine. Go finish your dinner," called Eddie.

Eddie stood bending over the sink while the doctor pulled bloody shards of shrapnel out of his back. The doctor dabbed betadine in the holes left by removal of the fine slivers.

"When was your last tetanus shot?" he asked.

When it was all over, the doctor gave Eddie a prescription for an antibiotic. Rachel's husband went straight to the pharmacy to fill it. When he came back, Eddie popped one in his mouth, sat down at the table, and said, "Now, for some cake."

THE END

ACKNOWLEDGEMENTS

This book is historical fiction; however, most of it is true. It is based on real people and real events, although I've changed some of the names. Many thanks to my historian husband, Kevin Boylan, PhD for making sure I kept my facts straight and for his selfless editorial assistance. Many thanks to my brother, Col. (Ret.) Steven Rotkoff and my sister-in-law Eleanor Rotkoff for their editorial assistance and patience. My mother Natty (Natalie Rotkoff) shared her memories with me of her life and of my father's.

I also want to thank my friends who have supported me in my writing endeavors. They are steadfast and true.

What Lips My Lips have Kissed by Edna St. Vincent Millay
How High the Moon by Nancy Hamilton and Morgan Lewis
The Rime of the Ancient Mariner by Samuel Taylor Coleridge
Jack O'Diamonds by Blind Lemon Jefferson

AUTHOR'S NOTE

The Blond Tiger is a true story based on my father's life. The book is my tribute to him. He was a wonderful father and I was a daddy's girl. I wish he was still around to read and comment on the book. But, in lieu of that, I've included some pictures of him, his wife of more than 60 years (Natty), and his family. While his story is not one of rags to riches (he never became rich), I think his life is a good reminder to me and perhaps, to you, that some people are strong enough to overcome many obstacles and not only survive, but succeed in ways that are far more important than riches.

A loving father and siblings made him strong. Friends, art, caring teachers, an astute coach, a mentor, a war, and a strong woman made him strong. If not for these people and events, if it had only been him and his hateful mother, he might not have become strong. I hope you have someone or something in your life that makes you strong. My father, Eddie, did it for me. He was a great success.

As Erma Bombeck said:
Success is outliving your failures

Eddie not only outlived his own failures but also his mother's failure to love him.

Sam and Gussie

Left to right in front:
Ez, Sam and Mac
Left to right in back:
Miriam, Gussie and Edna

Harry

Eddie in high school, showing off on the parallel bars

Eddie, the soldier

Eddie, the cowboy

Eddie and Natty
in their youth

Natty and Eddie

Eddie and Natty, engagement party

Natty and Eddie- Married!

Eddie, hamming it up

Natty and Eddie growing older together.

ABOUT THE AUTHOR

Leslie Boylan is a PhD prepared former academic scholar who has published more than 100 scholarly articles and 14 books. She has received three national "Book of the Year" awards and has served on several editorial boards for scholarly journals including one journal where she was associate editor. She lives in Maryland with her husband, a professional historian and currently works as a Nurse Practitioner. In her present role, she serves at a clinic for the uninsured and cares for immigrant patients from all over the world.